J·u·d·a·h
the Pious

Other titles available from G. K. Hall by Francine Prose:

Household Saints

J·u·d·a·h
the Pious

Francine Prose

G.K. HALL & CO.
Boston, Massachusetts
1986

This G. K. Hall paperback edition is reprinted by arrangement with the author.

First G. K. Hall printing, 1986.

Library of Congress Cataloging-in-Publication Data

Prose, Francine, 1947–
  Judah the pious.

  I. Title.
[PS3566.R68J8   1986]   813'.54   85-24902
ISBN 0-8398-2913-2 (pbk.)

TO BEA

J·u·d·a·h
the Pious

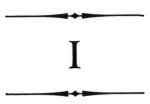

I

LEGEND has it that the heavenly gatekeeper actually raised his arms and danced down the steps of his golden watchtower to greet the Rabbi Eliezer of Rimanov; his passage was obstructed by the small angels who had had to climb up for a better view of the newcomer. It is said, too, that the celestial judges applauded Eliezer's freedom from all earthly vanity, his lifelong disregard for the style of his robe and the cut of his hair; these praises signified the elders' decision to ignore that one morning when the rabbi had been overcome by a spell of mirror-gazing, that morning when he had glanced into a glass for the first time in fifty years, and had seen fifty thousand images of himself standing before the King of Poland.

The palace in which this lapse occurred had been planned as a miniature Versailles; but the transcontinental journey home had so blurred the architect's memory of the French original that only a dim recollection of one glittering corridor remained. Therefore, mirrors had been installed throughout the royal summer residence—covering the walls, the ceilings, the bedposts, the windowsills, the shutters, and lining every surface of the magnificent audience hall where the king received official guests.

Faced with so many reflections of himself, the Rabbi Eliezer could not help gaping at how old he had grown, how his hair had turned the color of stained linen, and how the folds of yellow flesh hung from his neck like the skin of a boiled chicken. But soon a second thought made the old man grin. "Indeed," he chuckled softly, "a commemorative portrait of my visit with the king could extinguish the fire of patriotism in every Polish heart."

But of course, no artist would ever have been tempted to paint the scene which reappeared in mirror after mirror; it had none of the stirring grandeur of an emperor's coronation, or the mustering of a doomed battalion. Planted on the Persian carpet, the old man's grimy feet seemed like the base of some tasteless statue. His beard was greasy, his hair matted, his pock-marked nose drooped almost to the top of his thin, twisted lips. Apart from a mangy beaver hat, his only garment was a tattered robe of heavy black wool, not unlike the torn shrouds which sometimes hung from the backs of dying women in charity hospitals. In fact, his bright blue eyes appeared to be the only clean things about him.

If the Rabbi Eliezer was a dark smudge on the glass, then the young king and his advisors were the palace's natural jewels, for which the gilded mirrors could be the only proper setting. Concentrating on the king's reflection now, the old man decided that a painted wooden cherub must have descended from his perch on the enormous wall-crucifix to rest on the throne. Eliezer had never seen such a boy before; towheaded, blue-eyed, a bit plump, the king seemed to glow like the surface of a pearl. "A child of sixteen," muttered the rabbi, "and a young sixteen at that."

Gradually, the courtiers' faces grew contorted with fury at the old man's refusal to look directly at them. Clustered around their lord, they whispered excitedly until a sleek, mustachioed young colonel broke from the group and strode across the hall towards Eliezer.

Then, suddenly, he stopped.

The Jew had burst out laughing.

The nobleman's hand clenched and unclenched, as if it were grasping an imaginary riding crop. "What," he muttered, choking with rage, "just what in the court of the supreme ruler do you find so funny?"

"I am laughing at all of us," gasped the rabbi. "But, more than that, I am laughing with the amazement of finding myself where I find myself."

Rabbi Eliezer of Rimanov would never have found himself in such exalted surroundings but for a strange combination of circumstances.

That winter, two Polish noblemen had reluctantly

attended the funeral of the eminent Jewish doctor who had guided them back from that worldly purgatory known as the French pox. Unfortunately, however, the gratitude which had sent them on one last visit to their physician quickly vanished in the dilapidated cemetery. As the service wore on, the aristocrats felt increasingly cramped and uneasy, irritated by the bitter cold, the gibberish-like prayers, and the unrestrained tears of the mourners, whose very appearance offered a constant affront to their esthetic sense. Indeed, they would surely have bolted from the cemetery, were it not for their conviction that true gentlemen do not behave so rudely in the presence of death.

Thus, it was only an accident of courtesy which caused the nobles to remain until the end of the service, when, fixed in this uncharitable frame of mind, they chanced to find evidence of the barbarity they had been expecting all along.

The ceremony was over; the coffin had been lowered into the ground and covered with earth. But suddenly, on a signal from their leader, the black-robed Jews bent down, scooped up handfuls of frozen dirt, and tossed it back over their shoulders at the grave. Then they brushed off their hands and filed solemnly from the cemetery.

The two aristocrats stared at each other, confused by what they had seen. But after three hours, twelve steins of ale, and much debate, they finally agreed on the worst possible interpretation of that odd custom, an explanation which made their mouths run dry with horror.

It was obvious, they mumbled fuzzily, that the spiteful Jews were teasing their dead with a last sweet taste of soil; they were tantalizing their ghosts into coming back from the other world and stalking innocent people.

The news of this outrage rushed through the countryside, helped along by the tavernkeepers, who knew that indignation always afflicted their customers with a terrible thirst. Merchants peddled the rumor from town to town, and found their sales of crucifixes and lucky amulets doubling in volume. Even the washerwomen discovered that a few veiled references to the "funeral conspiracy" often served to distract their clients' attention from a frayed cuff or a stubborn stain.

Soon, everyone in Poland was whispering about the incident. All the old tales of poltergeists and hauntings were resurrected, and the people nodded in sudden comprehension. Tempers crackled like dead leaves, until at last, fearing a massacre, the court announced its intention to prohibit the Jews from further endangering the citizens' welfare.

Hearing rumors of this, the Jews shrugged helplessly and prepared to change their habits once again. There was nothing else to do, for who might they find to plead their case? Their great lawyers, skilled in the arts of persuasion, had become such strangers to the faith that they were no longer capable of conducting a

(7)

religious argument; their rabbis and scholars, intimate with the finest details of scripture and ceremony, were unaccustomed to convincing unsympathetic listeners. Besides, there was no one in the community who had really mastered the elaborate, highly figured speech of the court; and those citizens prominent enough to know how this language sounded were reluctant to risk their high positions in an attempt to speak it.

For all these reasons, the scribes had already resigned themselves to the task of deleting the final ceremony from the prayer books, when a second rumor made them pause and set down their pens:

The Rabbi Eliezer of Rimanov had volunteered to represent his people before the ruler of Poland.

Now the court nobles logically assumed that the Jews were sending their king, since no one but the chief defender of their faith could possibly perform such an important errand. But the Jews knew differently, for, with the apparent exception of the two old women who looked after his cleaning and mending, and swore that their master was the Messiah in disguise, nobody had ever heard of the Rabbi Eliezer.

Immediately, the community elders ordered a careful investigation into the origins and opinions of their newfound spokesman. But, even after their trustiest sources had been cross-examined, little information could be found. The rabbi, they learned, was a very old man—just how old no one knew. Since his arrival in Rimanov thirty years before, he had continued to live the life of a stranger, so that even his closest neighbors could only remark on the congenial way he smiled good morning, and on the tired stoop of his shoulders as he shuffled towards the bazaar between his two withered companions.

Despite his obvious poverty, despite his ill-nourished appearance and constant solitude, he consistently rejected all offers of charity and invitations to dinner, and, particularly, any overtures which might lead to the most innocent inquiry about his personal history. Occasionally, an enterprising gossip managed to corner him into commenting on the weather or on the coming holiday, but, as soon as the conversation turned ever so slightly from these formal topics, the rabbi would suddenly sag and stumble, as if he had just remembered that infirmity was an old man's prerogative.

Of course, there were many who actually preferred knowing nothing about their mysterious neighbor, for their total ignorance gave them total freedom to speculate about the rabbi's past. Poor men swore that he had once been fabulously wealthy, but had given up all his jewels, furs, and tasty delicacies for a return to the simpler pleasures. The rich burghers, on the other hand, took one look at his huge, now-emaciated frame, and concluded that he had been a free man, a traveling acrobat perhaps, wandering footloose over back country roads, finding adventure and indulging in wild delights with unspeakably exotic women. Thus, because his life had not been circumscribed by the city walls, Eliezer's past was forced to serve as a dumping ground for all the frustrated dreams and fantasies of the citizens of Rimanov.

All these fantasies were dutifully reported to the elders. Who could blame them for becoming alarmed? For all they knew, Eliezer of Rimanov could have been a dangerous heretic, or a foolish blusterer who might provoke the nobles and bring the wrath of the court down on thousands of blameless heads. Therefore, they hastily assembled a delegation of eminent men, and set out for the rabbi's home.

As soon as the distinguished visitors had bowed low enough to pass through Eliezer's tiny doorway, they began to congratulate themselves on their foresight, for it seemed that their worst suspicions had been confirmed. Shaking their heads, they realized that they had been lured on a fool's errand by an eccentric old recluse. The dinginess, poverty, and incredible slovenliness of the one-room hut struck them as truly unique. Prints, papers, cabalistic scribblings and books with disturbing, unfamiliar titles lay everywhere, scattered across the floor, completely covering the rickety table and the narrow bed.

The only space not taken up with worthless scraps was that occupied by the rabbi himself, who sat reading obliviously on a hard wooden bench in the center of the room. The investigators were of course impressed by his unattractive appearance and by his failure to offer them the chairs he did not have. Then, as if all this were not enough, they suddenly realized something which, even much later, they could scarcely believe: the Rabbi Eliezer of Rimanov did not appear particularly honored by their presence.

"So," he smiled, "you have come to see whether I am fit to address a king?"

Amazed that such an obvious lunatic could apparently speak perfect sense, the entire delegation was unable to answer this simple question. Determined to proceed with the investigation, if only for the sake of form, the committee members at last produced quills and notebooks from beneath their fur cloaks, and the chairman hesitantly stepped forward.

"There are a few questions we wish to ask you," he muttered. "Only a few questions," he emphasized, clearly still unsettled. Then, remembering the dignity befitting him as the man whose riches had built the main temple of Lublin, he raised his arm in a commanding gesture, and beckoned for the chief rabbi of Vilna to come up and take his place.

The ancient representative from Vilna shambled into position. "Eliezer," he intoned in a whining, nasal voice, "you call yourself a rabbi, yet we know nothing about your credentials. Could you possibly say a word or two about the source and nature of your training?"

"Everything I know," replied Eliezer pleasantly, "I have learned from life and from God. And as yet I have found no reason to criticize my school or my teacher."

A low murmur arose among the committee members, and the Vilna rabbi, unsure whether his question had been satisfactorily answered, knit his thin brows and smiled lamely until a famous scholar came forward to relieve him of his duties as inquisitor.

"I am certain we would all find it illuminating," began the learned man coyly, "if you would consent to cite for us Maimonides's well-known commentary on the fifth chapter of Genesis." The scholar pursed his lips together, and, after a weighty pause, continued. "Knowing, as I do, that the most brilliant minds are liable to their minuscule moments of forgetfulness, I will even go so far as to refresh your memory." And then, even the other scholars were frankly surprised to hear their colleague launch into a lengthy, tiresome recitation of the Genealogy and Age of the Patriarchs.

Throughout this performance, Rabbi Eliezer picked at a dirty cuticle, while the delegates basked in the hope that they might soon catch the old man red-handed in an attempt to conceal his ignorance. But they were quickly disappointed, for, when the speech was over, Eliezer only smiled. "I have never read Maimonides's commentaries," he said, speaking rapidly so as to thwart the scholar's efforts to answer his own question. "But, whenever I have had a specific problem to solve or a decision to make, I have always been able to think of an applicable portion of the Scriptures."

The scholar sneered, emitting a sharp, dry cackle, like the sound of rustling paper. Then, certain that Eliezer was faltering, a great lawyer rushed forward to help hammer the defendant into the ground; he pelted the old man with a barrage of questions concerning the flowers of rhetoric, while, all the time, the rabbi insisted politely that he knew only the art of plain speaking.

The lawyer moved his hand as if he were plucking fruit out of the air, in a gesture meant to imply that he had proved his case. "Well," he concluded, "if you have no hope of persuading the king, then perhaps you can at least work a miracle or two to win him over. Have you performed any miracles, Eliezer? Do you think you could do one on command?"

"In the words of the great Judah the Pious," smiled Eliezer, " 'There are thousands of miracles in the air above my head, but I have no desire to reach up and grasp them.' "

Perhaps it was at this point that the tide began to turn in Eliezer's favor; for, the committee reasoned, anyone who mentioned such a lovingly-remembered sage as Judah the Pious could not be all bad.

From then on, the delegates found themselves coming to feel that the Rabbi Eliezer might just as well satisfy his desire to address the King of Poland. His visit would probably bring no benefits, and do no harm; besides, no one else had volunteered to go. These conclusions also spared them the embarrassment of having to prohibit Eliezer from making the trip; so, quite content, they bid him a cold good-by and good luck, and departed.

Had their investigation chanced to uncover one grain of truth, the distinguished delegates would never have felt so comfortable and secure.

Instead, they might have trembled at the thought of

(13)

the rabbi's coming visit, but, on the other hand, would have been slightly more optimistic about his chances of success. For there were certain matters which the poor residents of Rimanov did not wish to discuss with such important men, certain subjects which, indeed, they rarely broached among themselves. Had these people been a bit less timid, a bit more articulate, they might have told the investigators this:

The Rabbi Eliezer was known to have a powerful, pervasive, and, some said, decidedly sinister influence over the thoughts and actions of young men.

Upon his arrival in Rimanov, the rabbi had initially attempted to support himself by giving lessons to boys whose parents could not afford to pay the fees of better-known teachers, but who still wished their sons to have some knowledge of their history, a love for the holy word, and the rudiments of a religious education. The Rabbi Eliezer asked only a penny per lesson; he was aged, obviously experienced and venerable. No one thought to demand the references of a Godsend.

Eliezer's hut grew steadily more crowded with eager pupils, who seemed to take so much delight in learning that their parents found it easy to overlook the first signs of danger. Mothers noticed that their boys were skipping meals, avoiding their former playmates, and spending their spare time staring out the window; the women clucked their tongues mournfully, and thrilled with secret pride to think that their darlings were simply studying too hard. Fathers searched their memories for basic facts on which to quiz their sons, met with blank stares, and decided that education had probably changed since their day. And the small children who pestered their elder brothers into revealing what they had learned in class were suddenly troubled by recurring nightmares; yet, when they rushed to their parents with grisly tales of demons, trolls and witches, they were merely scolded for letting their imaginations run wild.

Eventually, however, incidents of inexplicable behavior among the rabbi's students became so frequent that they could no longer be ignored. A respectable widow discovered that her son had written a poem containing terms and sentiments so indecent that the blush stayed on her wrinkled cheeks for two days. A moody youth contracted pneumonia by running out naked on a moonlit night to hurl himself into a snowbank. Three boys attempted to break their mothers' hearts by embarking on unwholesome diets of fruit and nuts, while four others infuriated their fathers by wearing dirty clothes and causing the neighbors to think that their families could not afford to dress them properly.

Reluctant to admit that education might have damaged their sons, the parents of Eliezer's pupils hesitated to discuss their suspicions with each other; thus, many private, repetitious family scenes had to be staged until they felt satisfied with their understanding of the old man's crimes.

At least, the parents sighed with relief, he had not physically or spiritually corrupted their children, nor led them into any sins which might cause their souls to roast in Gehenna. But he had done the next worst thing; he had filled their impressionable young minds with dangerous fancies and unrealistic longings. The citizens of Rimanov had prayed that Eliezer might make scholars of their sons, but he had turned them into dreamers.

One by one, the bewildered students were withdrawn from school, but it was already too late. Eventually, it became apparent that all of the old man's former pupils were somehow marked for life, set apart from their more predictable and easily contented neighbors. They drifted aimlessly from job to job, remained melancholy and dissatisfied for no reason. At weddings, they seemed to forget the wives they had lived with since their youths, and danced all night with graceful young women. Some had left town, and, every few years, sent back letters with mysterious foreign postmarks. A few even drank.

All this would certainly have helped the worthy delegates understand why the obscure rabbi might have felt any incentive or obligation to represent his people before the King of Poland. But of course such facts never appeared in the committee's official report.

These memories, however, had not been forgotten by the rabbi. And so, when he saw for himself the age and appearance of the small boy on the massive throne, a vision of the Rimanov school crept back into his heart, and gave him the courage to begin his interview with such a boisterous laugh.

II

KING CASIMIR of Poland had been dozing fit-
fully on his throne when the Rabbi Eliezer first
entered the royal audience hall. Shaken gently awake,
the king peered at his visitor through a nearsighted
haze, and wondered whether his advisors were trying to amuse him with another exotic ostrich brought
back from the wilds of Africa. But, when the black-
plumed bird threw back its head and laughed like a
man, the young sovereign began to recall that this was
the long-awaited day on which he was to meet the
Jewish holy man.

Squirming with excitement, the boy craned his neck
forward until it chafed against the jewel-encrusted
collar of his robe; then, disappointed, he straightened
back into the ramrod-stiff posture of a proper king.

Despite what Casimir had been taught as a child, no
diabolical horns sprouted from beneath the Jew's mat-

ted hair, nor were his yellow teeth stained bright red with the blood of innocent babies. Although he had known it would be this way, he still felt cheated. For, had Eliezer truly appeared a demon, a wild-eyed pagan with bones and boars' teeth woven into his beard, the king might then have been able to discuss certain matters which he had never mentioned to any of his courtiers—certain secrets so shameful that they could only be revealed to a man who was already damned.

No doubt, the good people of Poland would have been amused to learn the thoroughly mundane nature of the sins which so tormented their king. For Casimir, however, these problems were deadly serious. Unlike ordinary boys, who could share their growing pains with each other, the friendless young king could only conclude that his particular misery had never been experienced by anyone else.

Day after day, he brooded on his failings, cursed himself for his listlessness, his apathy, his sense of isolation, detachment, and general irritation. He daydreamed incessantly, inventing vivid fantasies concerning certain court ladies; then, he would censor himself, and walk around for hours with downcast, guilty eyes.

But the last of Casimir's troubles was the one which caused him the most anxiety, for it seemed the most perilous: he had begun to feel hopelessly estranged from the warm, protective arms of the mother church. All his life, he had been a true believer. But lately, his faith in the great Miracle of the Birth, the Passion, and the Resurrection had come to seem worthless, illogical, and silly; and he could not help thinking that God had not prevented him from losing his parents, nor from being locked into a position from which he could never escape. For these reasons, he felt his religion slipping steadily and irreversibly away.

What could be easier, he had thought in the days before the Rabbi Eliezer's visit, than to confess the loss of faith to a man who never had any to lose? And, once the major sins burst out, the smaller ones would be carried along, perhaps even ignored, like ripples in a swelling flood.

But Eliezer's thoroughly unexceptional ugliness had dampened the boy's hopes. There was nothing fantastic or exotic in the old man's appearance, nothing to suggest a reckless amorality; no scent of brimstone followed him through the hall. Now, all that Casimir felt was a mild revulsion for Eliezer's sunken cheeks and flabby skin.

Forcing down his distaste, King Casimir of Poland motioned for the stranger to draw near; but the old man's progress towards the throne was cut short by the same impatient nobleman who had just finished rebuking him for his inattention.

"How can you be so impudent?" cried the red-faced courtier, throwing his taut, massive body directly in the rabbi's path. "Or have you never heard that it befits swine like yourself to kneel in the presence of the sovereign?"

"I'm too tired to kneel," explained Eliezer. "And besides, I fear that hours of your precious time might be wasted in getting me back on my feet."

"A very funny old man," hissed the noble. "Tongues have been cut out for much less wit."

"Then do so," said the rabbi amiably. "I am eighty-nine years old, and that, as I see it, rather narrows your options. On the one hand, you can execute me immediately. On the other, should you feel inclined towards great kindness, you can keep me here in the castle, stuffing my thin belly with your finest wines and sweetmeats, and it would still be unlikely for me to last much longer. Now, while you are deciding to kill me and so shorten my life by a few months, I hope you will at least allow me to pass my last hours chatting pleasantly with your lord."

Waving aside the stammering nobleman, Eliezer shuffled forward until he stood within inches of the throne. Bending down, he winked merrily at the king and shrugged his bony shoulders.

"King Casimir," he whispered, "you can see for yourself that at this rate we will soon get nowhere. Meaning no disrespect, I wonder: have you ever tried to study the beautiful king bee when the hive was crawling with bothersome, useless drones? A waste of effort, I assure you. And as long as your worthy advisors continue to prattle about protocol, ceremony, bowing and scraping, my visit will come to nothing. Send these men away, if only for a while. Should you later have any cause for regret, I swear that I will pay

(20)

with a pint of my blood for every hour they are gone."

The king's clear blue eyes glimmered, then suddenly began to shine as he glanced into a nearby mirror and saw the nobleman stamping his foot in fury. Never before had Casimir seen his courtiers openly defied; no one had ever urged him to oppose their authority; it had never been suggested that he take a single action which had not been approved by centuries of court practice. The novelty of it thrilled him, and at the same time, calmed him by shutting his ears to the noise of his advisors buzzing about his head, mumbling about the dangers to his dignity, his prestige, even his physical safety. Sitting in the center of their swarm, the King of Poland was, for the first time, attempting to govern himself.

By making Casimir aware of his dependence on the courtiers, the rabbi's request had strengthened his desire to thwart them. But, each time he considered dismissing them from the hall, he remembered that, since his parents' death, these cold men had been his only family. And he knew that the old rabbi would eventually abandon him to the icy, reproachful glares which might remain on their faces for months. Thus, he wavered back and forth between rebellion and submission until his reason was exhausted, and inclined towards the easier course.

"I am afraid that I cannot in good conscience accede to your demand," said the king, frowning, raising his voice to drown out the courtiers' approving murmurs.

"I would prefer to be surrounded by men whom I trust, whose wisdom and experience have often kept me from reaching rash conclusions."

Rabbi Eliezer nodded. "Suit yourself, King Casimir," he smiled slyly. "But I feel I must warn you about the dangers of relying too heavily on the judgment of others; submission is a difficult habit to break. Who knows? You may soon begin to see the value of certain bits of wisdom which you have for some time been resisting. Perhaps you will finally agree to marry one of the frightful princesses of the realm— the rich, young duchess of the wens and boils, or the heiress whose hyena-laugh will certainly shatter all the mirrors in your palace. Then, if I may venture to predict, you will find that your courtiers are indeed so wise and experienced that none of them will ever volunteer to take your place in the bed of such a woman."

Gasping with surprise and indignation, the nobles closed into a tight knot around the king, as if to shield him from the rabbi's disturbing words; several broke from the group and began to move threateningly towards the old man. Then, a slow smile lit King Casimir's face. Calmly, with great dignity, he asked his courtiers if they would mind waiting in the antechamber until he rang for their return.

As the nobles reluctantly withdrew, King Casimir could not bring himself to look at the rabbi, but stared bashfully at the ground. When the last iron-tipped boot heel had clicked against the ebony doorstep,

Eliezer and the king simultaneously uttered deep, involuntary sighs of relief; catching each other at it, both pretended not to notice.

"Well," began Casimir at last, "I must say, that was a good trick, alluding to the duchess and such. But really, you must tell me how you did it. Surely, you are not going to pass yourself off as a great clairvoyant, capable of reading the secrets of the past and future at one glance. Admit it: it was just a matter of resourcefulness, a few pennies slipped into the apron pocket of a knowledgeable palace chambermaid."

"If I had money to waste on gossip," laughed Eliezer, "I would have eaten breakfast this morning."

"In other words," the king insisted, "you are saying that you knew it all beforehand, thanks to a few weeks of careful research into court affairs and the state of the noble families of Poland."

"Nonsense," answered the old man. "My secret is an empty head, purposely kept blank, so that the slightest tremor of an eyelid which passes before it can inscribe a story there, more accurate and complicated than anything I could have read."

Casimir raised his pale eyebrows and leaned forward, as if he were watching the old man work an elaborate shell game. "In that case," he said deliberately, "I suppose your mind must be equally empty of reasons why your people should be allowed to persist in their barbaric custom."

Turning his head slightly, Eliezer threw the king a sarcastic glance. "If there is one thing I admire," he said, "it is a young man who can beat me so effort-lessly in a battle of wits. But, I must admit, you have come much closer to the truth than you realize. Al-though that subject is exactly what I have come to dis-cuss, I really do not know of any arguments which I can count upon to convince you.

"Yet, be that as it may, one thing is certain: I have stood on my feet much longer than is usually consid-ered possible for an eighty-nine-year-old gentleman. Were there another chair in the room, I would never dare ask you to relinquish your throne. But, under the circumstances, I see no alternative. Besides, should you grow tired, your young body is still limber enough to lower itself down to the carpeted steps at my feet."

For the second time that day, Casimir found himself without a single precedent; certainly, no one had ever made such an unseemly demand of the King of Poland. His logic told him that the request was reasonable, for he could see the old man's skinny frame beginning to tremble. Still, it made him shudder to imagine the filthy, moth-eaten black robe pressed up against the embroidered cushions. And what a frightful scandal would ensue, should his advisors find him in such an undignified position, curled up like a disciple at the rabbi's yellow, calloused feet! Despite himself, Casimir looked furtively towards the door of the antechamber. It was this glance which irked him into standing up and offering the rabbi his seat.

"Thank you," nodded Eliezer, lifting his hem and weaving a bit unsteadily as he mounted the steps.

"You have a strong, young body. A boy of your age could probably stand for hours without growing weary."

Casimir, who had been just about to sit down on the steps, remained on his feet. He had never thought of himself as strong before; compared to his enormous, sinewy courtiers, he had always appeared as plump and powerless as a milk-fattened capon. He turned his head so that the old man would not see the flush of pride on his cheeks; by the time he looked back, Eliezer had settled himself in the imposing throne, as comfortably and naturally as if it were a simple bench offered him by a courteous ox-cart driver.

"Well," said Eliezer, after a short silence, "I suppose I might best begin by asking you the simplest question I can imagine: what, do you think, is in our minds when we throw those lumps of dirt on the huge mounds which the gravediggers have already heaped high enough?"

"That *is* a simple question," nodded the king, recalling the careful briefing he had received from his advisors. "You are hoping that the arc in which the soil travels as it flies towards the grave may form a bridge for your dead to pass over when they return to earth. Thus, they can revisit the scene of their lives, and, out of sheer malice, frighten blameless Polish people into joining them in the other world."

"Nonsense," shouted Eliezer, so loud that the muscles around Casimir's heart tightened for fear that the entire court would come running in. "Is this really the way bright young men reason these days? Do you honestly believe that we would disturb the sweet rest of someone we loved just to irritate a few men we do not even know?"

Still unsettled by the violence of the old man's response, the boy was beginning to feel empty-headed and stupid. "I am not sure," he stammered after a while. "If not for that reason, then why?"

"I will tell you why," said Eliezer, more gently. "But you must listen carefully, for I dislike repeating myself.

"Among our people, it is generally believed that a dead man's spirit accompanies his body to the cemetery, where it lingers like an uncomfortable party guest, seeking the proper moment to make an exit and a seemly manner of saying good-by. And it is not until the soul of the departed sees his loved ones turn their backs and cast dirt on his grave that he feels assured that life will go on without him, that he can depart in peace and begin to take his rest. So you see, King Casimir, our motives are actually just the opposite of what your nobles have been telling you. Really, does it not seem more logical to a young man of your intelligence that we should wish our dead to sleep quietly throughout eternity?"

"Nothing is logical," snapped Casimir quickly, to cover his uneasiness over the obvious good sense of the old man's argument. "The only certain thing is that my advisors are telling me one story, and you another."

"And which do *you* believe?" asked the rabbi.

Unaccustomed to being challenged in this way, King Casimir shrank from the old man's question. "My courtiers have done some painstaking research," he answered, "and, as a rule, tend to know what is best for the country. As for me, it is quite a different matter entirely; I hardly believe in spirits and such. Besides," he added hastily, "you yourself know that, given the public sentiment, a horrible slaughter would probably take place if the people caught you persisting in your custom."

"There will be no massacre if you prohibit it," shrugged Eliezer carelessly. "But why do you not believe in spirits?"

The king, who had been hoping that his remark had gone unnoticed, was taken by surprise. "Because," he began, then stopped, amazed at the tight, strangulated sound of his own voice. "Because I have never seen them."

"And you do not believe in anything you have never seen?"

"No," answered Casimir, feeling the word catch in his throat.

Rabbi Eliezer's face registered no emotion. "You must know that can often be a dangerous course," he said. "For when we refuse to believe in the possibility of impossible things, we can neither love all the unlikely beings which wish to do us good, nor be on guard against those which would harm us; we become like defenseless children, who do not understand what things should be feared, nor where they can call for help."

The boy, who knew by now that Eliezer had guessed almost everything, could hardly answer. "This skepticism is not a course I would have chosen for myself," he replied at last, bowing his head.

"And you would change it if you could?"

"Yes," nodded the king.

"I see," said Eliezer of Rimanov, "I see," and said nothing else for several minutes.

Taking advantage of the lull in the conversation, King Casimir attempted to restore matters to the straight, orderly path from which they had begun to veer. "At any rate," he began, keeping himself calm with the massive, almost-physical effort he had practiced as a small boy troubled by nightmares, "I do not see what my cynical turn of mind has to do with the burial customs of the Jews of Poland."

"Everything and nothing," answered Eliezer, smiling radiantly. "Everything and nothing. For it suddenly occurs to me that now, with things as they are, it would do neither of us any good if I remained here for an hour, improvising arguments for the innocence of our rites and the generosity of our motives. But, on the other hand, perhaps we could come to some sort of agreement, a bargain, if you will. Suppose I were to convince you once and for all of the fallacies in a system which does not allow for the unseen and the improbable? Would you then consider permitting my people to retain their custom—as a reward for me, or as the price of a lesson, to put it more delicately?"

"I will make you that bargain," replied Casimir readily, "with, of course, the understanding that I am very difficult to convince, and that I have never been able to maintain much interest or concentration in my lessons."

"In that case," smiled the old man, "it will not be a lesson, but, rather, an entertaining story—a story which, in fact, my father told us to help pass the hours before his death. But I must warn you, it is a rather long narrative, and perhaps you would be more comfortable here at my feet."

Without a moment's hesitation, King Casimir of Poland sat down on the carpeted steps, and the Rabbi Eliezer began his tale.

III

"LIKE ALL good stories," said the rabbi, "mine begins slightly before the beginning. For everything we know about a man's life means nothing unless we understand the circumstances surrounding his birth. By this, you must not take me to mean the position of the stars, nor any such thing; I would not wish to offend Your Majesty right off by flying straight into a skyful of superstition. No, we are talking science here, and what I am trying to say is this: I have often seen cases in which a man's whole life has been influenced by the thoughts and dreams in his parents' minds at the moment of his conception."

"So I have heard," snapped the king sharply, having no desire at that moment to picture either his own conception or that of his unborn children. "But everyone knows it has never been proved."

"Then this story will prove it," replied Eliezer,

equally brusquely.

"You will not prove anything unless you begin," growled Casimir.

"I am truly sorry," apologized the old man. "I had no idea your opinions ran so strongly on this matter. Now be patient, and I will try to find a more straight-forward prologue for my story." After a short pause, the Rabbi Eliezer cleared his throat and began again.

"In my father's village, three hundred miles from the city of Cracow, lived a brilliant scholar by the name of Simon Polikov. To those who knew him, the fact that he was a scholar seemed even more obvious than the fact that he was a man. For, if your best court artist were to combine all the traits and features tradi-tionally attributed to the diligent student, this improb-able caricature might well be an accurate portrait of Simon Polikov. He was short, skinny, and gangly, with a slack, toneless body. His thin face had turned a pasty blue-white shade, the color of dim lamplight in the late afternoon; his myopic eyes were the dead brown of plants which have died from lack of sun-shine. He was absent-minded, forgetful, timid, with-drawn; he squinted, and scratched his head perpetu-ally with a tense, irritated motion.

In fact, everything about Simon Polikov was spare and pinched, except for his heart, which was large and extraordinarily generous.

As a youth, the promising student had been hounded by all the Jewish families with marriageable daughters; but not a single girl could be found whose love for God and wisdom could reconcile her to the prospect of sharing a double bed with Simon Polikov. Sensing this, Simon decided that his bachelor's habits were already too well established to change, and, as gracefully as possible, hastened to remove himself from the marriage market.

Then, in his fifty-fifth year, he awoke one night with a searing pain in his chest and knew that none of his precious textbooks would be able to say the memorial prayers necessary to insure his soul's speedy entrance into heaven.

The next morning, his new-found determination to take a wife was reinforced by the realization that he already had one.

For almost five years, Simon's meager home had been conscientiously tended by an attractive middle-aged spinster named Hannah Bromsky, who, though not a charwoman either by necessity or inclination, did the scholar's cooking, cleaning, and washing as an act of charitable piety. To Simon, the fact that she had lived only a short time in the village seemed far less important than the fact that she had spent that time practicing for the job of being his wife. After due consideration, Hannah somewhat reluctantly admitted the seemliness of Simon's proposal, and opened her well-rounded arms to him.

Overjoyed at the mating of two such worthy people, the villagers danced for three days and nights at their wedding, then left the happy couple alone to go about the serious business of producing an heir.

The Polikovs put all their energy and concentration into this task; during the first days of marriage, Simon's eyes could hardly focus on the printed page, and Hannah's housekeeping grew careless and inattentive. Weeks passed, and the aging pair learned to integrate their strenuous efforts into a certain routine. Months went by; the couple was amazed at the tenderness developing between them, but still nothing came of it. At last, on the evening of their second anniversary, Hannah looked down and slapped the skin of her flat belly with anger and frustration.

She simply could not believe it might be too late for her, especially when all signs seemed to indicate the contrary. Nor could she understand why God might wish to punish her in this way, when, all her life, she had never committed a single sin worth fasting over. Like many women whose expectations for girlish happiness are awakened only late in life, Hannah had been sure that the satisfactions of her coming years would compensate for all the disappointments of the past; faced with the possibility of finding a fresh set of disappointments, she grew bitter and furious—so furious, in fact, that she resolved to force down her pride and seek a remedy for barrenness.

Immediately, the villagers began searching through their memories and their family almanacs for time-tested sterility cures; none of their suggestions proved too obscure or unpleasant for Hannah to try. Day after day, she immersed herself in ritual baths while swallowing endless philters, powders, and potions. She smeared her body with pastes and poultices, cut her hair and nails and buried the clippings, waded through bogs, cut the combs off roosters, and choked down mouthfuls of raw fish.

But, when the spring came round again, the scholar's wife resented it, and accused the earth of trying to taunt her with its fertility; for, by then, Hannah was worn out, dispirited, and still childless.

Fortunately, the sense of being cheated had not died in her, and, in a last kick of strength, this outrage pushed her to follow a course which was quite daring for a poor, no-longer-young woman. Hannah Polikov decided to travel alone, all the way to Cracow, to seek the advice of Judah the Pious, the most famous sage and miracle worker in all of Europe.

It was the end of April when Hannah set out on her pilgrimage; August had come and gone before she returned.

Naturally, the news of her imminent homecoming outraced her to the village; Simon put down his books and came out to greet his wife, whose true worth he had only begun to realize during the months of her absence. But, after one brief kiss, Hannah brushed past him, and, hurrying through the door, began to busy herself with the long-neglected housework.

Not a word was spoken between them for the rest of the day; an atmosphere of tense expectancy hung over their home, until, at last, lying close beside his wife in the narrow bed, Simon Polikov broke the silence:

"Tell me, at least," he said, trying to sound cheerful, "what the people of Cracow eat for breakfast in the morning."

"Plain tea," replied Hannah sensibly. "Just like us."

These few words were all that was needed to break the spell. "Listen," she went on quickly, glad to be getting to the heart of things, "I actually managed to get an audience with the great Judah the Pious. And even he—whose holiness and wisdom I could never begin to describe to you—even he needed a few days in which to comprehend the nature of my case. But, at last, it came to him: I am much too dearly loved, by you, and by our neighbors, so that certain of the spirits have become jealous and cursed me with barrenness in revenge. According to the holy saint, they will never be satisfied until I am dead and buried, and completely erased from the memories of all living men."

"But surely the spirits have never been so smart that they could not be tricked?" asked Simon.

"That is just what Judah the Pious suggested," beamed Hannah, proud that the years of study had made her husband so perceptive. "Since the spirits would never believe that you and all our friends have suddenly begun to hate me, our only hope lies in making them think that I am dead. You must put me in a simple coffin, and carry it out to the edge of the cemetery near the woods; then, with all the suitable prayers, place my casket in a trench. After that, I may be able to escape the spirits' notice for a few weeks, just long enough to conceive a child."

The wise scholar naturally had some reservations

(35)

about this idea, but his love for Hannah and his strong desire for a son kept him from expressing them. So, he contented himself with the thought that few men have the luxury of being able to choose a sunny day on which to bury their wives.

On the appointed afternoon, Hannah Polikov climbed into the wooden box, which was so rickety, so full of gaping holes and rough surfaces, that even the most unobservant spirit would have had no trouble spotting it for a fraud. Simon groaned loudly and struck his breast, urging on the neighbors who had volunteered to pose as mourners. Wailing a pitiful dirge, the procession wound through every street of the town, until at last it reached the cemetery.

The coffin was lowered into the shallow pit, which Simon had dug with his own hands; the prayers were dutifully chanted. But suddenly, just as the mourners had turned their backs on the grave and scooped up the dirt to throw over their shoulders, an unexpected thing occurred:

A band of unemployed mercenary troops, whom Hannah had hired in private, swooped down on Simon and the funeral guests. Shooting their pistols in the air, the soldiers scattered and chased all the terrified mourners in different directions, so that Simon was forced to lift up the hem of his robe and leap over the roots and fallen branches as he scrambled through the forest towards safety.

Thus, for just a few minutes, Hannah Polikov seemed to the spirits not only dead and buried, but also quite definitely forgotten by all those who might have remembered her.

Nine months later, Hannah gave birth to a son; they named the child Judah ben Simon—in honor of Simon's father, who had been called Jacob, and according to the Biblical fashion.

Everyone hailed the birth as a miracle. The people hesitated to rejoice too openly, for fear of attracting the spirits, who might try to compensate for their temporary negligence by harming the baby. Yet there was not one villager who did not awaken with a smile on his face every morning for weeks after the event; and, in the hazy obscurity of the May twilight, they tiptoed to each other's houses with bottles of sweet wine and platters of cake.

"You know," said Rabbi Eliezer, who realized that his listener's attention had begun to wander, "it has always struck me as odd, in a cheerful sort of way, that even the most downtrodden societies should rejoice so sincerely whenever another child is pushed head-first into the harshness of their world."

"Yes," nodded Casimir vaguely. Despite himself, he had been remembering his own pale, distant mother, who had spent her short life shivering like an aspen, whose death he had not learned of until she had successively missed four of her weekly visits to the nursery; even more distressing was the king's memory of his father, which, by now, consisted of only a few sensory images—the sweet, sickly odors of hair pomade and vodka, and the droning sound of long, tearful monologues on the pains of being sovereign.

"Tell me," murmured Casimir finally, "is this the case with all parents, that the desire for children drives them to stop at nothing? If babies start out their lives so loved and wanted, why are there so many unhappy men in the world?"

Rabbi Eliezer stared at him in disbelief until he realized that the boy was not joking. "I see now," said the old man softly, as if to himself, "why certain country people think the king's palace has its foundations built on whipped cream.

"King Casimir," he continued more loudly, "I am afraid that many people do not bear their children out of pure love. There are a few men who, fearing death, think they will be immortalized in a son; others, dissatisfied with their lives, are looking for an opportunity to start over again. But these things are so obvious that I need hardly go into them; you will find them out for yourself if you just live long enough, or have the good fortune to escape briefly from this—if I may say so—unreal court.

"Yet it is also true that there are men and women, like the two in my story, who develop a fierce love for their children before they are even born, and who continue to love them all the way into the other world."

"And were your parents of this sort?" asked Casimir.

Taken by surprise, Eliezer frowned for a second,

then turned to the boy with a newly open and unguarded expression. "That is something," he smiled, "which one can never definitely decide about his own case."

"Thank you," answered the King of Poland quietly. "That is mainly what I wanted to know."

Then, with the atmosphere in the room somehow indefinably lighter, the Rabbi Eliezer resumed his tale.

IV

THROUGHOUT the early months of Judah ben Simon's life, his parents awoke each day with the fear that their good fortune might prove to be a dream of the previous night. Every morning, they lay in bed warily, afraid to move until they heard the baby's first cries. Then they rushed to the crib and spent hours marveling at their son, until the scholar remembered to begin his prayers, and his wife went off to make tea. Simon Polikov had not been able to jump out of bed so effortlessly since he was a boy; Hannah was amazed that her dry, fallen breasts could, after so many years, suddenly give milk. Indeed, the old couple actually seemed to be growing younger.

In public, they did their best to keep from praising their son too immodestly; nevertheless, the neighbors had to agree that the baby was unusually beautiful. Visitors inevitably commented on the child's alert, affectionate nature; no one was surprised at how quickly he learned to walk and speak. After all, the villagers murmured approvingly, a boy conceived under such miraculous circumstances could only be expected to have an extraordinary childhood.

After a few years, however, people gradually became less free and casual in their references to the miracle, until at last they stopped mentioning it at all.

For, contrary to everyone's expectations, the boy's light hair had not grown darker. His small, sturdy frame already seemed stronger than his father's brittle skeleton, and his clear, handsome features gave him a dashing expression which neither of the Polikovs could ever have worn.

Fortunately, the townspeople were neither mean nor suspicious enough to interpret these signs as definite evidence of some complication in Judah ben Simon's paternity. They never began to gossip openly, nor even speculate about Hannah's innocence. It was just that they came to feel somewhat uncomfortable speaking reverently about the miracle which had taken place in their town.

Yet legends, as a rule, die slowly, and the story of the miracle was no exception. In fact, so well did the village remember the strange events surrounding the birth of the Polikovs' child that Judah ben Simon seemed to be the only schoolboy in the whole region who did not know of them.

It took the other children quite some time to discover Judah's ignorance, since, at first, they had no desire to taunt him about his colorful origins. Strong and skillful at all sorts of games, he was loved and respected by Jews and Poles alike; during his early years at school, he did nothing to single himself out for special praise or criticism.

Then slowly, inexplicably, the course of his life started to turn. Though obviously clever, he began to lag behind his classmates; his attention lapsed, and the fat, drowsy old rabbi who ran the Hebrew school began to nag and scold him. Like veteran prisoners, the other boys came to realize that the monotony of their terms might be safely and amusingly relieved by tormenting the convict who was most unpopular with the warden.

From then on, each time Judah ben Simon entered the Rabbi Joseph Joshua's dank front parlor after playing in the yard, the students smirked dramatically; speaking in stage whispers, they suggested that his mud-streaked appearance was perfectly appropriate for a boy who would never have been born if his mother had not wriggled her bottom in the dirt. At first, Judah knew only that he was being insulted, but did not understand precisely how, or why. Gradually, however, their constant badgering chipped away at his good nature, until one afternoon, maddened with fury, he confronted his former friends and threatened to beat them, one by one, unless they explained the meaning of their sly allusions.

As they stared at Judah's powerful fists, the schoolboys felt no overwhelming urge to fight—particularly when they knew that the battle might be simply and elegantly won by telling the plain truth. Giggling and snickering, they presented him with a somewhat exaggerated version of his mother's attempt to fool the spirits; only the few shreds of tact which they had inherited from their parents prevented them from impugning Hannah Polikov's honor before her son.

The subject was never mentioned in the classroom again. Somewhat remorsefully, the students realized that Judah would not soon forget the private history lesson they had given him that afternoon, and decided to leave him in peace; this noble resolution proved surprisingly easy to keep, for Judah ben Simon had stopped coming to school.

Each morning, he left his parents' house just as before, but instead of taking the road to the rabbi's home, slipped off through the muddy, garbage-filled back alleys; he did not stop running until he reached a sweet, pleasantly shaded grove in the forest—a spot not far from the site where Hannah's mock-burial had taken place.

There, day after day, he sat and thought, carefully rehearsing what the others had told him, trying to imagine the way it had really been. Closing his eyes, he could almost see his mother stuffing herself into the small, shoddy crate, struggling to reduce her ample body into a solid cube of flesh. He saw the mourners winking broadly at each other as they humored the old couple's pathetic folly. And, each time he pictured Simon Polikov jerking his skinny yellow shanks up and down in an effort to escape a bunch of drunken soldiers, Judah found himself shouting out loud to drive the image from his mind.

Although he was only eleven years old, Judah ben Simon felt that his childhood had been stolen from him. Regardless of what *he* thought, however, the Rabbi Joseph Joshua firmly believed that childhood was a span of time which lasted until the precise moment when the sun set on the evening of a boy's thirteenth birthday. Therefore, he paid no attention to Judah's desire to be left alone. Even though the old man had no particular wish to see his most immature and unruly student again, he felt compelled by a sense of duty to waddle across town and inform the Polikovs that they might just as well be throwing their good tuition money down the privy.

When Judah ben Simon came home for dinner on the evening after the rabbi's visit, his father did not ask him the usual questions about what he had learned in school that day. The house was totally silent, except for the sound of the ladle rattling unsteadily against the tureen as Hannah portioned out the soup. At last, when the blessings had been said, Judah looked up from his plate and saw tears in Simon's eyes.

"For the first time," said the old man quietly, "I am not sorry that my parents are dead."

"And why is that?" asked the boy, who knew exactly what was coming, although he had never met his grandparents.

"Because if they were still alive," the scholar answered, "they would die now of shame. It is very hard for me to believe that my own child would purposely keep himself away from books, away from all the beautiful things that have ever been thought and written down, and go out into the wilderness where there is nothing to see but magpies chewing worms."

Judah could not meet his father's stare. "What good will books do me?" he mumbled, concentrating on his hands as he attempted to scratch the soft dirt from beneath his fingernails.

"What good will they do you?" mocked Simon angrily. "They can make you wise, they can make you happy, they can bring you as close to heaven as it is possible for a living man to come; they can help you lead a life which will not look pitiful in God's sight. Is that good enough for you, or do you want something better?"

Judah ben Simon struggled to remain silent; but, despite himself, he was being carried along by his great desire to confront them with their own secret. "Will they make me so wise," he whispered tentatively, "that I will not make a fool of myself in front of the entire village when I am an old man? Will they make me learned enough to keep a woman from lying down in the dirt for no reason, smart enough to stand and defend myself against a gang of harmless mercenaries firing bullets into the air?"

Simon and Hannah looked at each other with amazement and reproach. They cursed themselves for all the fine scruples which had kept them from telling

(45)

their son the truth, lest he be damaged by the pride of being singled out by God; they regretted their unrealistic attempt to raise him in ignorance of the circumstances of his birth.

"Is that what put all those ideas about school into your head?" asked Hannah softly, when she could no longer stand the silence.

"Yes," answered the boy quickly, rushing to get the words out before he began to cry. "And another one of the ideas in my head is the notion that I can learn more by studying the animals and trees of the forest— which, at least, are *real*—than by reading books which try to make me believe in miracles which never happened, and spirits which never existed."

Then, with the tears of the argument still wet on his face, Judah ben Simon ran from his father's house. From that night on, he began to pass more and more of his time in the forest.

Naturally, the old scholar and his wife were disappointed and alarmed; eventually, however, they found a perfect means of weathering the crisis. First, they devised an explanation for the neighbors: their son was becoming a naturalist, which, as everyone knew, had always been considered a respectable pursuit for scholars. They boasted about Judah's notebooks, his sketches, his collection of wildflowers, and the hours he spent following deer tracks through the deep snow. They marveled at the fact that he had learned to walk so softly that the shyest animals would let him observe their most intimate habits. In fact, as Simon often said, the boy already knew more about the flora and fauna of the area than he himself knew about the holy word.

So genuine did their show of calm acceptance seem that Simon and Hannah almost came to believe in it themselves. They kept their son well-supplied with paper, inks, and pens, asked kindly about his progress, and never nagged or scolded him. But the fact was that most of their tranquillity rested on their conviction that there were many points left in Judah's life at which he might still change into a normal human being.

One of these expected crises was his thirteenth birthday; it came and went, apparently unnoticed by the boy himself.

Another was marriage.

Even before Judah ben Simon was fourteen years old, his parents had gone for a full discussion of the particulars with the village matchmaker. The broker was a stocky man with flowing white hair; he drank his tea very black, smoked huge cigars, and had the ability to change the tone of his laugh from a boom of unbelievable vulgarity to the most delicate, discreet, and confidential little chuckle. Expressing himself in a long series of ribald jokes, he assured the worried parents that such a highly respected scholar-father was a mark in Judah's favor, and that, unless things had changed radically since his day, no daughter would ever let her parents refuse such a strikingly handsome fellow.

No one mentioned the fact that Judah did not attend school.

As it happened, the matchmaker was right. There were many Jewish families in town who shared the Polikovs' faith that marriage could bring a boy to his senses—particularly such an attractive boy, from such a good family. And so, the invitations to tea began arriving at the scholar's house.

On the days specified in these carefully lettered notes, Simon dutifully trekked through the muddy woods to find his son and persuade him to come back. Realizing how few demands were made on him, the boy always agreed readily, and they stopped at home just long enough for Hannah to dry her tears and push a basin of soapy water towards her son.

In the modest, uncomfortable, rarely used front parlors of the town's middle class, the scenario always played itself out in the same way.

Half-suffocated by their constricting Sabbath finery, the parents of the prospective brides invariably looked at the unkempt boy with concern and dismay, until they remembered how much honor they would gain by showing their neighbors that they could afford to marry virtue instead of money. Their daughters, on the other hand, needed only one look at the tall, blond, handsome boy in order to be thoroughly convinced. Immediately, they began to fumble with the ruffles on their prematurely ample bosoms, and to vow that they would never allow their fathers to let this one slip by.

(48)

Naturally, the poor scholar and his wife had very little in common with the merchants and cornbrokers, so that the conversation over the tea often faltered. But, after a few of these visits, Simon and Hannah came to understand the strict conventions which governed these seemingly casual talks, and began to grow more relaxed.

It was really quite simple: every subject, no matter how innocent and irrelevant, inevitably made the proud parents recall one of their daughter's sterling qualities.

Thus, the fact that the weather had turned chill reminded them that their girl could brew the best samovar of gingered tea in all of Poland. A warming in the air made them smack their lips in anticipation of the preserves she would soon be putting up for winter. If the price of grain had gone up that week, their child could still bake the lightest and most economical rye bread in the world. And the current upheavals in the kingdom of Prussia would by no means stop her from attending to her household duties, for it was well known that she could sweep the floorboards so clean that a man might eat from them without the slightest hesitation.

On and on the parents went, listing virtue after virtue, praising and applauding their daughter's superiority, stopping occasionally to apologize for the fact that their honesty was temporarily winning out over their natural modesty. All this time, the would-be brides kept their heads lowered, bowed down partially by shyness and partially by the weight of their ribbons and ringlets, until at last they nodded, satisfied that their characters had been accurately and fairly represented.

The Polikovs smiled politely, but hardly spoke. They had no idea what to say about their son, except to assure their hosts that naturalists would soon be taking their proper place among the great scholars of the world. But, when the conversation had finally passed beyond resuscitation, Judah ben Simon would sometimes speak for himself.

"Your daughter is certainly a talented, beautiful woman," he would say, his brown eyes glinting merrily. "But tell me: does she know how to build an open fire in the woodlands without setting the countryside aflame? And, when the snow is on the ground and there is nothing else to eat, do you think she will be able to catch, cook, and skin a wild squirrel?"

The flustered parents remarked somewhat haughtily that their daughters would not cook *anything* prohibited by the dietary laws, and hastily went on to reiterate the specifications of the dowry. Still, try as they might, none of them could conceal the fact that something outrageous and irremediable had occurred. For, at these formal interviews, the boy was expected to appear as bashful as the girl. Even if he should be a garrulous type and have something to say for himself, who had ever heard of bringing a subject like the skinning of filthy squirrels into the terms of a marriage contract?

Needless to say, none of the proposed weddings took place. The matchmaker tried to comfort Hannah by reminding her how long it had taken her own dear husband to appreciate the joys of wedlock, and advised the Polikovs to contact him again in thirty years.

Eventually, Simon and Hannah gave up almost all hope. They no longer felt sure that they would live to see their son married, nor that they would ever succeed in reclaiming him from the forest, where he had begun to spend every night. "After all," smiled the scholar, "it does seem unlikely that a boy who lies down on top of a million flowers should give them all up for the body of one woman."

Still, the Polikovs continued to love their son, who, despite his pride and obstinacy, remained as gentle and good-humored as he had been as a child. Judah ben Simon returned their affection, but the shame and pain he had felt on hearing the story of his conception had not diminished. Indeed, his hatred of their superstitiousness was intensified by his love for studying and classifying the calm, predictable order of the forest. And both these passions grew steadily more powerful until the spring of his twentieth year.

"In other words," broke in King Casimir, "you are telling me that, because Judah refused all the matches his parents proposed, he lived out his life an unmarried man, without the companionship of a good woman, or the love of children to comfort him in his age?" The king's voice had grown tense and high-pitched, and his fair, smooth forehead was wrinkled with concentration and concern.

"I mean no such thing," replied Eliezer patiently. "If you will only calm yourself, I will explain more clearly."

But the boy's outburst had disrupted his thoughts, so that he was forced to wait several minutes before beginning again.

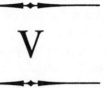

V

I T W A S a warm May morning," continued the Rabbi Eliezer. "The scholar's house smelled of freshly cut flowers, honey, and toasted almonds. Hannah Polikov was just beginning to prepare a cake for her son's twentieth birthday, when a knock on the door made her lose count of how many eggs she had broken into the batter. Glad that her husband had returned from the temple, she brushed off her hands, and raced towards the front of the house.

But, when the door opened, Hannah's smile of welcome cracked and fell from her lips; almost unconsciously, she wriggled her shoulders until she felt the protective cat's-tooth amulet bounce between her heavy breasts.

Standing on the threshold was a young woman, completely unlike anyone who had ever passed through the village. Tall, thin, delicately built, she carried herself with a graceful dignity which the local matrons would certainly have criticized as a sign of stuck-up notions. She was dressed in a purple wool shawl and a simple, bright green linen gown, which, despite the stains and creases of a long journey, still showed the fine quality that marked her as a city-dweller. Yet not even in the great city of Cracow had Hannah seen such a beautiful face, such flawless skin, such cleanly modeled features—"

"And tell me," interrupted the King of Poland, for whom certain images held special resonance, "did not this woman have firm, full, yet fragile lips, the color of red raspberries at the peak of their season?"

"Thank you for reminding me," smiled Eliezer. "Yes, she did indeed have a lovely mouth, though I am afraid that summer raspberries might have seemed a bit dull in comparison. Obviously, however, none of these traits would in themselves have made Hannah Polikov reach inside her blouse to check again for the amulet, were it not for a few other details which I have neglected to mention:

The young woman had a wild, unruly, waist-length mane of carrot-colored hair, which gleamed in the sunlight like a veil of fire.

From certain angles, her face appeared to have an exotic, foreign, almost gypsy cast.

And, when the stranger finally raised her heavy lids, the old woman suddenly perceived that her right eye was an incandescent sapphire blue, and her left a brilliant, emerald green.

These features offered Hannah Polikov conclusive proof that she was in the presence of a witch. Immediately, reason warned her to keep silent; she knew that any conversation with spirits was a trap which imprisoned one in their spell. Yet instinct forced her to speak, for, to Hannah, death itself seemed less fearsome than the shame of appearing inhospitable.

"Probably you have come to the wrong house," she stammered. "But what can I do for you?"

"I am looking for Judah ben Simon," the girl replied pleasantly.

"A plague on it," sighed Hannah, speaking rapidly now in an attempt to suppress her growing anxiety. "I should have known that my good luck would not last forever. I suppose there's no use trying to make you think I am dead again, the same trick never works twice. I must say, though, that it has taken you a long time to catch up with me; and I am grateful for all the years between now and the day I first managed to escape from your wicked surveillance."

"What in the world are you talking about?" asked the astonished young woman.

"Are you not one of the demonesses who tried to prevent me from conceiving a child?" cried Hannah shrilly.

"No," replied the stranger. "I most certainly am not —though I have often been called a witch by kind women like yourself, by people with so much faith in their God that they automatically interpret anything slightly odd as the work of the Devil."

"Is that so?" murmured Hannah, raising one eyebrow suspiciously. "Well, if you are not an avenging spirit, what do you want with my son?"

"With any luck," smiled the girl, "Judah ben Simon and I are going to be married."

"Oh my God," whimpered the old woman, hugging herself and rocking back and forth, "Oh my God. I have heard of this before, of the merciless succubi who marry human boys, drive them crazy with passion, then suck out their life's blood through the kisses of love."

For a few moments, Hannah trembled convulsively, then instantaneously grew calm. "Ah," she sighed, "if God's will demands that I have a demoness for a daughter-in-law, I guess I can bear it. At any rate, there's no use standing out here and talking philosophy. Why not come inside and sit down?"

The truth was that this invitation owed less to Hannah's kindness and pious resignation than to her sudden recollection of the fact that fresh eggs were reputed to be a particularly potent charm against spirits. "Just one look at a newly opened yolk," she could almost hear her mother saying, "and even Beelzebub himself will go shrieking up the chimney like a singed cat."

Hannah watched expectantly as the visitor sat down beside the flour-covered table; for good measure, the old woman cracked another egg into the bowl. But, instead of recoiling in horror, her guest only smiled. "It is good to be inside a home again," she said.

The implications of this seemed obvious to the scholar's wife: either her mother had been misinformed, or else the girl was not a demon at all. Now the ladies of Hannah's family had always been famous for the accuracy of their supernatural information; therefore, the old woman decided to give the stranger the benefit of the doubt, and, as compassion gradually cleared her vision, she noticed that the girl looked tired and worn.

"What is your name, and where do you come from?" she asked, more kindly than before.

"Rachel Anna," answered the other. "And I have just arrived from Cracow."

"Cracow!" cried Hannah. "I myself traveled to Cracow just before my son was born, to seek the counsel of that great wise man Judah the Pious."

"Oh yes," nodded Rachel Anna. "I have seen him many times in passing."

"I can hardly believe it!" gasped the old woman. "I can hardly believe that you too have seen him with your own eyes! Describe him to me, remind me what he looks like!"

Briefly, Rachel Anna spoke of the sage's striking appearance, his powerful grace, the eyes which seemed to gleam and crackle like summer lightning. All this time, Hannah Polikov kept her arms crossed across her breast, as if to contain in her heart that one moment when greatness has passed so near; finally, shaking her head as if to dislodge a dream, she interrupted.

"I am sorry for having been so impolite," she said.

(57)

"It is clear to me now that no evil witch could have survived within a mile-radius of that holy saint."

"It is quite all right," replied the girl. "You are by no means the first person to confuse my eyes with those of a demoness."

"I am sure," smiled Hannah. "But listen: even if you were an angel of paradise, it would still be out of the question for you to marry Judah ben Simon."

"Why?" asked Rachel Anna. "Rumor has it that you have been trying to find him a suitable wife for years, and that he has stubbornly refused each of the brides you proposed."

"Listen," pleaded the old woman. "Those were all girls who have been acquainted with my son since childhood, who would know, so to speak, exactly what they were getting into. But for you, this marriage would be like shooting blind into a crowd of men—aiming, for all you know, at a liar, a wife-beater, or a drunkard. Besides, what would people think? It is not really customary in these parts for a young lady to come out in her own behalf, without relatives to speak for her."

"It is not customary anywhere," said the girl. "And as for Judah ben Simon being a stranger, everything I have heard of him has convinced me that he is just the husband I am seeking. Anyway, it does not seem that you are being quite truthful—what are your real objections to the marriage?"

Hannah Polikov remained silent, reluctant to say that Rachel Anna did not at all appear the sort of woman who would tame her son's wild habits.

(58)

"Well," smiled Rachel Anna at last, "if you will not be honest, I will, and tell you this: not only is this marriage going to take place, not only will I win your son's love, but some day I will also gain yours. And now, I would be grateful if you would tell me where to find Judah ben Simon, for I do not wish to feed the idle curiosity of your neighbors by embarking on a public search."

Aware that she had no choice, Hannah Polikov sank limply into a chair and began to describe that part of the forest where her son stayed. So bewildered that she hardly noticed when Rachel Anna left the house, the old woman felt her head spinning as she tried to decide what to do, and how to explain the situation to Simon.

After a while, however, she recalled the rude manner in which she had first greeted Rachel Anna, and her face flushed with an odd mixture of embarrassment and hope. "Obviously," she told herself, "a woman who is always mistaken for a witch cannot remain ordinary for very long. And perhaps this singular girl will be able to influence our son in some unpredictably positive way."

This thought cheered her so much that, an hour later, she was able to present her husband with a sensible and by no means gloomy version of the morning's events.

But, later that day, as she straightened up the house for the evening meal, something in the general disorder of the kitchen caught her eye, and made a spark of doubt flicker across her mind:

There, on the floury surface of the table, where the girl had rested her left hand, were the sharp, unmistakable imprints of six fingers.

"I thought you were going to talk about a perfect beauty," broke in Casimir, his face clouded by disappointment.

"I am sorry," apologized Eliezer, "but the truth is more important. Anyway, you must admit that an extra digit is not nearly so terrible a deformity as a missing arm or a crooked spine. And indeed, just as Hannah Polikov was clucking in dismay beside her kitchen table, Judah ben Simon was calmly commiserating with the girl over the amount of superstitious nonsense to which her sixth finger had exposed her.

In the beginning, it had not seemed that Rachel Anna and Judah ben Simon would ever be holding such a civil conversation. For that morning Judah had been completing a painstaking sketch of a blue jay when his model was startled into flight by the sound of footsteps crashing through the brush. He wheeled around, saw the girl running towards him, and scowled with angry surprise; throughout his years in the forest, no one but his father and a few curious village boys had ever dared disturb his work.

"What are you doing here?" he shouted, his voice crackling with hostility.

"Making noise," laughed Rachel Anna. Then, closer, she stopped and stared at the young man who towered over her like the giant elms which surrounded them; she stood motionless, looking at his brown eyes, his generous mouth, his reddish-gold beard which flowed in waves down his broad chest, and she struggled to retain the composure which had never before threatened to desert her. "The truth is," she said finally, forcing up a small chuckle which died immediately at the back of her throat, "the truth is that I have heard a great deal about a man named Judah ben Simon, and I have come to see for myself."

"And what are all these wonders you have heard about me?" sneered Judah.

"I have heard that you already know more about the forest than the animals who can find their way through it in the dark. I have heard that you are becoming a great scientist who will someday be able to explain why the salmon swim upstream and die, and why the pine trees can laugh at their naked neighbors all through the winter. And," she added with a smile, "I have heard that you have blond hair."

"You have heard some exaggerations," replied the young man, pleased despite himself, "but no outright lies. And now that you have satisfied your curiosity, you can go back home."

"On the contrary," answered Rachel Anna. "Now I am less satisfied than ever, for all these things have only strengthened my desire to become your wife."

Suddenly, it was Judah's turn to stare, as he tried to understand why a complete stranger would come all the way out into the wilderness just to ridicule him.

* * *

"King Casimir," said the rabbi, "I would like you to stretch your memory until you can recall the time when you were younger, and still slightly uncomfortable in the presence of beautiful women."

"I will try," replied the boy grandly, wrinkling his forehead and puffing out his chest.

"Thank you," smiled Eliezer. "For perhaps you will be able to understand all the jumbled emotions which spun through my hero's mind, and perhaps you will not condemn him too harshly for the ungentlemanly way in which he received Rachel Anna's proposal. For it is unpleasant, but necessary, for me to admit that he snarled like a bulldog, hunched his shoulders, and asked the lovely young woman why in the world he should want to marry her.

"Because," smiled Rachel Anna calmly, "I am more obstinate than any woman you have ever met. And more beautiful."

Startled into seeing her fiery hair and jewel-like eyes as if for the first time, Judah ben Simon grew even more uneasy. "I have seen prettier women," he mumbled defensively, thinking of the boyhood hours he had spent speculating about the anatomy and love habits of a flirtatious, dowdy village washerwoman. "And the town is full of high-spirited girls," he added, remembering the bashful merchants' daughters whom, during those interminable afternoon teas, he had imagined lying in his bed, as foreign and repulsive to him as the carcasses of dead cows. Suddenly, he realized that this strange girl was speaking the truth, and confusion weakened his knees.

"Well," he muttered, "I can see that, having no intermediaries to speak for you, you have already begun singing your own praises. Then tell me: can you embroider pillowcases with so much skill that a man might mistake them for trappings from the temple altar? Tell me: can you brew a steaming samovar of sweet coffee with cardamoms? And can you polish a silver spoon so brightly that I might look into it and see my entire past and future?"

"I can do none of those things," answered the girl.

"Then if you cannot perform these simple household chores," persisted Judah ben Simon sarcastically, "how do you expect to learn all the complicated duties which might prove necessary for the wife of a woodsman?"

"I am not an idiot," snapped Rachel Anna. "Do you really think that I could not have learned to brew coffee if I had ever so desired? And I assure you, the minute I put my mind to building an open fire or making a mattress from pine needles, I will soon be doing these things better than you yourself."

Now the idea of a pine-needle bed had never occurred to Judah ben Simon, and the thought of it softened his heart. "So," he laughed, "I can see that I have got myself a nasty one. But, just for my personal information, I would like to know where in this country they allow a young lady to pass through her teens without knowing any of the domestic arts?"

"I come from the city of Cracow," replied the girl.

"So my reputation has reached all the way to Cracow?" asked Judah warily.

"Oh yes," nodded Rachel Anna. "Indeed, I first heard your name in connection with the great rabbinical court of that beloved saint Judah the Pious. All the sages there are fascinated by the reports which have reached them concerning your knowledge of the forest, for they truly believe that such a scholar may one day help them unravel the knots and intricacies of God's mysterious pattern."

"Then you can go straight back," hissed Judah ben Simon furiously, "and tell them that I already know God's plan, which has ordained that the so-called wise men of Cracow be exiled to the slimiest pits of hell."

And, before the astounded young woman could say another word, Judah ben Simon had turned his back and stalked off into the forest. He picked up his pens and brushes, and tried to work, but found it so hard to concentrate that, later in the afternoon, he headed slowly back towards the elm grove, telling himself all the while that he was only looking for the blue jay he had been sketching earlier.

Rachel Anna was sitting on the ground with her back propped against a tree, so that her orange hair fanned out against the rough bark; her purple shawl lay beside her, thrown carelessly on the grass. Hearing his footsteps, she raised her head and smiled; but, when he began to speak in the same angry tone, her expression turned to a look of wonder, as she marveled that his stubbornness was even greater than the rumors had led her to believe.

"I forgot to ask you," he muttered, "whether Judah the Pious also mentioned that brilliant piece of advice which he gave my family twenty years ago."

"No," answered Rachel Anna. "But your mother spoke of it this morning."

"Then you can surely understand my position," sighed Judah, sinking down onto the grass, exhausted by the battles he had fought with himself that day. "You can see why I wish to avoid all contact with superstitious, religious people, why I have come out here to bury my shame in the logical order of the forest. And you must realize that I could never pass my days with a woman—even such a beautiful woman— who has been to the court of Judah the Pious, and become the handmaiden of the world's greatest impostor."

In the fading sunlight, Rachel Anna looked back at him, too surprised to blush at the compliment. "I have also witnessed public executions," she said. "Does that mean I am a famous murderess? Listen, Judah ben Simon: having glimpsed the sage with my own eyes, I cannot deny that he is an amazing man. But, aside from that, I swear to you that my experience with superstition has been much more painful than yours. For it is likely that you were honored as a blessed miracle-child by your neighbors, while I have been scorned as a witch and a demoness all my life."

"Because of your eyes?" asked Judah.

"Because of my eyes," she nodded. "But also because of something else." Then slowly, cautiously, Rachel Anna raised her left hand, displaying the trump card which, she had always known, would someday help her win one game. And that was how Rachel Anna's sixth finger came to be discussed in the forest.

"And was he not disgusted by this?" cried the young King of Poland.

"Not in the least," grinned Eliezer. "In fact, he was so comforted by their common perspective on religion that he soon let himself be charmed into the web which Rachel Anna was spinning around them with her glittering conversation. Together, they talked of life in Cracow, and of all the things which Judah had learned in the forest. They spoke honestly and openly, bravely revealing all the secrets which they had always kept to themselves, though Rachel Anna seemed somewhat reluctant to dwell on the subject of her past.

"It is an old story," she smiled. "My father tried to marry me to an old man, whose body was as foul-smelling as his riches. I would not want to bore you with the details. But someday you will overhear me telling it all to our children, for I would not want them to think that their mother materialized out of nowhere."

"Let us not have any talk of children, or marriage, or even true love," laughed Judah, "lest our life be complicated by foolish expectations and constraints.

We should live together as friends and companions, coming no closer than that until we have as much faith in each other as we do in the sturdiness of that enormous elm."

"Agreed," said Rachel Anna, who felt so strictly bound by this bargain that, the very same night, she did not hesitate for a moment to creep beneath Judah ben Simon's blanket.

"And were they good at this business of love-making?" inquired King Casimir, who had been waiting for this part all along, and was hoping to obtain certain mysterious and precious bits of information.

"Very good," smiled the rabbi, then grew suddenly serious. "King Casimir," he said, "it has just occurred to me that there is nothing in the world more poetic, more romantic, more full of possibility than a love story of this sort, a love story which one virgin would not blush to tell another. On the other hand, there is nothing more preposterous."

"Why?" asked the boy bashfully, unable to meet Eliezer's eyes. "I do not see why a romantic love story cannot be just as believable and true-to-life as the most common anecdote. For surely you are not one of those who claim that love is merely a procession of shrewish women, grinning lechers, and cuckolded old men."

"Of course not," protested the rabbi. "But I am glad to see that you possess such a wise, comprehensive understanding of the nature of love."

"It is only a matter of experience," replied Casimir proudly. "I have been around, you know. I have learned that the onset of love is much like the terrible melancholy which creeps over one's whole body on a warm spring evening, and that the height of passion is something akin to the shivers which follow a cooling bath on a hot summer's day."

"Indeed," murmured Eliezer thoughtfully, staring at the boy in amazement. "King Casimir," he said, after a short pause, "there are many audiences which would make me quite uneasy at this turn in my narrative. But you have so reassured me that I no longer have any qualms about dealing with the delicate matter of love in your presence. Now, I must ask you to help me along, and together we will construct the story of Judah ben Simon's love. For we may be the only two men left in the world who might still believe it."

VI

"NEEDLESS TO SAY," smiled Eliezer, resuming his tale, "neither Judah ben Simon nor Rachel Anna wasted a moment of their first night together thinking of their neighbors in town; yet there were many villagers who, having once glimpsed Rachel Anna, dreamed of the beautiful young couple all night long. By the next morning, they had turned their dreams into a legend, which changed and grew as it spread through the countryside. In telling this tale, the young girls always emphasized the tenderness of Judah ben Simon's passion, while the married women seemed more concerned with his perfect fidelity; naturally, the scholars most enjoyed finding historical precedents for the idyllic romance, and began referring to the pair as 'the new Adam and Eve.' And there was one facet of the legend which inspired even the most sophisticated country bucks with a certain awe:

It was said that the handsome couple gave in to the urgings of love everywhere, even in the most unexpected and uncomfortable regions of the forest.

Oddly enough, this rumor owed its existence to the village children, who had come home from outings in the woods imitating the mysterious cries, murmurs and giggles which they had heard filtering through the screens of ferns and flowers. Their parents, many of whom had never uttered such noises themselves, still understood immediately what these sounds signified; nevertheless, they scolded their offspring for having wandered so near the child-eating woodland trolls that they had overheard their digestive grumbles, and forbade them to revisit the forest.

"And tell me," interrupted King Casimir slyly, "did these innocent children also happen to *see* anything in the places from which the noises came?"

"Possibly," shrugged Eliezer.

"For example?" persisted the king, driven to such boldness by his fear that the rabbi might otherwise overlook such essential matters.

"That, I suppose, would have depended on the season," replied the old man patiently. "In summer, they might have spotted the couple rolling through the sweet green meadows, or on the riverbanks, slippery with mud. In autumn, they may have seen them making love in heaps of fallen leaves; in winter, on the frozen crust of twelve-foot snow drifts."

"Twelve-foot snow drifts!" repeated the boy incredulously.

"Winters are stormy in those parts," said the rabbi.

"Amazing," murmured Casimir, who could barely stand to leave the palace during the colder months. "Such passion is truly amazing."

"Not necessarily," answered the old man sensibly. "After all, I must remind you that generations of children have been conceived in every season, long before the canopied bed and the silken sheet were ever invented. But, frankly, what *I* find amazing is the life which Judah ben Simon and Rachel Anna led in between these moments of passion. For, as I heard this story, the lovers never quarreled, or exchanged an impatient word, never grew tired or bored in each other's company—not even when the January blizzards kept them imprisoned in their tiny wooden shelter for weeks at a time. Soon, they learned to share the work which Judah had begun, and to order their lives so that they had no needs which the forest could not satisfy; they received nothing from the town, except for the few pennies and honey cakes which Judah ben Simon brought back from his parents' home.

By unspoken agreement, Judah always paid these infrequent visits alone. For as soon as the Polikovs had realized that Rachel Anna would never mold their son into a proper householder, they had lost all desire to hear her name. Still, they were invariably overjoyed to see their son, and to discover that the redheaded woman was not making him moody, sickly, or despondent.

Their neighbors, however, were not so easily contented; instead, they burned with righteous indignation when, two years after Rachel Anna's arrival, their children reported that the trolls were still giggling and panting in the underbrush. At last the burghers' wives managed to pressure the mayor into issuing an emergency edict, ordering the lovers to wed at once; for marriage was the only weapon which the villagers thought powerful enough to stamp out such unbridled passion.

Of course, such edicts were quite rare in a region where half the Christian marriages were based on informal agreements, and where none of the Jewish weddings had ever been recorded by the state; yet Judah ben Simon and Rachel Anna complied readily, indifferently. And so it happened that their wedding day came to replace the birth of Christ and the first day of Creation as the date from which the villagers measured the passing years.

"My father," sighed the Rabbi Eliezer dreamily, "was there to see it with his own eyes. It was, as he told me, one of those chilly, misty March days, when all the sadness of a lifetime seems to hover just outside the window. At precisely four in the afternoon, Judah ben Simon and Rachel Anna appeared out of the dense fog at the edge of town, and began to walk slowly down the main street. Families rushed from their houses to watch them; the children grinned, babies gaped, their parents smiled wistfully. For, in this town, where bridal garments were tailored sensibly, to be used eventually as shrouds, no one had ever seen such a couple before—not even, if you will excuse my saying so, King Casimir, when the royal party passed through, and the king and queen themselves peered briefly from the windows of their painted carriage.

Rachel Anna was dressed in the same bright green gown she had brought from Cracow; but now, it was decorated with ropes of violet crocuses, white daffodils, and golden forsythia. Dozens of live, blue-green iridescent scarabs were fastened in her orange hair; on top of her head was a lacy veil, woven from spiderwebs, which caught the moisture of the air in pearls, and hung down almost to her bright emerald-and-sapphire eyes. Judah ben Simon was clothed more simply, in a loose-fitting suit stitched together from soft, russet furs and honey-brown skins. With his saffron hair and wheat-colored complexion, Judah ben Simon reminded the merchants of their spice houses, and made the peasants remember their finest harvests.

Stringing behind the couple like tacks drawn to a magnet, the villagers followed them to the rabbi's door, then pressed inside, crowding the dank parlor so thickly that the startled schoolboys were forced to leap from their benches and press their backs against the wall to keep from being smothered. No one who could possibly squeeze a few inches of space for himself remained outside; even the Muslim carpetmaker stuck his head in the door, though he had always told his children that one whiff of air from a Jewish home could poison an entire flock of sheep.

Under express orders from the mayor, the rabbi

was easily convinced that Rachel Anna came from a fine, Jewish family, and that the union would not pollute old bloodlines. Of course, Judah's former schoolmaster had never entertained so many strangers before, and, in his excitement, accidentally omitted certain essential prayers from the ceremony, so that the service lasted barely two minutes. Then, he grasped the bride's shoulder, made a few references to her husband's youthful incompetence in the classroom, and sent the happy couple on their way.

The crowd burst out onto the street like sparks from a firecracker; there, they discovered that the sun had come out. Certainly, that is nothing unusual, the sun breaking through the clouds at the end of a March day. But when men are looking for a sign of heavenly benediction, almost anything will do. A cry of wonder went up from the crowd, and people smiled at the sky, praising God at the top of their lungs.

Who knows how celebrations begin? An old man drapes his arm around the shoulders of a friend, a young girl squeals with delight, someone whistles the opening bars of a polka. At any rate, a full-blown carnival was soon barreling through the town, pausing only to cheer the newlyweds as they slipped back into the woods; then, the procession doubled back through the sidestreets, engulfing everyone—the shopkeepers, the moneylenders, the clerks, gravediggers, and even the pinched-looking mayor, who could not help congratulating himself on the great political success of his new edict. Jugs of strawberry wine were passed from hand to hand; there were stacks of blinis, plum preserves, clotted cream. Snare drums kept up a steady dance rhythm, while fiddlers and piccolo players, vying to outdo each other in the sweetness of their melodies, played on past midnight. Neighbors forgot their quarrels, strangers linked arms and danced, enemies kissed.

Though the townspeople celebrated dozens of festivals each year, everyone agreed that there had never been such merrymaking before. Perhaps it was the beauty of the bridal couple which lightened their hearts; perhaps it was the coming of spring. Perhaps it was the absence of the couple's parents, whose presence at weddings always served to remind the revelers that their joy was emptying someone's wallet; for Simon and Hannah Polikov remained in their home all that day and night, with the curtains drawn tight.

By the next morning, however, the groggy villagers were more inclined to regard their nighttime gaiety as the product of a black magic enchantment. Yet, no matter how painfully their heads throbbed, no matter how fervently they repented their recklessness, they could not quite forget how happy they had been, nor could they keep from wondering if they would ever be so happy again. Thus, the day of Judah ben Simon's wedding came to be associated in the townspeople's minds with a bittersweet nostalgia which disturbed and dissatisfied them like the memory of a first crush. No one was surprised when a plague of broken engagements infected the town, and, years later, many would remember this period as the time when their parents first began sleeping in separate beds.

Aside from its devastating impact on village morale, the wedding accomplished nothing; despite the mayor's assurances, the lovers' shamelessness was never tamed by the humdrum rituals of married life. Rather, their passion grew constantly stronger, and might well have sustained them through a lifetime of uninterrupted contentment, were it not for the succession of jolts and tremors which undermined the foundations of their marriage.

"Wait," cried Casimir, his forehead wrinkling with concern. "I have scarcely had a quiet moment in which to enjoy your hero's happiness, and already you are telling me of his troubles."

"King Casimir," smiled Eliezer, "if I had a week to pass in your delightful company, I would cheerfully list all the small pleasures and tendernesses which brightened the couple's life together. But times of great peace are notoriously uneventful, and such niceties would add little to my story. Rather, you will simply have to accept my word about the quality of their happiness, and listen while I describe the beginnings of their sorrow."

One bright July afternoon, as Rachel Anna raised her face to the sunlight, Judah ben Simon suddenly noticed a pale scar, faded and flattened by the years, arching all the way across his wife's graceful neck.

"What is this?" he asked, running one finger along its jagged length. "A souvenir of some past duel?"

"Yes," laughed Rachel Anna. "Exactly. When I was three years old, I provoked a neighbor's boy into attacking me with a kitchen knife. I almost died; and even when I recovered, I could not speak for six months. But the odd thing was that the boy who injured me was also struck dumb, and did not recover his voice until weeks after mine returned."

"So you were a witch even then," teased Judah ben Simon.

"Be careful," smiled his wife. "For I dimly remember a remark like that sparking our childish fight in the first place." Then, laughing happily, she stretched out one arm and pushed her husband backwards, until the discussion ended in the dense, dark quiet of the forest floor.

But it did not end there for Judah ben Simon. Rather, it was continued in his daydreams, in which he repeatedly imagined the gleaming knife, the gaping wound, the two children tearing at each other's throats; and it went on in his nightmares, in which he saw crowds of redheaded little girls lying near death, drowning in quicksand, falling from the sky like rain. "For some odd reason," he told Rachel Anna, after he had failed to add a single word to his notebook for several days, "I am finding it difficult to concentrate."

Yet the reason was not really so odd at all: he had begun to realize that Rachel Anna was mortal.

Now the fact of death was nothing new for someone who had lived a dozen years in the wilderness, who had dissected carcasses, reassembled skeletons, and dessicated skulls; nor was it surprising to a naturalist who could predict the approximate life expectancy of a dragonfly, a dandelion, and a man like himself. But, until he had seen the scar, it had simply never occurred to him that his wife's life was as brittle as a length of bone, and subject to the same unchangeable laws which governed all living things.

For the first time, Judah began cautioning Rachel Anna about wandering too near the marshes, scrambling too quickly up the rocky hillsides, and failing to watch out for the poisonous snakes which nested beneath stones. Her disregard of these warnings only made it harder for him to work, for he was always listening tensely to make sure her footsteps followed closely behind his. Finally, even their lovemaking became for him a fearsome ritual, in which he was conscious of nothing but the light, quick beating of her heart.

Nor was he able to share his worry with Rachel Anna, since he did not wish to infect her with his fear. Unable to extract the truth from him, she finally interpreted his constant brooding as a temporary sadness of the blood brought on by the humidity, and waited for it to pass.

Suddenly, the Rabbi Eliezer jerked his spindly body to the edge of the throne and leaned forward. "Excuse me, King Casimir," he said, "but I have completely forgotten to ask your views on this delicate subject of death."

"I am quite resigned to it," sighed Casimir majestically.

"A healthy attitude," nodded Eliezer. "I only wanted to make sure that you were not one of those unfortunate people who make the entire journey to hell and back each time the matter is mentioned."

"I am not nearly so suggestible," said the king. "But still, I can understand Judah ben Simon's position; for if I had such a beautiful woman, I would also worry about losing her."

"Ah," murmured Eliezer. "Another soul lost in the Garden of Earthly Delights. But that is another matter entirely. As for now, I am quite pleased that you find it so easy to empathize with my hero, for perhaps you will be better able to understand the complex ways in which Judah's fears were to influence his actions during the rest of that summer."

"One night, early in August, Rachel Anna started suddenly from a deep, dreamless sleep. She sat bolt upright, her body tense and wary; then she began to sigh and toss about in a manner intended to wake her husband.

Judah ben Simon opened one eye and rolled over, murmuring the soothing, meaningless nonsense syllables which had always been sufficient to comfort his wife after a bad dream; but, this time, she was not so easily calmed. "Listen!" she whispered, her voice shaking with fright.

From the close, hot darkness near their shelter came the frantic, insistent shrieks of a terrified woman.

Judah ben Simon laughed. "It is nothing," he said. "You must be a very sound sleeper not to have heard those noises before. For that is the voice of an old admirer of mine, a lone wildcat who has come to visit me summer nights since my first year in the forest. By now, I am familiar with the most intimate details of her personal life; she is unmarried, childless, with a special taste for brown field mice. But I have never actually seen her, for, like many older ladies, she prefers to visit young men on the darkest nights, when the ravages of time are more likely to go unnoticed."

"Now you are making me feel like the jealous wife," said Rachel Anna, nestling comfortably against her husband's chest. Yet, as soon as she felt his regular breathing, and knew that she and the wildcat were alone together in the dark, all her uneasiness returned. Throughout the night, she stayed awake, trying to understand how a crying animal could terrify her so badly, telling herself that she was merely experiencing one of those strange, sudden nighttime fears which vanish with the first sign of dawn.

The next morning, Rachel Anna was still afraid. All day long, anxiety nibbled at the pit of her stomach, and, by nightfall, seemed to have bitten clear through: the cat had begun screaming again. Curled up in Judah's arms, Rachel Anna tossed, shivered, and wept.

Night after night, the wildcat returned, despite the flares which the couple burned outside their shelter, despite the burrs and thistles they scattered on the ground; each night, the shrieks seemed to grow wilder and more shrill.

"What is it that scares you?" whispered Judah ben Simon. "Is it the noise itself, or the darkness, or some frightening memory from your childhood?"

"I don't know," answered Rachel Anna. "I have never been afraid of anything before."

"And this terror," he persisted. "What is it like?"

"I cannot describe it," she replied, and began to tremble again.

Staring out the window at the blazing fire, Judah ben Simon decided that his wife had contracted his fear for her like an attack of plague. Assuming all responsibility, he watched guiltily as she grew steadily paler, more nervous and unhappy, until, one rainy morning, he looked at her face and saw the same brittle, redheaded skeleton which had grinned in his worst nightmares.

It was then that Judah ben Simon decided to poison the cat.

Until that time, Judah had never killed an animal, except when faced with starvation in the dead of winter; even the pelts for his wedding suit had been gathered from carrion. But now, convinced that his wife's life was at stake, he set to work brewing deadly mushrooms and berries into a colorless liquid, into which he dipped small minnows caught from the river as bait.

(81)

But, when it became apparent that instinct was protecting the wildcat against these natural poisons, Judah resolved to go into town and purchase some of the precious arsenic which generations of villagers had used against the rats invading their homes.

At eleven in the morning on a muggy August day, Judah ben Simon strode purposefully into the village. The town was quiet; the shutters were drawn against the heat, and the streets were deserted. Indeed, the only figure to be seen along the entire length of the main road was that of a stranger, leaning against the doorway of the apothecary shop. He was a large-boned man, with long, matted black hair and a beard streaked with red and gray. His ice-blue eyes had a wild, almost maniacal look; his skin was wrinkled, rough, and weatherbeaten. Had the foreigner not been dressed as a mountebank, in a velvet cloak embroidered with alchemical symbols and hung with bells, Judah would surely have taken him for a traveling holy man, one of the rootless mystics whom one occasionally encountered wandering towards the East.

Judah ben Simon looked at him curiously, nodded, and walked inside the store. Behind the counter was the apothecary's scrawny wife, the most pessimistic woman in the town. "Judah ben Simon," she intoned mournfully, "welcome to my shop. Tell me, has your marriage gone sour yet, as my tea leaves predicted on the day of your wedding?"

"No," muttered the young man coldly.

"Well, give it time," shrugged the woman. "What

can I do for you?"

"I would like a penny's worth of arsenic," said Judah.

"I knew it!" she cried, and ran off towards the back room in which the poisons were locked. Judah paid her with a coin he had received from his parents, picked up the parcel, and left. Then, just as he stepped out the door, someone grabbed roughly at the arm of his jacket; without looking around, Judah knew it was the stranger he had noticed before.

"Excuse my boldness," croaked the man hoarsely, "but I could not help overhearing your conversation, and learning that you are the same Judah ben Simon of whom I heard so much during my last visit to Cracow. I never expected to have the good fortune of exchanging a word with you, though it has often occurred to me that we might have much in common. For I am Jeremiah Vinograd, the famous herbalist and healer, something of a naturalist in my own right; we are, you might say, brothers of the trade. And in my travels I have met certain individuals and learned certain things which, I imagine, might be of interest to you."

Drawing Judah ben Simon away from the apothecary's open door, Jeremiah Vinograd talked without stopping for half an hour. Then, with a crazy laugh and a slap on the back, the mountebank sent the young man on his way.

Fascinated and upset by what the charlatan had told him, Judah walked slowly back through the town; just beyond the last house, he stopped short and headed back in the direction of his parents' home.

Inside the house, it was damp and dark. Simon Polikov was alone, huddled over the kitchen table, trying to read; he was eighty years old, nearly blind, and looked to Judah like a frail, grotesque dwarf. Simon looked up. "Hello," he said. "Your mother's gone to the next village to buy wool."

"At her age?" murmured Judah.

"She is not so old," frowned Simon. "How are you?"

"Fine," replied Judah.

A long silence fell, during which Simon peered intently at his son; suddenly, he recalled that this was the first time they had been alone together for more than ten years, and that there were certain questions which he had never been able to ask in front of Hannah.

"Tell me," he blurted out. "Did you really leave the school because of all those things that happened before you were born?"

"I was tired of school long before I heard about them," Judah answered quietly. "You yourself must remember how my attention kept straying out the window whenever I tried to assist you with the morning prayers."

"I remember," sighed Simon. "But all this love for studying the forest, did *that* come from finding out about the miracle?"

"No," replied his son. "The idea of doing research came to me suddenly, in the course of that first argument, as an excuse for myself, so you would not think I was just being lazy. But after that I set out to make the lie true, and began to study the plants and animals until my love for them became real."

"I see," said Simon.

"But my life *did* change when I learned about that so-called miracle, for I began to hate religion for having made a fool of you. Now I am older, I no longer brood about it, but it has left me with a powerful distrust for all superstition. And I still shudder each time I imagine that senseless mockery of a burial."

"If it is any comfort," whispered the old man, "I myself never had much faith in that miracle. Your birth was nothing but a lucky coincidence, that's all."

"Of course," agreed his son. "Yet *she* believed in it, and you indulged her foolishness. That is what I find difficult to forgive."

"Of course," nodded Simon, somewhat irritably. "I understand completely. But, unless your science discovers some way of changing the past, I cannot see any point in our discussing this. And now, since we are agreed, suppose we change the subject. Let me ask you: how is your wife?"

"Very well," answered Judah, feeling a slight pang of uneasiness. "I am on my way to her now." Then, during the silence which followed, he realized that there was nothing left to say; walking to the center of the room, he kissed the top of his father's head. "Good-by," he murmured, staring hard at the old man. "And say good-by to Mama for me." A moment later, Judah ran from his parents' house, fighting back tears, just as he had done so many years before.

"Good-by," sighed Simon Polikov, watching his son depart.

VII

"At five o'clock that evening," continued the Rabbi Eliezer, "Judah ben Simon accidentally encountered Jeremiah Vinograd once again. Preoccupied by the conversation he had just had with Rachel Anna, the young man would never have noticed the mountebank, had he not spotted his brilliant scarlet turban gleaming on top of a dry, sandy rise, beside the north-south road. Judah turned and climbed the barren hill until he stood directly above the herbalist, who was sitting cross-legged on the ground.

Jeremiah Vinograd remained staring straight ahead, lost in a deep trance. His back was perfectly straight, motionless; his hands rested quietly in his lap. All his energy seemed concentrated in his skinny toes, which were sticking out from the hem of his brown velvet robe and wriggling spasmodically in the dirt.

"Listen," hissed Judah ben Simon. "I could not persuade my wife to come with me, no matter how many times I told her what you said. I could understand her reluctance to go. She has been ill lately, plagued with insomnia, constantly exhausted; but still, her stubbornness so enraged me that I left our house in a fury. And I have decided to go alone."

"Ah," croaked Jeremiah Vinograd, emerging from his meditation. "Only this afternoon, you were positive that she would follow you to the furthest corners of the earth."

"I was wrong," replied the young man tensely.

"Perhaps it is for the best," mused the mountebank. "After all, it is said that the old fellow was once a great heartbreaker."

At this, Judah ben Simon raised one eyebrow and began to pester Jeremiah Vinograd with a series of eager questions; but the charlatan had fallen back into his stupor, and did not answer. After a few moments, Judah sighed. He returned to the road, hailed a passing ox-cart, and, six weeks later, arrived in the city of Danzig.

"Danzig!" cried King Casimir, whose memory of that town was permanently blighted by the dysentery he had contracted there as an eight-year-old prince touring his father's kingdom. "Are you telling me that this ruthless villain left his beautiful wife to the mercy of the wild beasts just to visit Danzig? Are you saying that this so-called scientist abandoned the fragrant wild thyme and parsley to study the stinking sewer lichen of Danzig?"

(88)

"No, I am not," replied Eliezer calmly. "And, in the hope that my hero will soon regain the sympathy which you felt for him just a moment ago, I will ignore the terms you use to describe him. No, King Casimir, Judah ben Simon did not remain in Danzig. How could he have stayed there, when he perceived the city as a raging battle in which the enemy surrounded him, hurled speeding carriages at him, threw buckets down at his head, rolled chickens and small children beneath his feet like cannonballs? Indeed, he struggled through the crowded alleys as quickly as possible, and, still following Jeremiah Vinograd's vague directions, left the city through the western gate.

Then, for the first time since the start of his journey, Judah ben Simon's heart ached with regret. He cursed the day he had left Rachel Anna, and the stupidity which had made him take the word of a crazy mountebank, who had sent him to seek his heart's desire in a region as empty and unpromising as the fields of the moon.

For the path which Judah followed across the bleak, sandy landscape seemed to lead nowhere. Snaking through the scrubby hills, it twisted so often, turned back on itself so unnecessarily, and branched into so many blind forks that it appeared to have been built to satisfy someone's peculiar whim, rather than to take a traveler to his destination. Seven miles from Danzig, the path ended at the base of a deserted, desolate ridge.

Judah ben Simon sat down on a mound of earth,

which crumbled beneath him, leaving him on the ground. At first, he felt only despair, but soon grew strangely elated as he began to imagine revenging himself on Jeremiah Vinograd, and returning to Rachel Anna. Smiling to himself, he could almost hear the questions she would ask about the Polish landscape, the streets of Danzig, and the rugged coast; resolving to see the ocean just once before going home, he stood up and headed into the sharp, briny wind.

Suddenly, halfway up a small hill, Judah ben Simon stopped. There, not far from where he stood, was an enormous mansion, perched on a steep cliff overhanging the sea. The house was executed in the classical style, to look something like Judah imagined the Parthenon. But the rambling wings and side buildings had so fractured the pure symmetry of the Greek model that the sculptured chariots seemed to follow each other aimlessly along the frieze, stumbling around the numerous corners, seeking some lost starting point. And the white marble columns and stone façade had obviously been defeated by the Baltic cold; they were chipped, weatherbeaten, overgrown with white lichen.

In many ways, this house resembled the mansion which Jeremiah Vinograd had described. But it was not until Judah looked up to see the astrolabes and sextants mounted on the flat roof that his knees almost buckled with excitement and relief. Immediately, he began to scramble up the gentler slope of the dune, struggling against the fine sand which slid back beneath his feet.

After almost half an hour, he reached the top of the

incline, and his heart leapt once again. For, surrounding the house was a spacious garden, landscaped without any shaded benches or granite sculpture, without any regard for comfort or beauty. Rather, the plot had clearly been intended as a sort of arboretum; the plants were spaced far apart in meticulously neat rows, and small, carefully lettered tags had been attached to each sapling.

This garden filled Judah ben Simon with so much pleasure that he scarcely noticed the fact that everything in it was dead. Grinning radiantly, he stepped over the grass which had been parched brown by the salt wind, past the shriveled vines which leaned limply against the trellises. And his smile grew even brighter when the bronze door, on which the Three Graces danced woodenly through the thick patina, swung open at his touch.

Judah walked briskly through the long corridors, passing in and out of the spacious rooms which were furnished with narrow wooden beds, straight-backed chairs, and cluttered worktables. "A student dormitory," the young man told himself happily. "An ascetic palace of the intellect." But gradually, as his eyes grew accustomed to the dim light, Judah began to feel the vague, aching discomfort which was to remain forever linked in his mind with that mansion near Danzig.

"King Casimir," murmured the Rabbi Eliezer, leaning back in the throne and surveying the mirrored walls around him, "I can think of no better setting than your lovely palace in which to describe that house. For here, surrounded by so many glittering reflections of ourselves, we should have no trouble understanding how an architect may come to discover all his plans dominated by a single motif.

Now the designer of that structure had suffered from just such an obsession; his taste, however, ran not to mirrors, but, rather, to the sort of illusionist murals which have since become quite the rage. No doubt you have seen them in your travels, King Casimir, those flat surfaces which are disguised to give the appearance of boundless three-dimensional space, of rolling sheep meadows, cloud-dusted heavens, and sublime mountain vistas.

Such paintings covered every wall and ceiling of the great house through which Judah ben Simon moved; as he went from room to room, he found himself leaving the misty moors of Britain for the crowded bazaars of the Levant, the starry vaults of paradise for the blazing pits of hell. At last, somewhat dizzy, standing on the threshold of a room surrounded by panoramic views of the centaurs' grove, he came upon a group of men.

"I sincerely doubt," mused the rabbi, "whether you have ever experienced the emotions which affected Judah ben Simon at that moment. For I simply cannot imagine a scene in which the King of Poland arrives to find his presence unexpected, unwelcome, positively ignored. Be thankful, Your Majesty, that you will never be able to comprehend the shame which overcame the young man when the ten scientists inside the room raised their heads, took one look at the newcomer, and clearly felt no need to honor him with a second glance. Without a word, they resumed their work, returned to the vials boiling over the open fireplace and to the thick ledgers half-filled with their cramped, even scripts.

"Is this the home of Dr. Boris Silentius?" the young man blurted out, fighting against his nervousness and embarrassment.

The scientists exchanged significant, slightly irritated glances, then turned to a thin man near the window, whose bald, bullet-shaped head was bowed low over an enormous book bound in red velvet.

Judah ran over to the man, and, pressing both palms on his desk, leaned close to him. "So you are Dr. Silentius," he cried eagerly. "You are the one who studied with the great Carl Gustavus Linnaeus, the one who traveled the world, applying his system to the white tigers of Bengal and the black orchids of the Amazon?"

"I am not Dr. Silentius," answered the bald man gravely. "I am merely Dr. Twersky, his student."

Mortified by his mistake, Judah wheeled around, seeking to find the master and beg his pardon; he peered at each scientist in turn, until Dr. Twersky winced with annoyance and spoke again.

"Dr. Silentius," he pronounced in a sepulchral tone, "has not left his room since February, when he was stricken with an attack of the tragic wasting disease which he contracted during his last visit to the tropics."

The young man failed to react to this for several minutes; then, his whole body suddenly became charged with tension and disappointment. Trembling violently, he was forced to press his fist against his mouth to keep from screaming. "So I have come for nothing," he muttered, his voice thick with suppressed tears.

The scientists, many of whom had never seen such raw emotion before, were thrown into confusion; squirming in their seats, they looked beseechingly at Dr. Twersky.

"Calm yourself," he said at last. "You have not come for nothing. You may stay here, at that empty desk, watching our research, listening to our conclusions, learning what you can. For surely you have not yet reached such a high level of advancement that only Silentius himself can help you?"

"Of course not," answered Judah ben Simon. "Of course not," he grinned, delighted by the generosity of the doctor's invitation. "I would be grateful for anything you could tell me, and for any fragment of your wisdom I might gain."

He hurried to the empty chair, and, for almost two years, left it only to eat the coarse oat porridge on which the scientists subsisted and to sleep four hours each night on a hard plank bed. There, he listened to the others with so much concentration that his mind had neither the time nor the energy to wander back to

Rachel Anna or his home. Scribbling as fast as he could, he strained to hear every word of their lengthy discussions on the subject of gorillas, Venus flytraps, armadillos, red-eyed salmon, and grizzly bears. He wrote down every statistic derived from the bubbling vials and rooftop astrolabes, transcribed and underlined every reference read aloud from the journals of Dr. Silentius, which were gathered in the velvet-covered volume on Dr. Twersky's desk.

Aside from these occasional citations, Dr. Boris Silentius was never mentioned; indeed, the only sign of his presence in the mansion came at six o'clock every evening, when one of the elder scientists carried a bowl of porridge down the hall which led to the invalid's room at the back of the house. Judah ben Simon first understood the meaning of this ritual a few days after his arrival, and inquired solicitously and somewhat curiously after the doctor's health; but he was rebuffed and silenced by the distant, impatient stares of his colleagues.

These detached glances were to set the tone for Judah's relations with the other scientists. They considered him an observer, an outsider, and were not particularly interested in his name, his religion, or his ten years in the forest. In a moment of lightheartedness, they nicknamed him "the enthusiast" because of the tears of joy which had come into his eyes when he had first heard them speak of the giant blue whales of the South Seas. They were serious, hard-working men, who conscientiously avoided all distractions.

Judah, on the other hand, could not help noticing certain things about his fellow workers. He soon understood that Dr. Twersky had been appointed their leader because he was the only one with any talent for practical organization. He saw that the fat, smooth-skinned mathematician on his left winced each time there was a mention of blood, though he had apparently been born into a long line of eminent surgeons. He learned that the withered old scholar to his right had ended his fifty-year career as an alchemist by being tarred, feathered, and driven from his home after having suggested that gold might never be refined from the baser metals. And he discovered that the bearded chemist who tended the beakers was a secret mystic, who awoke each dawn in the bed nearest Judah's, crying and pleading with the Holy Ghost to stop beating its wings above his head.

These observations did not at all dampen Judah's respect for the scholars, whose dazzling knowledge had made him come to revere them as gods; but, after more than twenty months, he began to notice something which reminded him that they were men:

One May morning, the scientists had fallen silent, and were struggling to comprehend the enormity of the great white-necked condor of Patagonia. "It is a gigantic bird," mused Dr. Twersky, "at least three times the size of the huge hooded crows which inhabit the woods due south of our own Cracow."

Having never participated in these discussions before, Judah ben Simon was extremely reluctant to draw attention to himself; yet, despite the apprehension which sapped all the strength from his body, he felt compelled to speak. "Wait," he whispered softly, "I myself have seen the hooded crows which live in the South, and they are quite small, not much larger than the magpie."

The scientists turned to face him, and a shocked, accusing silence fell over the room. "Well," muttered Dr. Twersky sarcastically, "it would seem that our young enthusiast has already learned so much during his short stay here that he now knows more than his teachers. But perhaps you will still accept the authority of Dr. Boris Silentius, who has written in his journal that the hooded crows of Poland are extremely large."

"I am sorry," replied Judah, bowing his head. "I did not mean to contradict."

Telling himself that the crows which had inhabited his neighborhood were probably stunted in stature, Judah attempted to forget the incident. But, during the next few weeks, he found himself taking a more active part in the discussions, and subtly trying to maneuver them towards the subject of the Polish woods. He grew restless, dissatisfied, without knowing quite why; until at last, on a hot summer night, lying on his unyielding wooden bed, he finally admitted the reason for his mounting uneasiness:

He had begun to realize that Dr. Twersky and his associates knew nothing about science.

Unwilling to accept this possibility, Judah jumped

(97)

out of bed and ran to his notebooks. But there, on page after page, was the damning evidence, the names of animals which had never lived in Poland, of plants which had never grown in the southern forests. The same creatures he had studied for ten years were unrecognizable in the scientists' descriptions of their color, size, and habits; the mushrooms he had eaten all his life were classified as deadly poisons.

"Perhaps," thought Judah desperately, "they are merely misinformed about their own land. Such things have been known to happen. Perhaps their research is better than their command of natural history."

But, when he had frantically added and re-added the calculations which had been drawn from the vials and sextants, he realized that the figures did not total, and suddenly recalled the brown, withered garden outside the house. By the time Judah ben Simon joined the others for breakfast, he even caught himself wondering whether such fantastic beasts as the gryphon, the sphynx, the garuda, and the hippopotamus had ever really existed.

"King Casimir," said the rabbi, "there are some men for whom disillusionment is far worse than illness, or the loss of love, or even death itself."

"I know," replied the king, in a mournful voice. "I myself have had some experience with disillusionment."

"Good," said Eliezer. "I knew that you would soon regain your sympathy for my hero. And certainly, you will now be able to understand the terrible anguish which overcame Judah ben Simon when he realized that he had wasted two years of his life among posturers and pretenders, who had spouted their half-truths and fancies, and had made him doubt the facts that he had observed with his own eyes.

It was then that the young man decided to return home. Later that night, when the others had retired, Judah ben Simon crept softly down the long hall which led to the back of the house, and, knocking once, pushed open the heavy wooden door.

The room into which he stepped was decorated and furnished more luxuriously than any other in the mansion. Its walls, however, were not covered with murals but, rather, with massive, mahogany bookshelves, filled with hand-bound volumes. One side of the room was taken up with a gigantic marble desk; elsewhere, there were comfortable leather-backed chairs, brass-hinged chests, cabinets, a red Persian carpet, and a long, lemon-colored divan beside the curtained windows.

On the divan lay Dr. Boris Silentius, a pale spider-monkey of a man—shriveled, spindly limbed, wizened. His shrunken, blotchy face was almost obscured by a pair of thick gold-rimmed glasses; four white hairs lay across the top of his head. Partially covered by a tattered bright gypsy shawl, Dr. Silentius was propped up against the arm of the couch, clutching a small volume in his long, trembling fingers.

After one look at the wasted old man, Judah comprehended the severity of his disease, and immediately understood his reluctance to go among men who had seen him in better days. Ashamed to have disturbed the sick man's rest, Judah was just about to leave the room when Dr. Silentius spoke.

"Who are you?" he whispered, in a hoarse, croaking voice.

"Judah ben Simon," answered the young man, realizing how long it had been since he had pronounced his own name. "I am sorry to have intruded this way. I would never have invaded your privacy had I not come all the way across Poland to study with you, and spent two years in your house without ever having seen your face. I only wanted to meet you once before I left."

"Think nothing of it," laughed the old man, sitting up with a surprising burst of energy. "It is delightful to have a visitor; I entertain so rarely these days. And I suppose you were sent to my home by one of your professors at the university?"

"No," murmured Judah uncomfortably. "I was referred to you by a shifty old peddler named Jeremiah Vinograd."

"Jeremiah Vinograd," repeated the scholar. "Ah, yes. What can I do for you?"

Suddenly, the young man could hardly remember why he had come. "I would like you to tell me about your scientific system," he stammered after a few minutes, "about the things you have learned in your travels through the world."

"Gladly," chortled the old man, his eyes dancing crazily. "Gladly. That is just what I am here for. But it has been so long since my teaching days that I hardly know where to begin. Let me see. . . . Perhaps you would like me to relate my experiences with the white tigers of Bengal. Yes, the white tigers of Bengal.

"When I was thirty-five years old," he began, "I conceived such a powerful desire to see the albino jungle-cats that I trekked six months, hoping only for a single glimpse of them. Then one day, just after the monsoon, I spotted one, a fine female it was, padding towards me through the brush, her pink eyes gleaming in the high grass. Instinctively, I backed away, and reached for my musket. But there was no need. Much to my amazement, the cat slowed down as she approached me, licked my hand, and led me back to her lair, waiting patiently for me as I stumbled through the jungle. There, in the hollow of an overgrown hill, were four young cubs and the carcass of a fierce male. I understood at once that the tigress had been seeking a head for her family, and had been attracted to the whitest beast she had ever seen.

"I stayed among them for three weeks, observing their habits, wrestling with the cubs, stroking their mother's silky back. Eventually, I could stand it no longer, for, despite what the poets would have us believe, one quickly grows bored living among the wild beasts. Early one morning, I slipped away. But for years afterward, I was constantly afraid to turn around, lest I find the she-tiger at my heels, stalking me across the earth like a wronged woman. And that is the story of the white Bengal tigers."

A pang of uneasiness passed through Judah ben Simon. "Fascinating," he murmured. "I myself have had some experience with possessive she-cats. But tell me, what do such unnatural attachments mean?"

"Ah," sighed Dr. Silentius, ignoring his question. "I can see that you are still unsatisfied. Is it that I am being too anecdotal for you, insufficiently scientific? If so, let me apologize, and try to make amends by telling you about the black Amazonian orchids. I must admit that this particular story is somewhat personal, but, in the interests of science, I will relate it.

"On my first journey through the South American jungle, I chanced to discover an entire grove of black orchids—mysterious, velvety, and rich. I had never seen such flowers before, though I could immediately identify them as belonging to the species *Galeorchis negris*. I headed for the nearest village, to see if anything was known about this strange breed; there, I was invited to pass some time, and informed of a most interesting local legend.

"It seemed that these simple-hearted people firmly believed that each of those inky orchids corresponded to the spirit of a particular village woman; it sprouted at her birth, blossomed during the week of her marriage feast, and withered at her death. Strangely enough, this improbable myth was accepted by everyone in the settlement, including the beautiful young girl who came out of curiosity to spend a few nights in my tent. In an attempt to convince me of the fable's truth, she even took me out to the grove and pointed out the precise flower which mirrored the stages of her life.

"You can imagine how my experimental spirit rebelled against such foolishness; therefore, when I left the village out of boredom with the savages—who were really no better than the tigress at the gentle art of conversation—I plucked and carried off my mistress's orchid, just to show them that she would still go on living."

"And did she?" asked Judah.

"Who knows?" muttered the scientist distractedly, as if the young man's question were beside the point. "I assume so." He paused, obviously considering the matter for the first time. "At any rate," he continued, "these are two of my favorite stories, for, between the tigress and the jungle goddess, they seem to cast me in the role of the great heartbreaker, a part which I played only these two times in my long life. But that is a fact," he wheezed in an undertone, "which I rarely add. Now tell me, have these stories not made your long journey worthwhile?"

"I am afraid not," sighed Judah. "I am afraid that I was not seeking to hear fascinating sidelights from your travels, but, rather, to find out what you have learned of scientific truth. Excuse me for failing to make myself clear."

"My fault completely," said Dr. Silentius. "I am not

surprised. People are always correcting me for being too anecdotal in my conversational style. Now, since you want to know the truth, I will tell it to you gladly: have you heard my insanity story? For that is the truth about my ailment, you know. There is no tropical disease chewing on my nerves. I am mad, an amnesiac, given to delusions. And I will tell you the truth about how it began.

"At the end of my last voyage to the Arabian sub-continent, I was feeling profoundly depressed by the monotonous desert scenery. Reaching the coast, I eagerly accepted a boatman's offer to ferry me to an island, several miles from shore, covered by lush foliage and populated by giant lizards. The local priest accompanied me as a guide.

"When we reached the sandy shore, the boatman headed back to the mainland, promising to return that afternoon. But, as we walked inland, I realized that there were no jungles, no lizards. The island was a vast leper colony, watched over by the curate, who knew that no important European visitor would have voluntarily come out to inspect the fruit of his labors.

"I am not a squeamish man; still, you can imagine my distress. I demanded to be taken off the island. But, eager for some funds he imagined me to have, the priest insisted on catering to my 'scientific interest,' showing me the stumps, sores, and stubs of his miserable patients. Yet, even with all my investigative spirit, I could not force myself to come within ten feet of those disgusting spectacles.

"Perhaps the priest was slightly mad; even after he saw my dismay, he did not allow the ferryman to return for seven days. When I stepped into the open hull at last, I was no longer myself: my mind was just as scarred as the skin of those verminous invalids."

Suddenly, Judah perceived that all the traits which he had interpreted as symptoms of physical illness could just as well be signs of extreme age and mental derangement. "I sympathize with your bitter experience," he stammered uncomfortably, heading for the door. "And now I will leave you alone, in peace."

"My boy!" cried the scientist, leaping up with a spryness which a sick man could never have mustered. "Why are you not thanking me for sharing my wisdom with you?"

Judah paused on his way out of the room, and turned. "Because," he shrugged sorrowfully, "what you have told me is not at all related to scientific truth."

"You are quite right," sighed Dr. Silentius, sinking back onto his divan. "Nothing to do with science, nothing to do with truth. You are very perceptive, I am amazed, you have caught me at my own game. Now, I can only hope to redeem myself by including both truth and science in a single explanation. I will give you the scientific truth, Judah ben Simon. And this is it:

"My master's system looks very simple in black ink on white paper, broken down into categories and subcategories, printed in neat charts and columns. But, in the natural world, applied to reality, it begins to reveal an entire network of mazes within mazes, false turns and twisting corridors. And it was at the end of one of those dark tunnels that I lost my way, and my sanity, so that now I hardly believe them when they tell me I am the great Dr. Boris Silentius, who once studied with Linnaeus and traveled the world."

"Can you tell me what you mean about the mazes?" asked Judah ben Simon, passionately eager now for the first time.

"No," replied the scholar. "But since you are such a perceptive young man, I will reward you by showing you my prize possession, my favorite work of nature —which I found, oddly enough, not far from our own Danzig." While speaking, he kneeled over a carved wooden chest, and began to take out wrapped objects, which he uncovered and assembled carefully on the figured carpet.

"This," he said proudly, when the skeleton was fully assembled, "was the body of a beautiful young woman, the most magnificent of all nature's creations. If only it had not taken me eighty-five years to learn that."

"Thank you for showing me," nodded Judah politely.

"You are very welcome," replied Silentius grandly. "You may go on your way now, and give my regards to your mother and father."

Early the next morning, Judah ben Simon headed back towards the city of Danzig.

VIII

UNFORTUNATELY," said Eliezer hastily, before the king could interrupt, "Judah never had a chance to give Simon Polikov the scientist's regards. For, by the time the young man left Silentius's home, the grass had been growing on his father's grave for eighteen months.

"On the night of Simon Polikov's death," continued the rabbi after a brief, somewhat melancholy pause, "Hannah had awoken to find him sitting bolt upright in bed. 'Wait!' he was screaming. 'Wait! I have something to tell you!' Only after lighting the candles did she notice how his breath sprayed the air with blood, and that his face was twisted in a look of unimaginable desperation.

The memory of this expression remained before Hannah's eyes for several days, and kept her from accepting any comfort from the neighbors, who advised her to thank God for Simon's sudden and painless end. "Nothing is painless," she had snapped, and it was truer than she could have known.

For what even Hannah did not realize was this: every night, for the past eight months, Simon Polikov had dreamed the same dream; every night, he had relived each moment of his son's last visit, dwelling on each of their words, their glances, their smallest gestures. In the mornings, he had awoken in a fog of discontent. Though pleased to discover that he was not wasting the sleep of his old age by inventing romantically distorted pictures of his youth, Simon still knew that God would not be sending him such meticulously accurate dreams if not to rebuke him for having let the boy leave without a final blessing. At the evening services, the old man always prayed for a happier ending to his fantasy; he never shut his eyes without hoping to see himself place one arm around his son's shoulders and fill his ear with sweet benedictions. Indeed, so badly did Simon want this vision that, at the moment of his death, he spent all his remaining strength in a struggle against the terrible muteness of dreams, and screamed after Judah's disappearing form.

The next morning, Hannah Polikov put on her husband's overshoes and slogged through the muddy forest to fetch Judah back for the funeral. Since Simon had never remarked on the odd finality of their son's last good-by, Hannah had naturally assumed that his failure to visit them for six months represented a clear cut victory for the redheaded demoness. This idea so infuriated the old woman that, when she finally discovered the girl lying on a heap of brownish pine needles in the half-dark wooden shelter, it was all she could do to keep from throttling her.

"Where is my son?" she demanded angrily, in a tone which implied that she expected to hear nothing but lies.

Rachel Anna, who had been studying a yellow spider spin its silvery web across the ceiling, was so startled by her mother-in-law's arrival that she was unable to respond for several minutes. "In Danzig," she whispered at last.

"In Danzig!" cried Hannah suspiciously. "Swear it on your mother's soul!"

An entire range of emotions passed across Rachel Anna's face before it assumed a somewhat shakier version of the composure it had worn during her first meeting with Hannah Polikov. "On my mother's soul," she answered softly, "he has gone to Danzig to study orchids and tigers."

"Then he really was crazy after all," sighed Hannah, sinking down beside Rachel Anna on the dried-out pine needle bed. "And now there is no one but me," she groaned. "For all Simon's success in finding a son to say the memorial prayers for him, he might just as well never have married me."

"Has something happened to your husband?" asked Rachel Anna.

"All deaths are the same," answered the old woman brusquely. "There is no point talking about it. Besides, what happened to Judah ben Simon is much more important, and that is what I have come to hear."

Rachel Anna, however, had no desire to narrate the story of Judah's departure, even though she had rehearsed it so many times in her mind. She wondered if she would be able to tell it calmly, without tears; it all seemed strange to her, unreal, as if she were being ordered to relate a nightmare. Stalling for time, Rachel Anna rubbed her eyes with her thin, work-callused hands.

Hannah Polikov recoiled in horror from the sight of the sixth finger. Soon, she perceived that the reality of it was far less gruesome than she had imagined, but, by then, Rachel Anna had already noticed—and, in that one look, had suddenly remembered what it was like to deal with other people.

"Late in August," she began, her clear, defiant voice ringing through the embarrassed stillness, "Judah ben Simon met a stranger outside the apothecary shop."

"The apothecary shop," murmured Hannah, her eyes widening with concern. "Which one of you was sick?"

"Judah was only buying poison for a troublesome cat," the girl answered.

"So that is what all his fancy science has come to!" snorted the old woman. "Killing cats!"

"It never proved necessary," replied Rachel Anna coldly. "The cat disappeared by itself right after Judah ben Simon left."

"And where did you say my son went?" cried Hannah, fearing that all these new developments would surely unhinge her mind.

"I am trying to tell you," said her daughter-in-law. "Now listen: that August afternoon, when I returned from gathering herbs in the forest, I saw him pacing back and forth in front of our house, twitching like a marionette. At first, I could barely understand the words tumbling from his mouth, but, gradually, I began to comprehend that a traveling mountebank had told him something about a great naturalist living near Danzig, teaching his precious scientific truths to anyone who might care to listen.

" 'Never trust a mountebank,' I had laughed nervously, trying to make a joke of it. 'They have been known to steal the silver from old women's hair.' "

"And right you were!" interrupted Hannah.

"If only Judah ben Simon had thought so," sighed Rachel Anna. "Two hours later, he had gathered together all his clothes and pennies; then, kissing me so violently that I almost fell over backwards, he set off toward the north-south road."

"Yes," nodded her mother-in-law, not without a trace of satisfaction. "When it comes to a choice between women and work, the good man will always choose one way."

"But it was *I* who made the choice," said Rachel Anna quietly. "Judah ben Simon begged me to go with him, but I refused."

Hannah Polikov could not have been more surprised had her daughter-in-law suddenly sprouted sidelocks and a full beard. "What was the matter with you?" she asked, staring at her in awe.

"Pride and obstinacy," replied Rachel Anna. "That is the plain truth, how else can I explain it? The journey which brought me here from Cracow was so tiresome that I swore never to embark on another. And I truly believed that no scientist in the world could lure Judah ben Simon away from me. Indeed, I believed it until the moment of his departure; then, watching him leave, I wanted to run after him, to hold onto him, to call him back. But pride and obstinacy were standing at my sides like two burly Cossacks, pinning my arms behind my back, stopping my mouth, rooting my feet to the ground."

"Who ever heard of such a woman!" hissed Hannah icily, shaking her head. "Not I, surely—not I, who would cheerfully have followed Simon Polikov into the grave itself! But why am I wasting my breath; it is said that stubborn wives never repent of their natures until they are singled out to drive the Devil's mules across the sticky, steaming swamps of Gehenna!"

"I have repented enough," Rachel Anna answered weakly; but Hannah Polikov was no longer listening. For the mention of her husband's name had reminded her of her own tragedy, which she had briefly forgotten in the minor drama of her daughter-in-law's abandonment. "You have no idea," sighed the old woman after a while, "how painful it is to see only one teacup on the breakfast table when there have been two for thirty years."

In the long, strained silence which followed, the two women looked searchingly at each other, glancing away whenever their eyes met. "She seems older," thought Hannah to herself, "paler, skinnier than a chicken. Her lips may still be that same crimson color, but now there is something sad and defeated lurking about the corners of her mouth."

"Surely this must have touched the old woman's heart!" cried Casimir, whose own heart had nearly been pierced by this last image.

"So it did," nodded Eliezer, ignoring the flush of embarrassment which overcame the king immediately after his outburst. "At that moment, in fact, an odd mixture of sympathy and self-pity made the anger drain from Hannah Polikov's body like a burnt-out fever, and her gaze grew steadier and kinder.

"So what have you been doing since Judah left?" she asked at last.

"Day-dreaming," replied the girl.

"What kind of life is that for a young woman?" demanded her mother-in-law good-humoredly.

"A fairly common one, I should think," answered Rachel Anna. "Except that most young women need not find their fantasies constantly interrupted by the harsh necessities of keeping alive through a winter in the wilderness."

"The winter," said Hannah Polikov, looking distractedly around at the rotting floorboards, the tiny fireplace, and the gaping chinks in the walls and ceiling. "I had completely forgotten about the winter," she murmured, flustered by the sudden realization that her own son had left his wife alone to face the icy blizzards and the snowbound isolation. "The winters out here must be unbearable; have you ever considered moving back to town?"

"No," answered the young woman. "I doubt whether I would be welcome there, and there are many things worse than a little cold weather. But," she added with a half-teasing smile, "if you are inviting me to come live at your house, then I would be delighted, for, quite frankly, I have had more than enough solitude to last me a lifetime."

"That is not what I meant at all," Hannah burst out. Then, mortified by the blunt inhospitality of her reaction, the old woman searched her mind for justifications and excuses. "My house is a small one, you have seen it yourself," she muttered. "Even if my husband's tiny pension could support us both, there would be no place for you to sleep in comfort."

"But certainly," replied the girl calmly, "there is enough room in your home for two teacups on the breakfast table."

Hannah Polikov looked up, startled, then nodded slowly, thoughtfully, knowing there was no need to discuss the matter any further. "Gather your things," she said, "and let us go. This forest air is dampening my bones."

And so Rachel Anna came to do her dreaming in Judah ben Simon's childhood room.

In the beginning, there were many delicate adjustments to be made. Hannah Polikov fumed constantly over a set of bad habits which irritated her mainly in that they were wholly unlike those of her late husband. Day after day, she bristled at the girl's too-frequent bathing, her late rising, excessive eating, and, particularly, at the way she got underfoot whenever she attempted to help with the household chores. And this was not the worst of it. For the old woman sometimes found herself unable to remember the days when her body was full of milk, and free of pains, scabs and creases; at such moments, Hannah would fall victim to black moods and bitter fantasies, and would turn on Rachel Anna, cursing her youth, and accusing her of having bewitched Judah into traveling to Danzig for the sole purpose of stealing jewels and engaging in devilish activities.

Her daughter-in-law weathered these storms without resentment; there were other facets of her new life which troubled her more. She hated going out into the close, crowded streets, hated the sight of headless rabbits dangling in the butcher's shop, hated the triumphant village matrons and their leering husbands. Nor was it always easy for her to remain indoors. The odor of chickens boiling in a closed room nauseated her, so that often, choking from the acrid smoke of the fireplace, she had to run all the way back to the forest before she could breathe easily again. And she was so accustomed to sleeping in the open that the thin stream of air filtering in through her one narrow window made her dream of huge animals breathing on her back. Occasionally, when all of Rachel Anna's minor sorrows became gnarled into a single knot of misery, Hannah Polikov truly had reason to complain of her daughter-in-law's withdrawn and surly nature.

"Then she should have left her in the forest," interrupted the king, who had already grown impatient with the subject of bickering women.

"No," answered Eliezer, "that is not true at all. For gradually, just as Rachel Anna had predicted so many years before, the two women came to love each other."

"Surely you are using the term 'love' rather loosely," smirked the boy. "For, if the ladies of my court are any measure, it would seem that women band together only to devise new methods of entrapping innocent males."

"King Casimir," the rabbi sighed patiently, "you can see for yourself that my heroines have little in common with your court ladies. However, it *is* true that, for several months, their only bonds were the absence of their men and a common sense of having been abandoned; at first, they shared nothing but the afternoons they spent watching for signs of return—the long hours Rachel Anna passed scanning the north-south highway, while Hannah crept stealthily around the cemetery for fear of making too much noise and exasperating her husband's spirit. At the end of these solitary vigils, the two women found only each other, walking slowly home at dusk. And the gentle, word-

(116)

less understanding which characterized these chance meetings slowly laid the foundations of something deeper.

Indeed, by the time the women had lived together a few months, they were already beginning to stay up late into the nights—drinking tea, sipping homemade currant wine, giggling like schoolgirls. Rachel Anna told bawdy stories she had learned as a little girl eavesdropping on her father's business conferences; Hannah sang songs about faithless lovers which made them weep with such melancholy that neither noticed when the old woman forgot the lyrics to entire verses.

Eventually, the warmth of their friendship gave Hannah such comfort that she no longer suffered the palpitations and night sweats which had plagued her since Simon's death. Rachel Anna, too, began to smile more, and to feel a certain resigned contentment. She ceased brooding about Judah's absence, stopped attempting to bargain with God for his immediate return. But, at the back of her mind, she knew that this new tranquillity was not without its price:

Rachel Anna was gradually growing to feel less comfortable in the wilderness. By late July, she went to the woods only to attend the community Sabbath picnics, during which she watched her neighbors sitting on the sweet, shaded grass as if each green blade were a separate iron spike. Nor did she feel the slightest twinge of embarrassment, or even nostalgia, when the apothecary's wife spent these outings bemoaning the days when the forest had been a bog of moral corruption. Finally, Rachel Anna found herself sharing in the general sense of relief when the chill October wind began to make these excursions unfeasible.

Occasionally, though, after Hannah Polikov had gone to bed, Rachel Anna would lie awake in her attic room, wondering what had happened to their wooden shelter. She would run through lists of wildflowers, conjure up visions of forest animals, and try to remember just how the pine needles had felt pressing into her bare thighs. All night long, she would torture herself with memories and regrets, until she was tearing at the edge of her embroidered linen bedsheets, and cursing herself, her fate, Jeremiah Vinograd, and Judah ben Simon.

It was on a chill December night, sixteen months after her husband's departure, that Rachel Anna fell asleep in one of these moods, and dreamed a strange dream:

In her vision, she was standing before the shelter, filled with the certainty that Judah ben Simon was about to return. She felt expectant, peaceful, troubled only by a vague sense that the forest seemed somehow unfamiliar, lusher and more exotic than she had remembered it: the entire ground was evenly carpeted with emerald green moss. Curtains of apple and cherry blossoms hung down from the branches. Copper-colored foxes gleamed in the bright sunlight as they chased iridescent blue dragonflies across the fields. And snow-white peacocks strutted among the thickets, staining their feathers with the sweet juice of strawberries.

"Perhaps I am in the wrong place," she thought uneasily. Then, attracted by a muffled noise, she turned towards the elm grove and saw Judah ben Simon, sprawled naked on the ground, making love to a woman whom Rachel Anna recognized immediately as herself.

"So this is what it was like," she thought, watching them with the unquestioning curiosity of dreams. "So those are our arms, our legs, the colors of our bodies." The next moment, she was no longer observing her double, but, instead, lay half-crushed by her husband's weight, feeling the warmth of his skin against her breast and the soft, velvety moss beneath her. "Yes," she decided happily, "this is exactly what it was like."

Locked together, they embraced again and again, without stopping—not even when the world around them began to change. First, the moss cracked and slid away in sheets, until they were left lying in the soft, slippery mud of a riverbank. The leaves turned yellow, red, brown, then floated gently down from the trees. The falling leaves grew thinner, lacier, lighter, and changed into snowflakes; frost appeared on the bare branches. At last, the soft earth hardened into a brittle film of ice, which cracked beneath the lovers; they fell deeper and deeper into the snowbank, holding each other tightly, crying out in fear and passion and joy.

In the midst of that cry, Rachel Anna awoke to find herself alone in her room, drenched with sweat, although, having kicked the blankets off her bed, she lay unprotected against the fierce December cold.

*　*　*

The King of Poland took a deep breath. "I do not see why that dream was so strange," he blurted out, regretting it immediately, and deciding that the dignity of his royal position demanded greater restraint in responding to the rabbi's story.

"You are quite correct," chuckled the Rabbi Eliezer. "Indeed, it is odd that Rachel Anna never had one like it before, especially during the eight months she had spent alone in the forest doing nothing but dreaming of Judah ben Simon. But I am afraid that you have misinterpreted me, King Casimir. For, when I referred to her dream as 'strange,' I was speaking not of its content, but, rather, of its consequences:

"Not long after that cold December night, Rachel Anna knew beyond a doubt that she was pregnant."

IX

N ow *that* is strange!" exclaimed King Casimir. "And what is even stranger," he continued, as his common sense gradually won out over his desire to think highly of the lovely young heroine, "is that you consider me naïve enough to believe yet another of your miracle stories. Unless I am mistaken, you have been speaking of a breathtaking woman, all alone in a village full of healthy men. And you honestly expect me to believe that she conceived a child in a dream?!"

"I suppose not," sighed the rabbi, obviously disappointed, "though your warmhearted response to the lovers' perfect happiness had led me to conclude that you were more of an idealist. Certainly, I would hate to think that Your Majesty's intellect was tainted with even the slightest trace of the pedestrian, the unimaginative, or the mundane. On the other hand, I would be equally upset to see the King of Poland automatically accept a story which was positively ridiculed by every peasant, merchant, landowner, apprentice, holy man, and idiot in Rachel Anna's village.

"For, as soon as the girl's pregnancy became apparent, wave after wave of gossip began to sweep through the town. Every male over twelve and under fifty was suspected in turn; stage whispers, obscene gestures, petty cruelties and vicious insults were exchanged in the market place. Families turned in on themselves to root out the culprit; fathers clamped tight curfews on their sons' late hours, and were in turn forced to deliver the house keys over to their wives promptly at midnight."

"But why the great scandal?" interrupted Casimir, feigning a certain bored sophistication. "Surely this was not the first love-child ever sired among the lower classes of the neighborhood?"

"Of course not," answered Eliezer. "The district orphanage was overflowing with such infants. But none of their cringing, guilt-ridden mothers had ever been so beautiful as Rachel Anna, nor so wild and headstrong as to stubbornly insist that her baby had been fathered in a vision.

Indeed, the whole case was so singular that even Hannah Polikov could scarcely understand it. Unlike her neighbors, she knew that Rachel Anna would never have chosen a lover from the bumbling ranks of village manhood. In the beginning, therefore, she simply refused to believe that the girl might really be pregnant. "Don't jump to any conclusions," she coun-

(122)

seled her. "Take your time. All this delay is just the cold weather freezing up your system."

Not until Rachel Anna's belly began to swell did Hannah finally come to see that something very strange and significant had occurred; then, thoroughly perplexed, she embarked on a solid week of worry and deliberation. At the end of these seven troubled days, Hannah Polikov issued her final pronouncement on the subject of the girl's condition. "Now I understand," she proclaimed proudly. "It would appear that miracles run in our family."

But the old woman never understood why this remark should have upset her daughter-in-law more than all of the village matrons' jeers. Actually, there were many things which Hannah and her neighbors failed to perceive: among them was the fact that the same proud girl who could offer such a calm, definite, consistent explanation of her pregnancy was actually more bewildered by it than anyone else.

For how could she possibly comprehend an event which contradicted all her knowledge and experience? She did not believe in miracles; she could never interpret her pregnancy as an instance of God's personal intervention, of His will moving in a new and unique direction. But she also knew that women do not ordinarily conceive in visions, and that she had not slept with any man outside her dreams. She refused to admit that a wonder might have befallen her; yet, at the same time, she realized that her condition could not have been caused by the sleight-of-hand and mirror tricks

(123)

which the Biblical fathers had used to divide the oceans, tame wild beasts, and halt the sun.

"King Casimir," said Eliezer, leaning forward eagerly, as if he were about to communicate something of the greatest importance, "would you be at all astonished if your palace suddenly sprouted wings and circled three times around the sky?"

The King of Poland nodded, smiling the silly grin of a young child being teased in a manner which he considers unduly babyish.

"Then I assure you," continued Eliezer, "that all your surprise at such a case would hardly amount to a fraction of Rachel Anna's amazement. For the marvel she was witnessing seemed even more extraordinary than a flying castle, because it was taking place not in the atmosphere around her, but, rather, within her own once-familiar body. The young woman found this notion so overpowering that three months of her term elapsed before she was able to devise the small compromise which made it possible for her to deal with it: she merely expanded her concept of natural law to include one additional fact: conception may occur within the course of a vision.

Once having decided on this new precept, Rachel Anna proceeded to defend it against disbelief, slander, insult, and even the threat of outright persecution—a threat which would never have been suggested had her pregnancy not happened to coincide with the local mayoral election. For the paternity of her unborn child quickly became the one important issue in an otherwise uneventful campaign.

In speech after speech, the reform candidate traced the entire scandal back to the incumbent's decision to order the libertines lawfully wed; his worthy opponent, he claimed, had only succeeded in installing the licentious woman in their town, when he should have been working to exile her from the entire region. If *he* were in office, promised the challenger, he would personally flush the moral poison from their town by banishing both Rachel Anna and her mother-in-law under the terms of the Fraud and Heresy Act, which had last been invoked against the followers of Sabbatai Zevi.

"A law which had been forgotten for thirty years," chuckled the Rabbi Eliezer, shaking his head from side to side. "What sweeter, more nostalgic music could have fallen on the voters' ears?" Two days after the reform candidate's election, Rachel Anna was directed to leave town at once, unless she consented to recant her story and name her partner in sin.

No one really expected this to happen, least of all Hannah Polikov, who knew her daughter-in-law's stubbornness only too well. The old woman lacked the nerve to even so much as hint that the girl lie. Yet she was still more reluctant to abandon the home she had shared with Simon Polikov—afraid that all her memories might somehow remain behind and leave her with as little to look back on as a bitter old virgin. Torn by these conflicting fears, Hannah began to pass more and more time at the cemetery, placing heaps of flowers on her husband's grave and pleading with his spirit to help her, to advise her, to tell her what he would have done in her situation.

At last, one foggy March morning, she heard Simon's unmistakable, adenoidal whine piercing through the clouds and filling the air around her. "Hannah!" it called out in a familiar, loving, yet peculiarly ceremonial tone. "The whole business is very simple. If you cannot make the girl change her story, then you must make the officials withdraw their charges. You know what authorities have the power to declare a man innocent of heresy."

"Of course I do, Simon!" exclaimed the widow, slapping her forehead. "How stupid of me to have overlooked that! How selfish of me to have bothered you!"

That afternoon, still murmuring these sincere apologies, Hannah Polikov set out on her second journey to the court of Judah the Pious at Cracow.

"As you may remember," said Eliezer, pursing his lips together somewhat impishly, "I told you that Hannah's first trip to that noble city took more than six months. Perhaps, then, you may be surprised to learn that, over twenty-five years later, the old woman covered the entire distance to Cracow and back in less than four weeks. And the dissimilarities between this expedition and the last did not end there; for Hannah's return was also wholly unlike the homecoming which had taken place so long before.

This time, crowds of onlookers lined the streets, telling their children the almost-forgotten story of Ju-

(126)

dah ben Simon's birth, and watching closely to see if the widow's return from Cracow might mean the beginning of more miraculous goings-on; but as soon as they perceived that her vaguely troubled face bore none of the beatific radiance of a woman about to experience one of God's wonders, they shook their heads and went home.

This time, too, Hannah Polikov did not wait until nightfall to reveal the results of her journey, but began talking the minute she crossed the threshold of her house. "Rachel Anna!" she called. "Bring me a warm towel and some hot tea. All that walking has made my feet swell like the limbs of a corpse.

"I am no longer a young woman," she sighed, collapsing into a chair. "Here, at home, I hardly notice, but out there, on the road, every mile introduced me to another throbbing nerve and aching muscle."

"Is that why you seem so unhappy?" asked Rachel Anna solicitously, filling her mother-in-law's cup.

"Unhappy!" cried Hannah, pulling herself up straight and twisting her lips into an artificially ecstatic grin. "Who's unhappy? I haven't been so joyous since my wedding day. True, I was somewhat disappointed at not being able to see the great Judah the Pious, who had just left on a pilgrimage to Jerusalem to weep for us all at the sacred Wailing Wall. But, aside from that, my trip was a total success; the treatment I received could not have been better. As soon as I declared my case an emergency, I was granted a private audience with Reb Daniel of Warsaw, acting head of the Cracower court during the beloved sage's absence.

"The moment I saw Reb Daniel, I said to myself: 'Nobody will ever call this one a saint.' But perhaps, God forgive me, my judgment was prejudiced by the scholar's unattractive appearance, by his fat, bandy-legged body, his pock-marks, and his slightly crossed eyes. For, when he smiled merrily and rose to greet me, a second thought almost made me cast this first impression from my mind. 'Certainly,' I decided, 'this man is so wise, so just, and so reliable that I would not hesitate to entrust him with the care of my mother's soul.'

"For this reason, I felt not the slightest embarrassment in relating your story, not even when it proved necessary to add certain details which no respectable woman would ever dream of discussing with a strange man. Yet despite all my faith in Reb Daniel, my heart still began to pound when he scratched his curly, black beard and told me that he could not possibly decide my case there and then, no more than a good physician would consider diagnosing the malady of a patient he had never seen. My palpitations increased when he and all his colleagues assembled to consult the spirit of their absent master, so that I thought the blood would come bursting from my veins by the time they pronounced their verdict."

Suddenly, Hannah stopped, and, fumbling in her bodice, produced a scrap of paper from which she proceeded to read aloud:

"Because of the unusual nature of this case, in light

of its capacity to open certain special avenues of philosophical discourse, the chief wise men of Cracow hereby announce that they will transport their entire court three hundred miles, in order to investigate and pass judgment at the scene of the petitioner's home."

"When are they coming?" asked Rachel Anna listlessly.

"In two weeks," replied her mother-in-law. "And then, if you are found innocent, you will be respected, perhaps even venerated, more than any other woman in Poland." The old woman paused, but, after several moments had passed without any reaction from the girl, she began to speak again. "I can appreciate your being disappointed," she said, "that Judah the Pious will not be back in time to officiate at this session. But still, I cannot understand why you are wearing such a long face, why you are not singing and dancing in ecstasy."

"Because," answered Rachel Anna, wondering how she would ever be able to explain her dealings with the Cracower court to Judah ben Simon, "because you have forgotten to drink your tea."

The ecstasy, as it happened, was reserved for the other villagers, who went half-crazy over the imminent arrival of hundreds of sages and scholars, with nothing to do but spend their generous stipends. For this would be the first time the village had ever been honored by anyone of importance or renown; of course—and again I must beg your indulgence, King Casimir—no one counted the official visit of the king

(129)

and queen, who had not bothered to step down from their carriage. The townspeople spent their evenings making elaborate plans for their new revenues, and their days in frantic preparations designed to impress the dignitaries. Families herded their children into one room, tidied the vacant bedchambers and lofts, and hung out signs offering space to let. Merchants doubled their monthly orders to the wholesalers, greengrocers begged the farmers to speed up the spring planting, and even the Catholic innkeeper stocked up on kosher mutton.

The breakneck speed with which these arrangements were made was not in vain. Only ten days after Hannah's return, the motley caravan of the Exalted Court of Cracow appeared on the edge of town.

"King Casimir," mused the rabbi, his eyes shining, "here, in this palace of mirrors, I could never make you understand how marvelous this procession seemed to the simple-hearted citizens of Rachel Anna's village. All at once, these provincial people—who never passed up a performance by a traveling mountebank or magician, who gladly walked thirty miles for one glimpse of an albino pony—found their main street mobbed with holy men and scholars, who had come from every part of Europe, Morocco, Araby, and the Ottoman Kingdom to study with Judah the Pious. There were mystical rabbis dressed in rags and feathers, community fathers in furs and diamonds. There were black-skinned Jews with kinkly sidelocks, desert patriarchs with turbans wrapped over their skullcaps.

Behind the sages came dozens of servants, loaded down with brass-bound coffers, enameled chests, cages of exotic birds, and other necessities of travel; the bearers coughed and spat continually, pausing only to curse at the eager students in frayed black coats, who trotted at their masters' heels, terrified by the thought of missing a single word of wisdom.

Near the market place, this chaotic band was obsequiously welcomed by the village rabbi, who had been appointed town representative in the case as a result of a campaign promise. The newly elected mayor had no wish to jeopardize his budding political career through imprudent dealings with prominent Jews—who might, at any moment, be denounced as traitors by the central government. The rabbi, however, had accepted the position eagerly, more than happy for a chance to show himself before the chief scholars of Poland in a distinguished light; and his first official act had been to prohibit Hannah Polikov from coming out to greet Reb Daniel, lest the great celebrity be offended by such unholy presumption in a woman.

Thus, it was not until the first session of the assembly that Hannah was able to get a good look at the court of Judah the Pious. Seated beside Rachel Anna in the front row of the women's section, the old woman was in an ideal location to smile back over her shoulder at several kind faces she remembered from Cracow, and the fortunate few neighbors who had been able to squeeze into the narrow aisles of the synagogue. For a small crowd of local Jews was already milling around the scholars' pews, filling the air with the smells of milk, sweat, salami, and attar of roses. Mingled among them like pillars were the village Christians, standing stock-still and gaping at the temple which they had never entered before.

Suddenly, Hannah saw Reb Daniel push his way down the main aisle until he reached his seat at the center of the dais, directly in front of the ark, surrounded on both sides by a row of elders. She was relieved to discover that his round, pitted face emitted the same magnetically cheerful radiance, despite a night spent sleeping among the poorest students on the synagogue floor. She began to nod frantically at him, until he looked towards her, grinned, and rose from his chair.

Rocking back and forth on his heels, Reb Daniel led the Cracower court in chanting the prayers for wisdom and success in their venture, then spoke for the first time. "We have come here," he pronounced deliberately, in a rich, deep voice, "to decide the case of a woman who may or may not have conceived in a dream. As is our custom, we will listen to the accusations first; now, we will learn the grounds of the fraud and heresy charge from the man whom God has chosen to best serve His people in the region—Rabbi Joseph Joshua."

At this signal, the village rabbi waddled up to the dais, where he stood woodenly, with both arms stiff at his sides, in such obvious discomfort that the members of his temple—who had watched him dozing in that same spot every Sabbath—feared that he was becoming the victim of an apopleptic attack.

"It is an overwhelming honor," he began shakily, "for a humble man like myself to have the opportunity of addressing the greatest minds of the Western World. On the other hand, it is a source of unspeakable grief for me to have to use this opportunity to vilify a member of my own flock—a girl whom I myself joined beneath the bridal canopy with her poor, betrayed husband, one of my most promising students." The rabbi paused and lowered his tear-filled eyes. "But all of us know," he continued, his voice swelling theatrically, "what just one drop of sour curd can do to a gallon of fresh milk. And it is in the interest of the pure souls of my congregation that I stand before you today, to save them from the corrupting influence of this vile young woman. It is only for their sake that I denounce her.

"For how can this community not be ashamed before God when every one of its innocent babes knows the whole history of this sinful wench—how she came to our town seeking refuge from a wicked past, departed for the wilderness in order to indulge in shameful excesses with her lover, then returned to our bosom to break our hearts, to weaken the moral fiber of our families. And now, now that the fruit of her transgressions has begun to ripen, she asks us to believe that her filthy bastard child was conceived in the spotless chastity of a dream!

"Is this logical?" cried Joseph Joshua, casting his

eyes towards heaven, turning his palms upward, and shrugging dramatically. "Has such a thing ever happened before, even in the wondrous era of the Prophets? Did God ever warn us of the coming of this miracle? Can this be anything but heresy and fraud?

"Unless we answer these questions with a resounding 'No!,' I fear deeply for the future of our women. What will happen to their modesty, their honor, and their reserve when they learn that all their secret sins can be blamed on mischievous dreams? And now, gentlemen, at the risk of sounding unduly learned and esoteric, let me conclude my deposition with a quote from the wisest sage of all: 'For who can find a virtuous woman; her value is more precious than rubies.' "

The villagers' thunderous applause did not cease until long after Joseph Joshua had regained his seat. Then, a hush fell over the room as Rachel Anna went up and stood behind the lectern.

The Cracower scholars were glad that they had insisted on seeing the dreamer herself; their students could only blink in amazement, exchange sheepish grins, and lower their eyes modestly to the floor.

With quiet self-assurance, the young woman outlined the history of her life in the forest and the town, and assured the court of her sincere desire to remain there with her mother-in-law. When she had finished describing her first months in Hannah Polikov's home, a three-hour recess was called; during this time, the two women conducted several sharp-eyed sages on a tour of the dreamer's room, where the wise men failed to discover any positive evidence. Finally, that afternoon, Rachel Anna discussed the details of her dream in a private session with Reb Daniel and the chief elders.

It was from then on that the real testimony began. One by one, the holy men and scholars spoke on the nature and power of dreams. They cited the Torah and the Mishnah, the Kabala and the Apocrypha, argued over the meaning of Jacob's ladder, Pharaoh's cows, Nebuchadnezzar's four kingdoms, and Daniel's wild beasts. The antiquarians brought in examples from ancient history—Constantine's cross, Nero's swarm of ants, Xerxes' false victory, and the visions which warned Caligula, Tiberius, and Domitian of their imminent deaths. Of course, the modernists insisted on updating this discussion with the mention of more recent cases, such as that of the long-buried treasure unearthed at Tours the previous week on the basis of information received in a milkmaid's fantasy. Nor did the legal scholars forget the famous "dreaming judge" of Budapest, whose infallible verdicts depended on a night of restless sleep. And there was even some gossip about the chief rabbi of Coblenz, reportedly killed by a murderous hag who appeared only in his worst nightmares.

In the course of the hearing, every imaginable authority on the subject of dreams was quoted, debated, refuted. Some swore by the theories of Gabdorrachaman, while others preferred those of Artemidorus, Synesius of Cyrene, Theophrastus Bombastus, and even the Hindu King Milinda. There was talk of true and false visions, of divine and prodromic dreams, of symbols and contraries, of fantasies brought on by overeating, fasting, and excessive use of spirits.

These debates lasted until twelve each night, and resumed again promptly after the prayers at dawn; the clerks dutifully transcribed all that was said. Every member of the Cracower assembly had ample opportunity to speak his mind; a few beginning students, desperate for a chance to participate, even interpreted their own dreams according to the most elementary Talmudic guidelines. The entire court of Judah the Pious was growing steadily more exhilarated by its own scintillating display of wit and erudition. But gradually, as the discussion progressed, rising and falling in intensity, turning and circling back on itself, repeatedly straying from and returning to the main issue, it began to seem increasingly obvious that none of the wise men of Cracow could think of a single example, or general principle, which might explain the case of a woman impregnated in a dream.

For this reason, Reb Daniel called the session to an arbitrary halt at the end of seven days. "Enough time has gone by," he sighed wearily, interrupting an old Yemenite's discourse on the proper interpretation of visions involving date palms and vultures. "If this debate continues much longer, I am afraid that all the dreams of our coming years will seem stale and conventional, like jokes told a thousand times before. Go home now; I wish you a night of dreamless sleep. To-

(136)

morrow we will announce our verdict."

The next morning, the synagogue was again crowded with local peasants, most of whom had stopped attending the sessions out of boredom with the interminable discussions. Rachel Anna watched her neighbors file in, their faces smug and self-righteous in the expectation that they were about to hear their suspicions officially confirmed. She felt detached, casual, as if all this were part of another dream. She wanted to be found innocent, but only as a matter of principle, and because she did not want to see her mother-in-law unhappy. As far as she herself was concerned, the case had been decided the minute she walked into Judah the Pious's court; she had lost Judah ben Simon's love and respect, regardless of the verdict. Besides, during the week she had spent listening to the passionate arguments which rarely mentioned her name or her vision, she had almost forgotten that the subject they were debating had anything to do with her.

Now, with great calm, she held her mother-in-law's sweaty hand, and watched Reb Daniel rise to speak. After a few moments, she knew that the villagers had won.

"None of our learning," sighed the unusually solemn scholar, "none of our common experience, and none of our books tell us anything about a child conceived within a dream. We have no evidence to show that such a thing ever happened, or ever will."

An excited murmur raced through the synagogue,

followed by a short round of applause.

"But!" cried the chief disciple of Judah the Pious, holding up his hand, "that is a judgment on our knowledge, not on the dreamer or her dream. And all that judgment means," he continued, brightening slightly, "is that we cannot name a place or a time when such a thing happened before. Now, since we have been unable to find such an easy solution to the puzzle, perhaps it would be better to attack the problem differently: let us, for just a moment, forget about the reality and meaning of visions, their purpose, their function, their influence on our waking lives. Let us, rather, do something much simpler—interpret *this* dream, and speak of *this* dreamer."

"Here," Reb Daniel went on, "we have a woman who has imagined herself and her absent husband indulging their desires in the wilderness. The fact is that such a vision is classified by the Talmud among the Blessed and Lucky Dreams. The forest setting is a sure symbol of peace and tranquillity; the return of a traveling man always speaks of trust and fidelity; and to dream of physical love with one's mate cannot mean anything but many years of harmony and contentment for the married pair. On the basis of her dream, then, we must naturally conclude that this young woman can look forward to a lifetime of pleasures and joys.

"Now our Holy Books tell us plainly that God never sends happiness where there is no virtue; furthermore, even my beginning students could cite that section of the Mishnah in which it is categorically

(138)

stated that Lucky and Blessed Dreams are forever de-
nied to wicked sinners. All of which leads us to our
second conclusion: there is absolutely no way that
Rachel Anna could be guilty of the filthy, sluttish
crimes of which you accuse her.

"And now, just to clarify this point, I must beg permission to ask your esteemed rabbi one question.

"Tell us," inquired Reb Daniel, leaning over the dais
towards the front row, "whom you and your neighbors have found to be the natural father of this
woman's child."

The entire audience was amazed to see the anger
and determination in the scholar's eyes—which, because of their slight cast, had always worn a somewhat
whimsical and abstracted expression. Beneath their
steady gaze, the Rabbi Joseph Joshua appeared to melt
like a lump of butter. "We are still searching for the
culprit," he stammered.

"This is a very small town," sneered the acting
head of the Cracower court. "Such a treasure must
be difficult to keep buried in a village of this size—particularly when everyone is digging for it.

"Let me put it more simply," continued the chief
disciple, without removing his attention from the
rabbi. "Unless you have some actual evidence to sup-
plement your narrow-minded suspicion, there is no
way we can declare this woman guilty of fraud.
Therefore, I suggest that you allow her and her
mother-in-law to remain in your village, and, next
time, be less hasty to accuse someone of trying to stain
your spotless virtue."

As another rush of murmurs sounded through the hall, Rachel Anna smiled at Hannah Polikov. "You were right about this man's wisdom," she whispered.

"Yes," sighed the old woman. "But, compared to Judah the Pious, he is like the dimmest star beside the sun."

"As for our purposes," Reb Daniel began again, turning to the members of his court, "we are still faced with the question of whether or not a child has been conceived in a dream. And now that we have thoroughly exhausted all our knowledge and our powers of debate, we can only look at the plain facts. We see before us a woman who is obviously honest, and just as obviously pregnant. She claims she has not known a man for two years except in one dream; we have no evidence to the contrary. What can we do but take her word? After all, if everyone agrees that the chief rabbi of Coblenz's life ended in the course of a vision, why cannot the life of another be so begun? And finally, who among us can read the Pentateuch without realizing that more wondrous things than this have been known to happen in the Kingdom of God?

"I am sorry," Reb Daniel said, after a brief pause, "that we could not have arrived at this decision through brilliant turns of logic, feats of scholarship, and bursts of impassioned discussion. But, nevertheless, the judgment seems clear. Let it be written in the ledgers of the court of Judah the Pious: at this time, in this place, a woman conceived a child by her husband, who appeared to her in a dream."

(140)

For just an instant, as the verdict was pronounced, Rachel Anna had the strange sense that it had been issued a long time ago, perhaps even before the Cracower court had arrived in her village. But the impression was a fleeting one, and vanished quickly in the deafening uproar which filled the synagogue. A few townspeople, of the sort who automatically accept any official judgment, were already cheering; as in any crowd, there were many who simply enjoyed the feeling of joining in the general applause. Still seated in the front row, Rabbi Joseph Joshua was snorting angrily and tapping his foot; a few of his close associates were shouting in outrage. And the Cracower scholars only added to the chaos by standing up and calling across the room to their servants, ordering them to begin preparations for the homeward journey.

Encircled by the warm, embracing arms of Reb Daniel, the two women hugged each other and wept. The old woman blessed the chief disciple a thousand times for having made it possible for her to remain in her home. Rachel Anna thanked him too, but the truth was that her gratitude had little to do with the actual verdict. Only after the three of them were almost alone in the emptying synagogue did Rachel Anna begin to understand that all her relief and happiness stemmed from one source: Reb Daniel's interpretation of her dream, and its promise of a long, happy life for herself, her unborn child, and Judah ben Simon.

X

A<small>ND IS THAT</small> what happened?" asked the King of Poland, trying to sound delighted that the lovers' troubles had come to such a prompt and painless end. "Did Judah ben Simon return home from Danzig, claim his wife, accept his child, and settle down to a life of modest contentment?" In fact, the boy was bitterly disappointed, certain now that Eliezer's story was just another of those worthless legends about princes and princesses who must overcome the requisite obstacles in order to reign happily ever after— those fairy tales which had always infuriated Casimir, who knew the truth about kings and queens, about his father's trembling hands, and the terrible silence in his mother's wing of the palace.

"Unfortunately," replied the rabbi curtly, interrupting the boy's reverie, "that is not what happened at all. It would seem, King Casimir, that your fondness for my hero and heroine has led you to form an unduly optimistic image of their future. Or perhaps you are merely being facetious, perhaps you have decided that it is your turn to accuse me of being commonplace and unimaginative?"

"Oh, no," protested Casimir, terrified lest the old man take offense and refuse to reveal the remainder of his tale, "your story could not be more fascinating and delightful!"

"Then maybe you have let your fascination carry you away," suggested Eliezer of Rimanov. "Maybe *that* explains your unrealistic prediction. Maybe your delight has kept you from listening with enough concentration and care."

"I swear," cried the young king indignantly, "that I have been paying closer attention to your words than to anything my advisors have said in—" He stopped in mid-sentence, blushing deep scarlet, aware that he had finally overstepped the last bounds of decorum. Yet, in doing so, he had spoken the truth. For the last sections of Eliezer's narrative had made Casimir feel pliant, witless, torn between his natural romanticism and his inherent practicality, until he no longer knew which side of his personality dominated, nor by what standards he might assess and judge the old man's story. For this reason, he had been hanging on the rabbi's every word, searching frantically for some clue which might help him solve the intricate puzzle.

"I am grateful for your receptive ear," smiled Eliezer, ignoring the king's embarrassment, "I only pray that your heart may remain just as open, always ready to change your position on the possibility of impossible things, and to declare me the winner in our bargain."

"Our bargain," murmured Casimir, in the cold, abstracted tone of a wealthy lover suddenly recalling the old fear that his mistress's ardor may derive from some ulterior motive. "I had quite forgotten our bargain. Well, I will tell you, you have not made a true believer of me yet. So you had better continue with your fable."

"That is exactly my intention," replied the rabbi, and began again.

"Three weeks after Rachel Anna's child was born, Judah ben Simon returned to his village. It was a chilly September midnight; Judah had been traveling steadily for over two months, constantly pushing himself forward as if the time he saved going home would somehow make up for all the hours he had wasted at Dr. Boris Silentius's mansion. And perhaps, King Casimir," said the Rabbi Eliezer, "you will comprehend the extent of my hero's exhaustion when I tell you that the presence of a light in Hannah Polikov's window convinced him to pause for a while on his way out to find Rachel Anna in the forest.

Of course, he never doubted that Rachel Anna was still standing before the woodland shelter where he had last seen her. Being a normally self-centered young man, Judah ben Simon firmly believed that, during the two years in which he had stopped thinking of his wife and mother, their lives had also stopped, remained unchanged and static, like a play which cannot resume until its audience returns from intermission. Therefore, when he opened the door to find Hannah sitting at the kitchen table, all he could see were the new wrinkles in the old woman's face, and the two small changes which had altered the room's appearance since his last visit. He noticed the memorial candle flickering beside Simon's old armchair, and saw that all the books had been put away, piled in neat stacks, in a cupboard formerly reserved for his great-grandfather's finest prayer shawls.

All at once, Judah ben Simon understood why his mother was up alone so late at night. "How long ago did it happen?" he cried, striding across the room and pulling the old woman out of her chair in a tight embrace.

Hannah's first reaction was to thank God for having returned her son; her second was to brace both hands flat against his broad chest and push him roughly away. "You mean Simon's death?" she shouted, her voice shrill with outrage. "Your father died nineteen months ago, and, for all I know, his spirit is still floundering around in limbo for lack of a son's prayers."

"I am sorry," muttered Judah, releasing her and stepping backward. "But there was somewhere I had to go."

"Where?" cried the widow. "To Danzig, to study orchids and tigers?"

"Yes," nodded her son.

"So what now?" demanded his mother. "Can you sell those orchids in the market place? Can you ride there on the back of those tigers? Are you one step closer to making a living and supporting your poor abandoned wife than on the day I bore you?"

Judah ben Simon bowed his head and kept silent, waiting for the flush to leave his mother's cheeks, and her chest to cease heaving. "So you have seen Rachel Anna," he said quietly, when she seemed calmer.

"Rachel Anna!" screamed Hannah, rising to a new crest of fury. "How can you pronounce that unfortunate girl's name without glancing over your shoulder for the thunderbolt about to strike you down? Of course I have seen her, she has been living with me ever since your father's death. Day after day I have seen her, pining away for love, waiting for one word from you, just one word to tell her you were still alive. And now—now, after all that, you drop in her lap like manna from heaven; you expect to pick up everything exactly where you left off, to resume that crazy hand-to-mouth life in the forest, as if nothing had happened? Frankly, I will be surprised and disappointed if your woman takes you back, for even I am having trouble forgiving you—even I, your own mother, who let you suck the milk from my breasts and leave me with these two dry bags of wrinkles!"

"Is that why you are crying?" asked Judah ben Simon. "Because you cannot find it in your heart to pardon me?"

"No," replied the old woman, sinking back into the chair and burying her head in her arms. "I am crying because I cannot find it in my heart to remain angry."

Watching his mother weep, Judah realized that the moment for reconciliation had arrived. He knew how easy it would be to grasp her thin shoulders, to confess all the sorrows of his journey, to make her recall the joys of having a loving, dutiful son. But, just as he approached her bent form, Judah ben Simon heard a noise which made his heart begin to pound at the pit of his stomach.

From the attic loft, ringing out in unison with the widow's sobs, came the sharp, insistent cries of a newborn infant.

"Whose child is that?" he scowled.

"Yours, may the Lord keep it from harm," answered Hannah Polikov, so cheered by the thought of her beautiful grandchild that she was able to smile through her tears. "How could I have gone on so long without telling you, unless I assumed that everyone in Poland knew by now. But I see that you are as innocent as that babe upstairs, so I will explain.

"One night, not long after your wife came to stay with me, she dreamed of you. You know the sort of dream I mean; God forbid, a woman should discuss such things with her own son. Now listen closely: nine months later to the day, Rachel Anna gave birth to your spit and image, a fine, healthy boy, just what one would expect from the child you fathered in the course of that vision."

Too stunned to reply, Judah ben Simon struggled

to perceive the meaning which, he believed, must lie hidden beneath his mother's explanation. Again and again, he considered each of her words, as if they were elements in a code he could somehow decipher, but all his efforts only intensified his confusion, and his despair. "So," he murmured sadly, after a long time, "I sired a baby in a dream. Surely that must have been counted as something of a miracle?"

"Of course," nodded his mother brightly. "But the greatest wonder was yet to come. For, when those plodding drayhorses who call themselves our neighbors refused to believe Rachel Anna's story, the entire court of Judah the Pious traveled all the way from Cracow just to convince them that she was telling the truth."

"I see," muttered Judah, his eyes narrowing in fury, "the holy beloved saint has seen fit to play with my life once again. And indeed, it would seem that his judgment has remained admirably consistent over the years. Really, one cannot help but agree: a child born of a dream is no more improbable than an infant fathered by the filthy worms and maggots of the village graveyard."

Stung by the unexpected cruelty of her son's reply, Hannah felt all the energy drain from her body, so that she could not prevent her shoulders from sagging, nor her frame from assuming the brittle angles of a tired old woman. Searching her mind for a suitable reply, she raised her smarting eyes to see Judah climbing the ladder which led to the attic. In her agitation,

Hannah Polikov could only echo a phrase which she had often heard Simon use in reference to their child. "With all your knowledge," she called after him, "you still know nothing."

But her son was no longer listening. On every rung of the ladder, he was busily inventing another suspicion, another accusation, another method of extracting the truth from Rachel Anna. He felt quite certain that no one but his mother and the fools of Cracow could possibly believe this fable about babies conceived in visions. Briefly, he allowed himself to speculate on the identity of his wife's lover: had he been cuckolded by a gray-whiskered merchant, or by one of the young men with whom he had attended Rabbi Joseph Joshua's school?

What disturbed him most, however, was the question of why Rachel Anna had lied to the villagers—lied in a manner designed to contradict all the principles which the two of them had always held most sacred. Perhaps she had done it out of spite, in the hope that her outrageous claim would reach him in Danzig. Perhaps the months of loneliness had disturbed her reason, shaken her wits. Perhaps she has gone mad, thought Judah ben Simon, and suddenly, the memory of Dr. Boris Silentius's glittering eyes made him almost afraid to reach the attic.

Yet as soon as the young man entered his childhood room, Silentius's eyes dimmed and vanished from his mind like two fireflies extinguishing their lights. Dumbly, Judah stared at Rachel Anna, who was sitting up in bed, dandling the tiny pink infant to make it stop crying; even in the pale candlelight, he saw at once that his wife was far more beautiful than he had remembered. Her red hair, grown longer and thicker over the two years, fanned out against the pillow and down over her shoulders; the tears of anger in her blue-green eyes only made them shine more brilliantly. She was dressed in a lace-trimmed nightgown of fine, yellowing silk, which had once been the pride of Hannah's trousseau, and which—the old woman had once confessed over a third glass of wine—she had never found any reason to wear to bed with Simon Polikov.

Judah ben Simon stopped several feet from the bed; his head felt empty, dizzy, he could think of nothing to say. He and Rachel Anna stared at each other in silence until the baby ceased its yowling and permitted them to speak.

"Welcome home," she said at last, smiling uncertainly. "How was your stay in Danzig?"

"Useless," he answered grimly, "utterly useless."

"I cannot believe that," teased his wife. "By now, you must know more about the ways of nature than God himself."

"The only thing I learned," replied Judah, deadly serious, "was the importance of trusting my own judgment."

"Then I am sorry your time could not have been more profitably spent," said Rachel Anna. "I myself learned exactly the same thing, and I did not need to travel all the way to Danzig."

(150)

He knew that she was challenging him to resume the conversation he had begun downstairs, to express the same disbelief and scorn he had been heaping on his mother. But he simply could not bring himself to start so soon; his second wind had gone, and had left him with an aching desire for a few moments of peace.

"So this is your baby," he said, smiling, sitting on the edge of the bed and hesitantly running one hand over the child's head.

"Yes," she replied, relaxing slightly.

"Good strong lungs," murmured Judah ben Simon.

"Of course," Rachel Anna said pointedly, looking hard at her husband.

But still, Judah could not begin asking the obvious questions. "Tell me," he said, trying to approach the subject indirectly, "have they made it very difficult for you in this town?"

"After the departure of the Cracower court," she answered, without taking her eyes from his face, "the people were very kind. I like to think that they actually accepted the scholars' authority, and at last believed my word; but perhaps it was only the money they made during the sages' visit which sweetened their doubts. At any rate, the village women soon began besieging me with friendly advice about pregnancy and childbirth, and well-intentioned warnings about the deformed infant they feared might result in my particular case. The apothecary's wife confidently predicted that I would follow in the unfortunate path of the famous Frau Elisabeth of Bremen, who, in the space of one night, gave birth to twelve children, three dogs, two roosters, and a spotted boar."

"But none of their predictions came true?" asked Judah anxiously. "The baby is completely normal?"

"As far as I can tell," replied Rachel Anna. "But, nevertheless, everyone in town has been terrified of me since the birth."

"Why should that be?" murmured her husband, almost afraid to hear her answer.

"Because," she replied softly, "I did not make a single sound during the entire eighteen hours of my labor."

"How could you have done that?" Judah ben Simon asked in amazement.

"The answer to that is simple," said his wife. "It was not so terribly painful. After all, women have been giving birth for centuries, in places where a single cry might ruin the hunt and so starve their whole tribe. But the question of *why* I did it is far more difficult to answer. Maybe I did not want the townspeople listening to my suffering like a concert, telling each other that I was finally being punished for all my shameful pleasures. Maybe it was the fault of the village midwife, who advised me to shriek as loud as I could, telling me that tears were a woman's lot, that they would help me ease the agony.

"Yet, whatever my reason, the outcome could not have been more certain: 'Animals and witches give birth this way,' pronounced the midwife solemnly, 'not human women.' And, ever since, our neighbors have avoided the house, and have taken to saying that this innocent baby is the offspring of an enchantress and her demon lover."

As Rachel Anna spoke these last words, Judah could no longer meet her gaze; he shut his eyes, and knew that the time had come. "Rachel Anna," he whispered, "who is the father of the baby?"

"You are," she replied deliberately. "You came to me in a dream."

"Whose child is this?" repeated her husband.

"Yours and mine," she said.

"But that is impossible," he exploded. "I cannot imagine," he continued, when he had regained his self-control, "how you could have forgotten the years we lived together, and all the things we believed in. Rachel Anna"—Judah's voice took on an almost pleading tone—"listen to me: I swear that I love you still, I swear that I will forgive you for this and raise the child as if it were my own. I will not even ask you to reveal your lover's name. Just tell me the truth, tell me that you do not really subscribe to this lie, to this superstitious nonsense about fantasies and visions."

"What can I say?" sighed his wife. "I conceived this child by you and no one else, one December night, in the midst of a dream."

"But you are asking me to believe in a miracle!" the young man cried desperately.

"No," she answered, "I am asking you to believe in a scientific fact, but you are simply too close-minded, too stubborn, too narrow in your notions of science.

"Suppose you had never seen a bird, Judah ben Simon, and I told you there were large animals capable of coasting and gliding on the breeze. Certainly, you would accuse me of talking miracles, and scorn me for telling superstitious fables about things which have never happened in nature. And yet—"

"That is exactly the point," Judah broke in. "With my own eyes, I have seen wrens flying through the air. Therefore, I know that they exist. But I have never yet seen a child conceived in a dream.

"I can accept only what I know for myself, Rachel Anna; the only meaningful fact I learned at Dr. Boris Silentius's home was the etymology of the word 'science,' which comes from the ancient root meaning 'eyes.' I have seen children born from the mating of men and women, not of women and dreams. Unless you tell me that you slept with a living man, nine months ago, you are asking me to believe in a miraculous work of God."

"All right, then," snapped Rachel Anna. "Hold on tight to those unshakeable truths of yours. If you insist on thinking that the conception of our child was a miracle, then I am talking about a miracle."

"But you are lying," he shouted.

"I am telling the truth," she replied, without the slightest tremor of doubt.

Judah ben Simon rested his head in his hands. "In just a few days," he said quietly, "I could have overcome my jealousy of another man; I could have resumed living with you as happily as before my journey. But I could never adjust to sharing my life with a woman who believed in miracles. I would rather exile myself from the entire region, far away from all memories of you."

Rachel Anna said nothing as he rose from the bed and walked slowly from the room; an instant later, her voice rang out so loud that the chickens in the outer courtyard woke up and fluttered their wings.

"Wait!" she screamed, in a manner which allowed her husband no choice but to turn back. "I knew," she began, as soon as she saw his face again, "that I had married a stubborn man, but I was unaware that I had married a stubborn fool. I am disappointed, I would have expected better from you. But I cannot make up lies to keep you, not even though I know you are about to leave the house and depart from the village forever."

Rachel Anna paused for a minute, and, when she spoke again, her voice was thick with tears. "You are so obstinate," she whispered, "there is no way I could ever convince you that I am right. I can only ask you to promise me this. Swear to me, Judah ben Simon, that you will return to me immediately if you should ever see, with your own eyes, something stranger than a child conceived in a dream."

"I promise to come back with the story of my first miracle," he muttered, and left the room for the second and final time.

XI

IN THE WORDS OF Judah the Pious," said Eliezer, aware that the young king was attempting to conceal some new anxiety, " 'Speak your heart and rob the physician of his fee.' "

"All right, then," sighed Casimir at last. "What bothers me is this: I believe that I can now foresee the outcome of your narrative; and I am wondering how I can sustain my interest when I already know that Judah ben Simon must eventually encounter some great miracle and return home to seek his wife."

Rabbi Eliezer of Rimanov laughed out loud, then raised his eyes in an expression of suffering patience which the boy had last seen on the painted martyrs in his royal chapel. "Even if you are right," he said, "what then? I can assure you, there is no reason to fear boredom or disappointment. It is true that my hero will discover untold wonders as my story nears its finish—but why should that upset you? Do you think that a single one of your subjects finds his enjoyment of the Easter plays diminished by the knowledge that they must necessarily conclude in the Passion, the Resurrection, and the Life?"

The king was too stunned by Eliezer's presumption to reply.

"You see," continued the old man, interpreting his listener's silence as a sign of agreement, "it is not such a terrible thing to know the end. Indeed, I am proud of you for having perceived it so soon, and I would hate to punish your foresight and perspicacity by interrupting my narrative in the middle. Therefore, with Your Majesty's permission, I will resume my tale again.

"Soon after Judah ben Simon left his mother's house," continued the Rabbi Eliezer, "he found himself roaming the deserted streets and alleys of his village. He passed by the Rabbi Joseph Joshua's schoolroom, by the town bakery, the market, and the empty lots in which he had dug for treasure as a boy. He walked out towards the woods, then, thinking better of it, merely skirted the edges of the forest; he revisited the cemetery where his mother had been briefly interred so long ago, and where his father now lay for eternity. Judah did not cease his wandering until daybreak, when the shopkeepers who came out to open their shutters began to whisper and point at him. Then he broke into a run, and instinctively headed back towards the highway from which he had come the previous night.

Just outside of town, Judah ben Simon gazed absentmindedly towards the hill where he had last met Jeremiah Vinograd—and spotted the embroidered brown velvet cloak and the red turban. Making his way up the incline, Judah noticed the familiar matted hair and streaked beard; but this time, he saw, the mountebank seemed so alert and cheerful that his face appeared to glow with merriment in the pale dawn light.

"Hello!" shouted the herbalist, recognizing the young man at once. "Did you ever succeed in killing that wretched cat?"

"What cat?" asked the other.

"The last time I saw you," explained Jeremiah Vinograd, "you were leaving the apothecary's, where you had just bought some poison for a wildcat whose screams were annoying your wife."

Staring down into the mountebank's maniacal, ice-blue eyes, Judah ben Simon suddenly realized that he no longer wanted revenge for the years he had wasted in Danzig. "Ah, the she-cat," he sighed, so exhausted that he could not refrain from sinking to the ground beside the old man, "the poor she-cat seems to have been forgotten by everyone. At any rate," he continued, unable to resist an urge to reproach the charlatan, "I must remind you that our last conversation did not take place outside the apothecary's, but here, on this very spot, as I was on my way to visit your friend Dr. Boris Silentius."

(158)

"Oh yes," murmured Jeremiah Vinograd, tapping his forehead, "perhaps we did exchange some words about the good doctor. But I regret to say that I cannot remember meeting you here on this lovely hill. I hope you will pardon my forgetfulness; that summer was a particularly stormy time in my career, during which I was much given to brief trances and sudden fits of aphasia. But now I am completely recovered, thank you, and absolutely overjoyed to remake the acquaintance of a fellow scientist." The old man paused. "And a former student of the great Dr. Boris Silentius?" he added questioningly.

"Yes," nodded Judah, "a former student of the great Dr. Boris Silentius."

"How wonderful!" exclaimed Jeremiah Vinograd. "Since you have studied with Silentius," he said, watching to ascertain the young man's reaction, "you may be interested in an article I have in my possession, an object which may have a certain—shall we say— sentimental value for you. But before I exhibit this treasure, let me first explain the reasons why I bother to drag this souvenir of Boris Silentius around with me from town to town.

"In addition to being a man of science and a thespian," declared the mountebank proudly, pulling himself up straight and brushing some sand from the front of his robe, "I am also something of a collector and a connoisseur. But I am not at all like your typical collector: I refuse to be classed in the same league with those misguided old women who squander their leisure hours and spare pennies just to cram their cupboards full of glass bottles, bits of old lace, tea cosies, balalaikas, and butterflies.

"No," he continued, "*I* am a collector of collections —or, to be more exact, a pilferer of selected objects from the collections of others, from the most meticulously assembled and catalogued collections in the world. I can neither understand nor explain why this hobby should so fascinate me; the trickery and theft involved are truly my only vices. But whenever I behold the prize of a lifetime's effort, or the one perfect specimen necessary to complete an entire series, I find it impossible to resist.

"For that reason," said the herbalist, reaching into the enormous canvas bag which lay on the ground beside him, "I have here, direct from the Paris thieves' market, the one pair of pincers which the Marquis de Lyons needed in order to possess all the favored instruments of Torquemada. I am also the proud owner of the jawbone of Saint Isidore, specially obtained for me from the vaults of Toledo by a greedy young friar. This piece of tattered cardboard is The Ruined Tower from an ancient tarot deck—assembled, card by card, by a penniless Syrian widow. And this torn parchment is the final page from an Anglo-Saxon law book, which I collected from a British scholar, whose life's work involved the completion and repair of this very manuscript. Nor am I overly scrupulous about borrowing from my fellow mountebanks; otherwise, I would never have gotten Genghis

Khan's pillbox from a colleague of mine who chanced to save such things.

"But enough of this boasting," concluded Jeremiah Vinograd, when his sack was half-empty, and an incongruous assortment of objects littered the earth, "what first set me on this track was my desire to show you one item from the worthy collection of Dr. Boris Silentius. And this is it!" he announced, again reaching into the bag, "the entire pelvic girdle from that lovely skeleton which the doctor unearthed near the Danzig coast. Surely you must have noticed its absence from his arrangement?"

Judah ben Simon shut his eyes to avoid looking at the heavy, butterfly-shaped bone. "I am no longer interested in Dr. Boris Silentius's pathetic, twisted mind!" he cried angrily. "The sight of that skeleton made me suffer once—what good did you hope to accomplish by reminding me of it?"

Suddenly, Jeremiah Vinograd jumped to his feet, and, glowering in fury, thrust his face down towards that of the young man. "Where are your manners?" he shouted. "Only a boy your age could be so cocksure, so boorish, so lacking in all graciousness. Not only did you neglect to thank me for showing you my treasures, but now you dare address me in a tone which a gentleman would never use, not even to reprimand a thieving servant. Let me remind you: I am the one and only Jeremiah Vinograd, scientist and mountebank, artist and magician, master of illusion and reality. Which is to say: I have been practicing my

(161)

craft for fifty-five years, Judah ben Simon, and I know more about every aspect of life than you have learned from all your gazing at the trees.

"Indeed, if you had *any* of the makings of a genuine scientist, you would have thought to examine these bones for hidden clues about the eminent student of Linnaeus. And, in time, you might have discovered a fascinating story, a tale which might have proved important in guiding your thoughts and your future— the history of my first encounter with Dr. Boris Silentius."

Realizing that the herbalist's accusations were not unfounded, Judah ben Simon bowed his head in shame. "You are right," he admitted. "I apologize for my rudeness, and would very much appreciate hearing about your relationship with the doctor. Perhaps there is something we might learn from our common experience."

"Something *you* might learn," the mountebank corrected him, and, instantly recovering from his rage, smiled and sat back down on the ground. "Ten, eleven, maybe twelve years ago," he began, his voice assuming a reflective and nostalgic tone, "I had the misfortune to spend several months in the prison at Padua. It was an unspeakably insanitary place, which I would never have graced with my presence but for a certain misunderstanding about the nature of my trade.

"Fortunately, a true soldier of fortune like myself can quickly adjust to the most dismal surroundings;

but, just as I was beginning to feel at home in my cell, my privacy was rudely invaded by a skinny, frenetic chatterbox of an old man—you know the individual to whom I am referring.

"It soon became apparent that my fellow prisoner, who identified himself as the great Dr. Boris Silentius, was to be the butt of our jailer's cruelest jokes and insults. For his crime was a peculiar and unsettling one: he had been found guilty of robbing graves, of rooting up cemeteries from the northern Alps to the southern Apennines.

"In the course of his ceaseless conversation, my cell-mate defended himself to me, arguing that his so-called sin was merely another misunderstood aspect of his experimental research. All he had been doing, he claimed, was studying the structure and significance of human bones, comparing them with those of animals, and investigating the relation between these skeletons and the spirits of their dead owners.

"But who could believe him?" Jeremiah Vinograd demanded of his listener. "With his madman's eyes, his smooth skin, and his long, trembling fingers, the old fellow certainly looked the part of the midnight ghoul. And none of his scientific prattle ever explained the reason why his researches were apparently re-stricted to the frames of beautiful women who had died at an early age.

"Yet gradually, as our friendship deepened, I had to admit that Boris Silentius was certainly no simpleton when it came to the subject of nature; he could talk for hours about orchids, tigers, elephants, and jungle begonias. Indeed, I had never seen a plant or animal in all my travels which the doctor could not describe in the most intimate detail. And, if this alone had not convinced me, there was also the fact that Silentius could blather away in Latin, naming species, classes and kingdoms as if they were lullabies learned at his mother's knee.

"At any rate, I finally came to believe that my poor cellmate was actually what he claimed: an accomplished naturalist and a onetime disciple of Carl Gustavus Linnaeus. Besides, I reasoned at the time, I myself had been imprisoned on false charges, by men who could not distinguish between a master herbalist and a petty swindler. Had fate not intervened, I might well have accepted the doctor's invitation to join him at his family home in Danzig, to which he planned to return after his release. But, be that as it may, the moral of my story should still be clear to you, young man: it is not always easy to tell the true scientists from the graverobbers, the criminals, and the madmen."

"But did you not realize that Boris Silentius was a lunatic?" cried Judah ben Simon. "Surely you must have known that you were sending me to learn science from a crazy man? How could his circular chatter, his impossible stories and his bones not have struck you as unmistakable symptoms of insanity?"

"Perhaps I suspected that the doctor was a bit eccentric," replied Jeremiah Vinograd, clicking his tongue sympathetically. "But I would never, *never* have ventured to pronounce him insane. My long life has taught me to be extremely cautious in making such definite and final judgments. I have learned that, aside from a man's heart, nothing can deceive and make a fool of him like his own two eyes.

"Let me show you an example," continued the mountebank, taking yet another object from his bag and handing it to Judah ben Simon. "How would you identify this fine specimen?"

The young man examined the limp, withered petals, noticing their purplish-red color and their heavy, perfumed scent. "It is a wilted rose," he said, embarrassed at having to declare the obvious.

"Right!" nodded Jeremiah Vinograd, taking back the flower. "Now, on the basis of all the wilted roses you have observed with your own two eyes, tell me: how long do you think it will be before these poor petals begin to drop from the stem?"

"The plant is nearly dead," pronounced Judah confidently. "It will surely begin to decompose within a few hours."

"Wrong!" cried the mountebank. "Watch and see." The old man passed his palm over the flower, carefully tracing its outline from the base of its stem to the tips of its petals. Then, suddenly, the rose burst into full bloom, assuming the bright, healthy color, round shape, and sweet fragrance of a blossom newly opened on the bush.

"But that is impossible," Judah ben Simon stammered in amazement. "Only a moment ago, that flower was withered and shrunken."

"Do not be upset," murmured the herbalist, with a whimsical smile, "just because your empirical knowledge has failed you. Any man of good judgment would have reached the same conclusions as you did.

"And there we have it!" Jeremiah Vinograd concluded triumphantly. "If an intelligent, experienced naturalist cannot even determine the prognosis of an ailing rose, who among us has the authority or the perception to define the limits of sanity? Perhaps I am the crazy one, perhaps you are; perhaps your most respected neighbors should really be chained to the asylum wall and allowed to satisfy their frustrated desires to scream out loud and howl at the moon."

"In other words," suggested the young man, more confused than ever, "you are telling me that you doubt your own sanity?"

"Maybe," snapped the mountebank, offended once again by his listener's bluntness. "But, crazy or not, I am still sufficiently in touch with reality to be able to discern that you have just had another disagreement with your wife."

Words of angry denial sprang to Judah's lips, but, when he looked into the charlatan's face, he knew that there was nothing he could say. "It is true," he admitted, as tears of misery welled up at the corners of his eyes, "I can no longer continue living with her. Now, I must leave this town, but there is nowhere for me to go, and nothing for me to do. How will I support myself?" he asked desperately. "How can I keep myself from starvation?"

Jeremiah Vinograd rested his chin in one hand, and, shutting his eyes, thought for a long time. At last, he spoke. "Despite your boorishness," he said, "you are obviously a goodhearted boy, and so I will give you some sound advice. Why not take up my trade? Become a mountebank, and travel the country dispensing remedies and cures. A life fit for a king, I assure you. How many other men can still say that after fifty-five years at the same job?"

"Thank you for your opinion," shrugged the young man disconsolately. "But, after all that has happened, I somehow cannot see myself becoming an itinerant magician and a quack."

"Who is a magician?" demanded the mountebank, his entire body twitching with indignation. "Who is a quack? Not I, certainly. I am a scientist, a student of nature, an experimenter and scholar, just like yourself. Of course, the necessities of my occupation have dictated that I also become something of a performer— and an excellent one, at that. But, if you can only master that part of the business, the work is absolutely perfect for you. You can see the world, and, at the same time, continue with your research by merely shifting your attention from botany and zoology to the equally important science of medicine."

"But I have no head for finance," argued Judah ben Simon.

"If you become rich enough," argued the herbalist, "you will not need a head for finance."

"No," murmured Judah, "the whole thing is not so simple."

"It is as simple as this," declared Jeremiah Vinograd. "Your heart's noblest ideal put to its most practical use. Pure science employed to cure the sick and entertain the healthy. Fame, glory, and economic remuneration.

"You must realize," continued the old man, "that I would never be urging you this way if I did not so adore my job—a fact which, in itself, should be sufficient recommendation. But, more than that, the thought of your ideal suitability for this work pleases me as a well-matched couple warms the heart of a matchmaker. Indeed, I am so taken with the idea that I will make you an unprecedented offer:

"The morning has hardly begun. Stay here in this field with me for the rest of the day. I will teach you all the necessary rudiments of the art of bench-mounting, performing and debating, or vending herbs and dispensing ancient remedies. And I will even reveal my time-tested method of reviving a wilted rose."

"You do make the work seem attractive," admitted Judah ben Simon, whose curiosity was sorely tempted by the prospect of seeing Jeremiah Vinograd explain his trick. "And, if you taught me the trade, I would lose nothing by giving it a try, and discovering its virtues and drawbacks for myself. But," he went on, his eyes narrowing suddenly in suspicion, "what do you charge for all this knowledge?"

"My price is a reasonable one," the mountebank answered coolly. "A simple tuition fee, which need not be paid unless you decide to take the work: for one year, and one year only, set aside one-eleventh of your earnings. Deliver it to me, on this very spot, in exactly twelve months' time."

"That is hardly too much to pay for a lifetime's livelihood," said the young man.

"Of course!" boomed Jeremiah Vinograd, laughing jovially. "So, now, are we agreed?"

"Yes," replied Judah, after a brief moment of doubt, during which he felt as if all the dreams of his boyhood were slipping away. "However," he added, as he gradually began to identify the pain gnawing at his heart, "there are personal reasons why I cannot return so near this village next year."

"That is merely a technicality," smiled the herbalist. "We will meet along this same highway, precisely one hundred miles to the south."

"And so it happened," continued the Rabbi Eliezer, "that Jeremiah Vinograd came to teach Judah ben Simon the mountebank's trade. The lesson began at six in the morning, with three hours of instruction in the general theory of healing and herbal medicine.

Speaking so rapidly that Judah could not allow his attention to lapse for an instant, the old man explained the principles of the Mysterium Magnum, the Protoplastus, the Iliaster, and the Arcanum. He discussed the issue of Affinities, debunking the modern idea that "like may be treated with like," and upholding the old notion that "contrary cures contrary." "There is no weapon against a moist disease," he swore passionately, "like a dry medicine." He went on to contrast the relative virtues of Galenical and Paracelsian cures, to enumerate the laws of diagnosis, and to outline the broad categories of cases which invariably call for stimulants, purgatives, emetics, diuretics, and aphrodisiacs.

Jeremiah Vinograd did not stop talking until the village church, tolling matins, drowned out the sound of his voice. Then, he opened his sack, extracted two worm-eaten apples, and offered Judah ben Simon breakfast. But, when the young man allowed the brownish parings to fall into the mud, his instructor flew into a rage, screaming that fruit peels should always be saved, dried, powdered, and used as a cure for fever blisters. "Yet how could I have expected you to know," he sighed at last, "when I have not yet spoken on the subject of prescription." And, with these words, the mountebank resumed his lesson.

"I will run through this quickly," he said, "and you must listen well. For, in this short time, I can only list the most important and basic remedies; as for the fine points of medicine, you must discover them on your own. With these few, simple cures, you will certainly be able to handle the majority of cases which come your way. Should you encounter an entirely unfamiliar ailment, you will still know enough potions to try out, and will have a sufficiently impressive pharmaceutical vocabulary to keep yourself from appearing the fool. And, I can assure you, the ability to avoid seeming ridiculous is the true mark of the successful mountebank.

"But," Jeremiah Vinograd reminded himself, shaking his head as if to dislodge some impediment, "I am dealing in generalities again, when I have promised you specifics. And now, if you will accept my apology, I will do my humble best to compensate for the time I have spent chatting.

"In case of ulceration," he began, jumbling the words in his great haste to get them out, "dose the patient with moss grown on top of a skull. For hemorrhage, nothing works like children's fingernails boiled in a kettle by a blue-eyed man. Frogs' eggs will prevent a wound from festering; a spider hung round the neck will keep away the ague. Vitriol works wonders against epileptic seizures, arsenic against the French pox. Human blood draws lost sheep and cattle like a magnet; viper fat and feathers will make a lover more attentive. Azoth of the Red Lion is remarkably effective against convulsions. Mummy powder, as you probably already know, cures absolutely everything, but, in these advanced days, has become somewhat hard to come by. Still, a passable substitute can be obtained from pigeons stuffed with spices and pulverized to a fine paste."

Late that afternoon, Jeremiah Vinograd concluded his lecture on prescription. "And now," he proclaimed, "I will reveal my own personal secret of secrets, a trick which I would never disclose if not for my unselfish love for medical science: black helle-bore, the only plant which flowers in the midst of the deepest winter snows, has, according to its nature, miraculous powers of rejuvenation, of restoring the bloom to the white cheek of age."

"Is that right?" murmured Judah ben Simon dubi-ously, wondering how many of the old man's remedies were the result of cautious experimental investigation, and how many were merely the product of some hap-hazard folk chemistry.

"Yes, that is right," replied Jeremiah Vinograd, slower to anger now that he had filled ten hours with the music of his own knowledgeable voice. "But I am fully aware that your know-it-all skepticism, your stupid insistence on proving everything for yourself is, at this very moment, preventing you from accepting the wisdom I have offered here today. 'Why should I believe in this old fool's home remedies,' you are ask-ing yourself, 'when I have never seen them in action.' Well, Judah ben Simon, what can I say? You will simply have to trust the experience of my years until you have the opportunity to test my theories in prac-tice. And for a start," said the mountebank, his wild eyes gleaming with significance, "let me suggest that you investigate the effect of a few drops of hellebore's essence on the petals of a wilted rose."

Judah ben Simon lowered his eyes, and made no further comment.

"Very good!" cried Jeremiah Vinograd, smacking his lips in evident satisfaction. "Now, since we are on

(172)

the subject of tricks and secrets, perhaps I should at least present you with a short dissertation on the Arcane Mysteries of Mountebankery, the Three Principles of Performance, Self-Promotion, and Publicity —which, if the truth be known, can make or break the most highly skilled pharmacist and diagnostician.

"I am afraid that these may well be the most difficult skills for a serious and studious young man like yourself to master. Perhaps I should assure you that I, too, had no easy time learning the fine art of vending my wares.

"But now, in my old age, it is truly the one aspect of the work which pleases me most, which alone offers constant promise and surprise. Let me explain it this way: not once in my entire career has tincture of laudanum ever failed to put a patient to rest; by now, I know that, after administering the proper dosage, there is precisely enough time for me to drink one cup of tea before I must go back and check on the sleeper's tranquil pulse. Yet fifty-five years of experience have not enabled me to predict whether the members of my audience will greet me with cheers and acclamation, or whether they will pull me down from my platform and drag me through the outer gates of their town.

"This uncertainty is what amuses me, Judah ben Simon. But it is absolutely certain that a novice like yourself will earn only tar and feathers for your efforts, unless I teach you those few flourishes of style which I myself learned from Father Time—and which, after all these years, allow me the occasional luxury of a warm reception.

"Of first importance," said Jeremiah Vinograd, grinning with pride at having accumulated such priceless information, "is the matter of names. Invent yourself a professional title under which you can travel with due pomp, elegance, comfort, and speed. I myself have ten or twelve appellations, all with a certain exotic flavor, from which I pick and choose, depending on my mood. I am the Sowdain of Babiloun, Count Fibanaccio, the Knight of the Gilded Scalpels, Absalom the Jew. And, when I am in a comical frame of mind," he giggled, "I blacken my face with pitch and bill myself as the Moor of Tours. At any rate," he continued, growing suddenly serious, "I would advise you to find a suitable name as quickly as possible, and learn to turn around when someone uses it to call you.

"But names are only an opening," sighed the herbalist, "a foot in the door. Once you have introduced yourself, then the real work begins. If only I had not left my equipment with a friend in Warsaw, I could show you how to twirl the bench three times around your head before stepping up on it; as it is, you will simply have to practice on your own.

"But listen: as soon as you have mounted the platform, spread your arms out wide and start talking. Use only the most dramatic gestures, the longest words, the most obscure pharmaceutical terminology. Speak as loud and as fast as you can; make your listeners think they are observing a scientific genius, and a master of elocution. Spend your first wages on a figured cloak, some bells, a fur hat, perhaps even a trained monkey; that way, those who do not like your face will at least have something to look at. Memorize a few jokes, some ribald stories for the evening crowd; simple feats of prestidigitation are always useful in convincing an unsympathetic audience. And, while we are at it, let me give you a short list of handy expressions and turns of speech which may add some spice and color to your presentations."

Just as the autumn sun began to set, Jeremiah Vinograd finished dictating these catch phrases, and commenced a lesson on what he termed "spiritual medicine"—the petty lies and falsehoods which, he swore, were regrettably but absolutely necessary for the recovery of one's patients and the furthering of one's business. "Always prescribe *lots* of medicine," he was saying. "Nothing strengthens a sick man like an armload of glass bottles. Always tell your customers that the gingerroot you stole from their neighbors' gardens has been specially imported from the far reaches of Cathay. And, when a character of great social importance fails to recover after two weeks under your care, leave town by the fastest possible route. Do you understand what I mean?"

But, if Judah ben Simon understood, he gave no sign, for he was already standing up and rubbing his stiff, cramped limbs. "Thank you for the instruction," he said, interrupting the herbalist in mid-sentence. "I assure you that I will put your knowledge to good use."

"I knew that this last part would not please you,"

laughed Jeremiah Vinograd. "That is why I saved it for the end. Nevertheless, if you manage to remember half of what I told you today, your business will be a profitable one. And I sincerely hope that our bargain will be among the things you remember. I am sure that you are an honorable man, Judah ben Simon, and that you will keep it in mind: one-eleventh of your earnings, a year from today, one hundred miles to the south."

"I will keep it in mind," said the young man, and walked slowly back towards the north-south road.

XII

O N A C H I L L, September morning," continued Eliezer of Rimanov, "precisely one year and seven days after his meeting with the mountebank, Judah ben Simon arrived to find that the hundredth milestone south of his village was lodged between the elegantly-worked railings of a tall iron fence.

Beyond the bars was a forest of dark pines; across the highway, wheatfields stretched towards the horizon. Nowhere in the wet, gray fog was there any sign of Jeremiah Vinograd. Judah paced the mile-long fence until he spotted a scrap of paper impaled on a spiked ornament; but the crude, hand-lettered public notice only identified the enclosed property as the estate of the exalted Prince Zarembka, and went on to list the unwary trespassers, each of whom had forfeited six fingers in payment for his crime.

"No wonder Jeremiah Vinograd decided not to

spend a week awaiting me in this inhospitable place," thought the latecomer uneasily. "Perhaps I should re-examine the milestone once more for good measure, then continue on my way."

But, as Judah ben Simon neared the smooth granite tablet, he was startled by the loud notes of a tune which he immediately recognized as "The Dove"—a sentimental folksong which the girls of his village used to sing until they collapsed from weeping.

"The poor white pigeon," a man's voice was bellow-ing, "Shot down by the hunter/ Is in no more pain/ Than a lady abandoned by her lover."

"That vile croak could only belong to one man," laughed Judah happily, and, summoning all his cour-age, squeezed through the space between two railings. Emerging from a dense curtain of tall firs, he reached a circular clearing where, as the fog alternately thinned and thickened, he began to perceive the elements of a strange spectacle.

The vale had been landscaped according to the tastes of the Old Nobility; the artificial pond, grassy banks, and lacy, white-pillared pavilion all seemed in-credibly small, delicate, and perfectly proportioned in contrast to the massive, sinister pines which sur-rounded them. At one time, the dell might well have been a favorite trysting place for aristocratic lovers; but it had clearly fallen into disuse, so that a thick scum of green algae floated on the surface of the pond, blending fuzzily with the lower borders of the mist.

On the steps of the gazebo, a beefy soldier—whose

unkempt uniform identified him as a member of the royal guard—was placidly coughing up phlegm and spitting into the lake. "So this is the fellow who sings like Jeremiah Vinograd," thought the disappointed young man. "He is not what I would call a ferocious type, but, nevertheless, that notice on the fence suggests that there may be some sharp teeth behind that dumb grin." With this in mind, Judah ben Simon was just about to slip back into the woods, when a momentary break in the fog permitted him to catch sight of the pond's far shore—and of Jeremiah Vinograd, who was sitting quietly near the water's edge.

Even from a distance, the herbalist's face seemed heavier, firmer, alight with the complacent smile of a man used to feasting on wine and fine meats. He was dressed in a quilted cloak of rich maroon velvet, stitched with gold thread; his scarlet turban had been refurbished, bordered with a rope of bells and a band of black mink. On his feet were low-cut shoes of tooled leather, turned up at the toes. Surprised by the charlatan's new splendor, Judah ben Simon grew even more amazed when he realized that Jeremiah Vinograd's magnificent garments represented only a fraction of his recent acquisitions.

Directly behind the old man, a white mule grazed peacefully beside a covered gypsy cart adorned with carved woodwork and painted all over with brightly colored symbols, hexes, birds, flowers, spells, and incantations. The wagon was balanced on high, light wheels with orange spokes; its front end, covered by a heavy black curtain, tilted down towards the ground.

As soon as Jeremiah Vinograd noticed Judah ben Simon at the edge of the forest, he jumped up and began to wave both arms in the air. Casting sidelong glances at the white pavilion, the young man inched forward, until the mountebank laughed, motioned deprecatingly towards the guard, and came out to greet his visitor.

"What took you so long?" boomed the herbalist, slapping his former student on the back.

"An error in judgment," murmured Judah evasively. "I am sorry for having made you wait."

"Think nothing of it," said the mountebank graciously, ushering his guest around the lake until they stood within inches of the gypsy cart. "There is nothing I enjoy more than a leisurely week in my own sweet haven of refreshment and relaxation."

"Your haven!" cried the young man incredulously, wondering if he had perhaps underestimated the charlatan's sensational good fortune. "Do you mean to tell me that this grand estate is yours?"

"Be reasonable, my boy," laughed Jeremiah Vinograd. "Would the owner of a paradise like this spend fifty-one weeks a year cramming leaves and roots down the throats of ignorant peasants? I should say not; indeed, I should say not. I meant only that I consider this setting uncommonly soothing and inspirational, and that I would sooner lay my head on this sweet bank than on the finest silk pillow in Poland."

"And have you no fear of the penalties for trespass?" inquired Judah, peering anxiously at the soldier, who seemed to be picking lice from his shaggy blond forelocks.

"It is obvious that you have not been a mountebank for very long," smiled the old man patronizingly. "Otherwise, you would realize that the prince's men— who have guarded this estate for the fifteen years since his lordship's death—are, like all members of their class, hopelessly superstitious fellows; they simply cannot tell the difference between a scientist and a warlock. More than a decade ago, when I first discovered this lovely glade, they were afraid to evict me, petrified lest I curse them with some sort of black magic enchantment; since then, we have become fast friends. Is that not right, Corporal Svoboda?" yelled Jeremiah Vinograd, directing a jaunty salute towards the man on the pavilion steps.

Corporal Svoboda raised his head and grinned, revealing a set of wildly irregular, tobacco-stained teeth.

"But surely," continued the charlatan, "you must have encountered certain symptoms of this superstitious awe among your own patients?"

"Whenever possible," the young man replied coldly, "I try to discourage that sort of thing."

"So much the worse for you," declared Jeremiah Vinograd. "But, while we are on the subject, let me ask you: how have you been faring in this business of mountebankery?"

"I have no cause for complaint," answered Judah ben Simon. "Indeed, you were quite right: my study

(181)

of the healing art affords me even greater pleasure than all my observations of woodland plants and animals. For medicine is really three fields of knowledge in one—the purely physical sciences of physiology and pharmacology, and the more abstract science of human behavior. And the truth is that I most enjoy my research in this last area; just a year ago, I had not the dimmest notion that all the thoughts and actions of men derived from a fixed set of rules and regulations— a complex version of the systems which govern the habits of fish, birds, and beasts."

"And what are these immutable laws?" asked Jeremiah Vinograd.

"I could list them for days on end," replied the young man proudly. "But I will name only a few, to show you what I mean.

"All matrons wish to eradicate the signs of age," he began. "All grandmothers refuse to admit that they are ill. All unmarried boys are troubled by sleeplessness. Fathers of grown children suffer from stomach complaints; childless women are prone to headaches. Old men become either tightfisted or prodigal with their money. Every bride weeps uncontrollably at some time during the first year after her wedding; every young girl has fits of uncontrollable daydreaming—"

"So that is human life," interrupted the mountebank. "A closed system of actions and reactions, like the principles of prescription and recovery."

"With a few exceptions," nodded his former pupil, "that is it."

"Then I must beg to differ with you," smiled Jeremiah Vinograd knowingly, as if he were about to disabuse a child of some illogical and preposterous misconception. "The most wondrous thing about our fellow men is the fact that they are so unique, and unpredictable."

"Their unpredictability is only a façade," frowned Judah, "masking the inescapable pattern which controls them. I assure you that a genuine and complete deviation from my system is rarer than a robin migrating north in winter."

"Yet certainly you must have had some odd and unusual experiences in a year of travel," insisted the herbalist. "Surely you must have witnessed some interactions among men which you would never have expected to see."

"Of course," replied Judah ben Simon. "I met an old peasant woman who, all her life, had shared her bed with a dappled gray drayhorse. I treated a fanatical nun who had blinded herself in order to rid her eyes of lust. I even watched a madman kill his brother, rape his sister, and begin to babble in tongues. But none of these events was so extraordinary that I would ever have termed it impossible."

"In other words," sighed Jeremiah Vinograd, "you have still not encountered anything as remarkable as a child conceived in a dream."

Judah ben Simon looked at him sharply, then shut his eyes. "No," he answered tensely, "I have not."

"At any rate," said the mountebank hurriedly, trying to rekindle the warmth which had suddenly gone out of their conversation, "one thing is clear: a man must treat a great variety and number of patients in order to observe the entire range of human behavior. And therefore"—the old man's eyes began to glow like those of a child anticipating some gift brought back from his father's travels—"I assume that financial success has fallen into your lap like a lady of the evening."

"I am afraid not," mumbled Judah uncomfortably, growing even more embarrassed when he saw the look of disappointment which crossed the herbalist's face. Unable to meet his teacher's searching look, he focussed his attention on a tightly laced leather purse, from which he slowly extracted ten small silver coins.

"Here is one-eleventh of my year's wages," he pronounced solemnly. "Three of these pennies were earned last week. For the truth about my tardiness is that I spent these past seven days in a frantic round of bench-mounting and oration, in a desperate effort to collect enough money to present you with an honorable fee."

"I appreciate your efforts," nodded Jeremiah Vinograd, receiving the coins in his outstretched palm. "But I cannot understand why your pocket should have remained so empty. I certainly would never have taken you for a lazy type."

The young man blushed. "I will tell you a secret," he whispered, staring miserably at the ground. "I work very hard, but the major part of my business is transacted with women. As soon as I ascend my platform, the ladies start edging towards the front rows so that they might stand near me; they invent imaginary ills and ailments just to visit my lodgings. But they can only pay me out of their meager pocket funds and household allowances, for I have never met a man who was eager to place his wife or daughter in my care."

The mountebank glanced up and down his former student's strong young body, noting how the blue physician's caftan set off his blond hair and beard. All at once, he began to laugh uproariously. "I should have known," he gasped, struggling to contain himself. "But tell me: just how near do these women come when they come near?"

"What difference does that make?" cried Judah indignantly. Then, remembering how insufficient his tuition money had been, he felt himself grow calmer, humbler, more eager to please the leering old mountebank.

"I have a story which may answer your question," he said at last, his voice slow with reluctance. "When I was in the southeastern part of our land, I had occasion to treat a young foreigner, a Persian woman, who came to me complaining of violent pains behind her eyes. At first, I blamed her malady on the carpet-weaving with which she filled her leisure hours; but gradually, it became apparent that these seizures only came on after my patient had been scolded by her husband—a crass, impatient old man, who trafficked in imported spices, brass, and turquoise.

"As it happened, the lady was disarmingly beautiful,

(185)

with bright, almond-shaped eyes and olive skin. How could I have resisted her advances, the sincere and simple effusions of her gratitude? Nor was she a stupid wench, for she gave evidence of a sharp intelligence in the clever plan which she devised to keep our liaison from being discovered.

"Whenever her husband was scheduled to spend the day in a neighboring village, my mistress would work late into the night, weaving the figure of a dove or a lily into her prize tapestry. In the mornings, when I saw her loom on the porch, I would know that it was safe to visit her."

"But such signals between lovers always miscarry," interrupted Jeremiah Vinograd, smiling with pleasure at the classic story which the young man was telling as if it had never been told before. "Either the old cuckold changed his mind and decided to remain home after the weaving had already been displayed, or else he returned unexpectedly to find you locked in the embrace of Venus."

"No," replied Judah, somewhat offended, "we were much too wise and cautious to make such crude errors. No, we were undone by something which we could never have taken into account.

"For how could my lady have foreseen that love would transform her from a mere craftsman into a great artist? During the few short weeks of our relationship, her tapestry grew by several inches of unearthly beauty, unequaled in the finest carpets of the shahs. Her husband immediately suspected that something was amiss, and locked her in her bedroom until she agreed to explain her sudden attainment of genius. And so I was obliged to leave that place with nothing to console me but a new principle for my systematic scheme of human nature: true love can never be concealed."

"My God!" laughed the mountebank. "What a change in you! Just one year ago, you were telling me that you could not abide a woman who did not subscribe to your lofty ideas on miracles and religion. And now you are jumping between the sheets with every pagan rugmaker who comes your way."

"I was only sharing my bed, my body, and a bit of my heart," protested the young man angrily, "not my entire life. A man need not spend every moment alone in order to retain his integrity."

"Of course not," chortled Jeremiah Vinograd good-humoredly. "I was only joking, I swear. I hope you will not take offense, for I myself could not be in a more mellow frame of mind. In all honesty, your story has delighted me more than a hundred pieces of silver, so that I am not at all displeased with you for having failed to fill your wallet. Besides," he continued, looking down at his heavy robe, "this has been an exceptionally good year for me, profitable beyond my wildest hopes."

"And how do you explain your success?" Judah asked eagerly, anxious for some useful advice.

"Oh," replied the old man, in an affectedly casual tone, "I have merely obtained some new equipment, and, in my old age, have learned a few new tricks. Why, in this little wagon," he went on, affectionately stroking the side of his cart, "I now carry certain tools which have permitted me to amass a small fortune."

"May I see them?" inquired Judah ben Simon.

Jeremiah Vinograd shook his head. "Twelve months ago," he said, "when you were still my student and protégé, I was only too happy to teach you everything I knew. But now that you have officially enlisted in the army of my competitors, how could I disclose the secrets of my success without feeling a pang of anxiety and resentment? At any rate," he added, looking across the pond towards the gazebo, "there are some strange and imposing objects among my new possessions, and I fear lest the mere sight of these marvelous articles might strain my warm friendship with Corporal Svoboda."

"I understand," nodded Judah ben Simon, and forced himself to stop staring at the cart.

"But wait," said Jeremiah Vinograd. "Even though I myself have survived some hard years, and profited by the experience, I am still deeply troubled by this financial embarrassment of yours. I would hate to think that I bore any responsibility for the failure of a young man who had voluntarily placed himself under my tutelage. Therefore, I will extend a hand to assist you in climbing out of the grim pits of impecunity; I will give you a piece of advice which is even more finely tailored to your individual needs and talents than mountebankery itself.

"Let me put it as diplomatically as possible: this year, your difficulties appear to have resulted from a surfeit of poor, powerless women. The solution to this problem could not be more obvious: next year, go out and find yourself some ladies of wealth and power."

"Obvious indeed," smiled Judah ben Simon. "I have reached the same conclusion many times over."

"Perhaps," nodded the old man. "But, without my aid, you would never have found the perfect means to implement this notion. You would have remained unaware of a fact which may well change your entire future, of a priceless bit of gossip which has long been a favorite topic for speculation among Corporal Svoboda and his colleagues. Listen well, Judah ben Simon:

"Not far from the eastern border of our land is the town of Kuzman, the home of the late Prince Zarembka's lovely daughter. Now Kuzman is an unusually lucky village which boasts not one, but three, unmarried ladies—beautiful, isolated, aristocratic women, who have absolutely nothing to do with their gold coins but melt them down into rings for handsome young mountebanks. Surely, Judah ben Simon, your eventual home in paradise might well be modeled on this place."

"Then I will have to wait until I see it in heaven," replied the younger man. "I thank you for your generous advice; but I have no intention of roaming the swampy marshlands and rocky hills of the East just to bilk rich women of their patrimonies. No, my plans for the coming year are somewhat nobler, and more expansive: I will winter on the Bay of Tangiers, summer in the forests of Norway, spend spring on a sunny Aegean isle. I will observe distant lands, strange men, and foreign cultures; I will test my principles of behavior among the peoples of the world. And maybe my fortune will improve when I escape from the dull and stonyhearted citizens of my native land."

"Maybe it will," agreed Jeremiah Vinograd cheerfully. "In any case, I admire your energy, your courage, and your ambition; I wish you the best of luck. And, when we meet again, it will be your turn to instruct me, to enlighten me concerning recent trends in international mountebankery. For I myself have not stepped beyond the borders since my unfortunate sojourn in Padua."

"I do hope we see each other," said Judah, preparing to leave, "so that I can finally repay my debt by telling you all the latest news from abroad."

"Do not worry," smiled the mountebank mysteriously, "our paths will cross at least once more." Then, with tears streaming down his cheeks, he bid his former student a warm and heartfelt good-by.

As soon as Judah ben Simon left the clearing, Jeremiah Vinograd strolled around the lake and exchanged a few words with the drowsy corporal. Circling back, the old man hitched up his mule, glanced once inside the curtain to make sure that all his treasures were still intact, and led his tiny caravan out towards the opposite edge of the estate.

* * *

"And what was in the gypsy cart?" asked King Casimir of Poland, no longer able to restrain his simple curiosity.

"I am very glad you asked that question," chuckled the Rabbi Eliezer. "In Jeremiah Vinograd's wagon, behind the thick black curtain, sat Rachel Anna and her infant son."

XIII

THE KING OF POLAND did not stop gaping until he noticed his foolish, dumbstruck gaze reflected in a thousand mirrors. Then he clamped his lips shut, and adjusted the corners of his mouth into a sly, knowing grin. "You need hardly bother to explain," he said, faking an elaborate yawn. "Even a child could see that Jeremiah Vinograd was actually a spy, hired by Rachel Anna's family to retrieve their lost daughter. Why, as soon as the old man entered your story, I suspected that his so-called mountebankery was merely a ruse designed to trick Judah ben Simon into leaving his wife at the bounty hunter's mercy."

"A noble effort to outwit me at my own game of turns and surprises!" cried the Rabbi Eliezer. "Unfortunately, you have overshot the mark. For, with all due respect, I must inform Your Majesty that the real reason for Rachel Anna's presence in the gypsy cart was far less contrived than that which His Highness has suggested."

"And what might that reason be?" asked Casimir, as his bright, self-satisfied expression gradually collapsed into the sheepish smile of a chastised schoolboy.

Eliezer of Rimanov reached out, grasped the king's shoulder, and gave it an affectionate shake. "You need only be quiet and listen," he said. "And I will tell you:

"Two months after Judah ben Simon left his home for the second time, Rachel Anna awoke one morning to find her mother-in-law dead on the kitchen floor. One look at Hannah Polikov's face enabled the young woman to determine the cause of death. Trembling with fear, she rocked her baby to sleep in the attic room, then watched beside the body until she had summoned enough courage to inform the neighbors.

But the village elders who came to arrange the widow's funeral were quick to assure the grieving daughter-in-law that her panic had been unfounded. "A simple case of heart attack and brain fever," the mayor declared grimly.

"All those miraculous carryings-on finally proved too much for her," added the Rabbi Joseph Joshua, who was still smarting from the sting of his defeat before the Cracower court. "It is not uncommon for the Lord to punish evil sinners by striking down their loved ones."

"Nonsense!" snapped Rachel Anna. "You know the meaning of those boils, those swellings, those fiery sores!"

"God's will be done," mumbled the elders, and rushed out into the street, where, strangely ill-at-ease in each other's company, they soon parted ways. For the truth was that every one of them had recognized the plague's hideous signature, tattooed on the dead woman's forehead. But their memories of the last outbreak—which, after thirty years, still haunted their grisliest nightmares, would not allow them to admit that another epidemic had begun. Therefore they tried desperately to convince themselves that Hannah had really died of brain fever, and labored to suppress the rumors which had already begun to surround the widow's sudden death.

At first, their efforts succeeded in calming the terrified villagers, who drew comfort from a superstitious notion that the pestilence might somehow be rendered powerless by the elders' refusal to acknowledge its presence. Yet this faith vanished when it became apparent that the town council planned to invoke an obscure technicality of birth and residence, which would prohibit Hannah Polikov from being buried near her husband—in the public cemetery in which she had rested once before.

Thus, all things conspired to make Hannah's funeral an unusually tense and somber event. Obliged to honor the memory of a woman who had twice played such a wondrous role in local gossip, everyone in town trooped out to the barren Pauper's Field. But the atmosphere was so grim that no one referred to Hannah's more joyous past, nor did anyone think to compare this burial with its lucky predecessor. Indeed, there was no mention of better, bygone days during the course of the ceremony, nor were there any of the sighs, sniffles, tears, downcast looks and involuntary smiles of relief which normally accompany the burial of a well-known citizen.

Instead, there was nothing but strain, worry, and icy preoccupation until the very end of the service, when the dirt was being tossed on the coffin. Then, as several mourners—like theatergoers who habitually exit five minutes before a performance's end—rushed over to offer their half-distracted condolences, Rachel Anna turned on them in fury. "Save your sympathy!" she cried in a clear, ringing voice. "Go home and make ready, for Hannah Polikov has become the first victim of the black plague."

Now this was the first time that the word "plague" had been spoken aloud in public; the mere sound of it was enough to make each citizen imagine himself surrounded by a crowd of dying human bodies. Immediately, pandemonium broke out—and, for the second time, the scholar's wife was totally erased from the memories of living men.

"If Judah the Pious had been present at this scene," chuckled the Rabbi Eliezer, "he would surely have interpreted it as another instance of divine intervention. 'Once again,' he might have said, 'the Lord is finding it advisable to divert the spirits' attention from Hannah Polikov—to prevent them, in this case, from hindering

(195)

her soul as it leaps toward heaven.' But, by then, the panic-stricken townspeople would never have accepted such a warm and benevolent vision of God's plan, not even though it had come from the greatest mind in Europe.

For, that very afternoon, just as he had finished quieting his neighbors and convincing them to return home, Rabbi Joseph Joshua felt the telltale soreness in his groin and armpits. He died the next morning, and was followed into the earth by three other victims. After these first burials, when it was announced that mass cremations would begin, old women wept all night, bemoaning the fact that their grandchildren would now come to know that terrible, burning smell, wafting in from the Pauper's Field.

At the start of the plague, the streets were ominously quiet. No one strolled or chatted in the alleys; no one lounged in the doorways. The shutters remained closed at all hours, keeping out the harmful light, muffling the groans, sobs, and cries. But, when ten heaped-up corpses went down the main road with no living company but that of the terrified waggoner, a time of general panic began. During these frantic weeks, men mumbled the same prayers, chanted the same incantations, and danced the same devil dances which their fathers had done thirty years before; almost instinctively, they burned the same incense which, for centuries, had proved worthless as a disinfectant.

There were the same public accusations of witchcraft, and the same private hurry to ask the alleged witches for help; every opinion on the epidemic's cause and cure was heard and evaluated. Prominent citizens jotted down the babblings of madmen and infants, and studied them for secret meanings. The apothecary's wife discovered that her long-ignored tea leaves were suddenly in great demand, and, with a grim face, interpreted their pattern as a prophecy of the town's imminent devastation; shortly thereafter, she herself succumbed to a mild case of the disease which no one expected to prove fatal. In the desperate search for help, every eccentric monk and wizened hag in the entire area was consulted, until the residents of neighboring districts closed their borders.

Finally, when everything else had failed, it was suggested that someone approach the filthy old charlatan who had been haunting the north-south highway for six months, whose sporadic attempts to sell herbs had met with ridicule because of his outlandish and disreputable appearance.

Forty minutes later, Jeremiah Vinograd strutted down the deserted main street. Entering the market place, he leaped up on a deserted counter, and began to shout so loud that he was soon surrounded by all the villagers brave enough to venture out.

"Ladies and gentlemen!" the mountebank cried. "In all the world, you could not have found a physician better suited to your needs. For I alone am Simon Magus the Samaritan, sole possessor of the only guaranteed remedy for the black death, the bubonic plague, the nightmare pestilence—"

"Tell it to us!" shrieked the townspeople, who had never heard anyone make such an astounding claim.

"Do you imagine that I give my secrets away for free?" asked the herbalist. "No, kind sirs, I must remind you that my livelihood depends on such things. However, in keeping with my regular policy of 'great wonders at low prices,' I am asking only one thin silver coin for every man, woman and child in your fair town. Should you decide not to implement my remedy, I will cheerfully refund your money. Should my plan prove ineffective, I will repay this sum a thousandfold."

"Ah," murmured his listeners, almost in unison, "a claim like that could only be made by a man who has never failed."

"Precisely!" declared Jeremiah Vinograd.

"Then you have succeeded in eliminating the plague?" inquired an eager young woman.

"Unfortunately," the mountebank replied, "my system has never been tested. For it involves a certain calculated risk, which no one has ever had the courage to undertake."

The mayor glanced around to gauge his constituents' mood, then stepped forward. "Do you really expect us to pay good money for some harebrained scheme of yours," he demanded, "some foolish, private theory which has never been tried?"

"No, I do not," answered Jeremiah Vinograd. "Rather, I expect you to meet the same fate as all those

(198)

other unfortunates, who—like you—suffered from the fatal combination of pestilence and pride." And, with these words, the mountebank swung the corners of his cloak in a manner which clearly indicated his readiness to jump down from the counter and abandon his audience to the merciless scourge.

In the uproar which greeted this gesture, someone proposed that Simon Magus be tortured into revealing his secret; an impatient young man even offered to gather the coals and brands required for his execution. But the majority of citizens had no desire to injure a master of the demonic arts, a wizard who appeared to offer their last defense against death. Therefore, after a long, hesitant silence, the people voiced their willingness to pay the old man's bill.

"A wise decision!" said the mountebank. "And now, I will commence my treatment by reminding you that the sooner I receive my payment, the sooner your relatives stop dying."

At six o'clock that evening, Jeremiah Vinograd was sitting on the same countertop when the mayor tossed a heavy bag full of coins at his feet. "Thank you," nodded the herbalist, climbing back onto the platform, "thank you for the generosity which you will never regret. For, without any further delay, Simon Magus of Samaria will reveal to you his marvelous cure for the bubonic plague—the remedy which was taught him, in the course of a dream, by the renowned Sybil of Damascus."

Still facing his dumbfounded audience, Simon

(199)

Magus slowly rotated his body, extending his arm to include the entire town. "Burn it down," he commanded, in a dark, meaningful whisper.

The angry scream of an old woman shattered the ensuing silence. "Burn down our village!" she cried incredulously. " 'Calculated risk' is hardly the term for these crazy ravings!"

"On the contrary," smiled the mountebank. "My plan is based on an eminently sane and logical principle. For, according to the blessed Sybil, epidemics only occur in villages which have been built on unlucky ground."

"But the pestilence strikes everywhere," protested a schoolboy.

"Every place becomes unlucky sooner or later," replied Jeremiah Vinograd. "That is how the wheel of Fortune turns. But, before I become sidetracked on the subject of that powerful wheel, let me give you one last word of wisdom.

"Rebuild your homes on that high, sandy rise, on which I have camped for the past few months. For it impresses me as the only lucky place in the whole neighborhood, the only location which may be able to save you from contagion."

"Now you are truly betraying your lunacy!" shouted the mayor. "How can you even suggest that we destroy our lovely homes and relocate on that desolate land, which can support nothing but wild grass? How can you advise us to live on that rocky soil, which cannot even satisfy the simple needs of a rose bush or a flea. I am afraid that your 'cure' is really too absurd. As one gentleman of honor to another, I must ask you to refund my neighbors' hard-earned money."

"As you wish," murmured Jeremiah Vinograd. "When you are all dead, I can return and fill my pockets with as much silver as they can hold."

Of course, the sack of coins remained with the herbalist. Four days later, a young father witnessed the cremation of his infant son, then went home, ushered his wife out into the street, and tossed the first torch in through his front window.

Within a week, Jeremiah Vinograd's cure had already begun to produce dramatic results. The families which pitched their tents on the dry hillside developed no new cases of the plague; nothing more was heard from the few stubborn neighbors who refused to abandon their homes. Finally, the survivors revisited the dank, corpse-littered streets of the abandoned city, and obliterated all traces of their old community. Then, when they had sent Jeremiah Vinograd on his way with all the proper honors, gifts, and praises, they returned to the side of the north-south highway to begin rebuilding their lives on lucky ground.

Slinging the heavy moneybag over his shoulder, Jeremiah Vinograd walked out through the cemetery and into the woods. After a brief search, he discovered Rachel Anna and her child, huddling in the ruins of a ramshackle wooden shelter.

"You must be the famed and lovely Rachel Anna," the herbalist declared gallantly.

Tightening her cloak around the shivering infant, the young woman glared up at him. "And you are Jeremiah Vinograd," she whispered furiously.

"I am Simon Magus the Samaritan and none other," replied the mountebank, "though I would dearly love to be that fortunate gentleman for whom you mistake me, whose name alone can elicit such powerful emotions from your heart."

"Jeremiah Vinograd," she repeated, in a voice which shook with hatred. "You are a liar and a fraud."

"You have managed to penetrate my latest and greatest disguise," declared the herbalist. "Your intelligence must surpass your extraordinary beauty. Yes," he admitted, with an acquiescent shrug, "Jeremiah Vinograd is one of my many names. But I am most definitely not a liar or a fraud. After all, did I not save your neighbors from the ghastly black death?"

"I suppose you did," she nodded reluctantly. "But you are still a monstrous villain, whose irrational malice has succeeded in destroying Judah ben Simon, his wife, and even his helpless child. You knew that I would be unable to rebuild a house for myself, that no one would offer to help me; you knew that I would be forced to seek shelter in the forest at the start of winter. And yet you pressed on with your senseless, fiendish plot to ruin our family."

"You misjudge me, Madam," protested the old man. "Your stupid husband brought on his own misery, though I did everything in my power to help him. First, I sent him off to Danzig in the hope that crazy

Boris Silentius might teach him a lesson. Then, when it became clear that he intended to persist in his folly, I taught him a trade which would keep him from starving.

"And as for you, Rachel Anna—only an idiot or a lunatic could want to hurt such a lovely woman; by now it should be apparent that I am neither of these. Could a fool have rescued you from the plague, as I did? Would a madman have the common sense to advise you against remaining here, awaiting a husband who may never return?

"No, my dear lady, I have no desire to harm you. Indeed, I am so concerned with your happiness and well-being that I am about to make you a remarkable offer: why not wander the country with me, as part of my act? I am a rich man now, I can afford an assistant. And my audience will doubtless appreciate the brilliantly allusive symbolism of your presence, for everyone knows that Simon Magus did not travel alone."

"Simon Magus roamed the world with Helena, his whore," whispered Rachel Anna, shutting her eyes in sudden recognition. "So you expected me to come with you all along?"

"You need not complicate matters with your coarse language," replied the mountebank, ignoring her question. "I am inviting you to be my helper, my fellow showman, my business partner, and nothing more."

"Then what will my duties be?" asked the surprised young woman.

"You will have no duties," smiled Jeremiah Vinograd. "Only pleasures—the simple joys which are the thespian's constant companion. You will have the satisfaction of a gracefully executed pirouette, of a song sung on key; you will know the pride of seeing tears roll down your listeners' cheeks when you tell them how my miraculous plague cure pulled your community from the jaws of death. What could be easier? In fact, it would not surprise me if you turned out to have a natural talent for such things."

Suddenly, the old man noticed the squirming lump beneath Rachel Anna's cape, and, struck by a fresh and entrancing notion, he smiled. "For the benefit of those who are not sufficiently overwhelmed by your story, we will exhibit the leprous Baby Lazarus, whose hideous disease—a lumpy creation of flour and water —will be instantly and painlessly washed away by the aqueous medicine in my magic vial."

The herbalist paused, his eyes gleaming with visions of untold wealth. "Rachel Anna," he said, "we cannot fail to make a fortune. So come now, what do you say to the idea of food, clothing, shelter, and all the luxuries you desire?"

"I have no choice," sighed Rachel Anna. "If I stay here in the wilderness, my baby will surely die before the winter ends."

"Exactly," boomed the mountebank jovially, and helped the young mother to her feet.

And so it happened that Rachel Anna came to practice the charlatan's trade with Jeremiah Vinograd. Soon their partnership was working smoothly.

Though dazed into numbness by the sudden changes in her life, the woman was nevertheless pleased by the respectful, almost formal courtesy with which the herbalist treated her, and by the kindness which he bestowed on her baby.

"Simon Magus" was positively delighted by the huge audiences which flocked around to stare at the beautiful hair and eyes of his "Helena of Tyre." He enjoyed the tears of gladness which flowed over the recovery of the leprous Baby Lazarus, and basked in the murmurs of awe which greeted his assistant's description of her neighbors' salvation. But, most of all, he loved the endless rain of coins which showered at his feet, which could buy him gold rings, fur pillows, a painted wagon and embroidered robes without depleting his ever-deepening pool of silver.

Indeed, Jeremiah Vinograd's fortune seemed to be improving each day. For several weeks after his meeting with Judah ben Simon, he noticed that Rachel Anna's listeners appeared doubly moved by the trembling voice in which she told her tale of suffering, doubly inclined to recall their own miseries, and to buy the medicines necessary for their cure.

For the truth was that his assistant had become so bored and familiar with the lines of her act that she could repeat them mechanically, automatically, while her mind ranged elsewhere; eventually, out of confused, half-conscious motives of her own, she began to concentrate all her mourning for Judah ben Simon and Hannah Polikov into the few hours each day during

(205)

which she performed.

Thus, it was this genuine sorrow, glimpsed through the tired sentences of Rachel Anna's monologue, which brought her audience so low that they could think of nothing but their own bouts of melancholia; and it was the grief which the abandoned wife felt as she recalled the conversation in the Prince Zarembka's estate which invariably convinced her listeners that only a good purgative could save them from the deadly sin of despair.

"Ah," sighed King Casimir, interrupting the rabbi, "if only Judah ben Simon had been wiser, *he* could have been the one to make use of Rachel Anna's talents, to combine true love and happiness with financial success."

"Perhaps," murmured Eliezer thoughtfully, "though one might well inquire whether a contented woman is likely to sell as much patent medicine as a sad one. Nevertheless, one is tempted to assume that Judah ben Simon could have benefited from any assistance, no matter how trifling. For, as Jeremiah Vinograd was climbing toward the peak of his success, his former student was slipping further and further into poverty and failure."

"Then it was wrong for him to think that his fortune would improve in distant lands?" asked the king, who had often been attracted by the same notion.

"Yes, he was," nodded the rabbi. "So wrong, in fact, that it took him less than a month to understand the extent of his error. Judah ben Simon needed only to cross the Hungarian border and hear the strange yawp of the Magyar tongue in order to realize that he would probably starve before he could learn how to advertise his products. He cursed himself for having overlooked this obvious obstacle, for having failed to consult his teacher about the rudiments of other languages.

Still, hoping for some burst of enlightenment which might suddenly enable him to solve the puzzle of Czech, Bulgarian, Serbian, Croatian, and Italian, he continued with his foreign journey, sleeping in the unfamiliar forests, and barely subsisting on his dwindling resources. Finally, at the end of a long, frozen winter, the traveler found himself at the foothills of the southern Alps—penniless, hungry, asking in sign language for the road back to Poland.

It was then that Judah ben Simon resolved to conquer his pride, and to try his luck among the aristocratic ladies of Kuzman.

XIV

The morning of Judah ben Simon's arrival in
Kuzman," began the Rabbi Eliezer, "was filled
with sunlight and the scent of May flowers, all the
clarity of winter and all the sweetness of spring. The
traveler stood in the outskirts of the settlement, feeling the cool, fresh wind on his face, gazing up at the
pine-covered mountains, and wondering if he had actually stumbled in upon his future home in paradise.

But, as his glance moved downward, he soon realized that heaven would never quarter its celestial hosts
in a town which had made such a pitiful attempt to
hide its squalor beneath a thin veneer of quality and
comfort. The ramshackle huts were plainly visible behind their false fronts, paneled doors, and carved shutters; even a shell of new masonry could not conceal
the crumbling wooden shingles of the ancient Ortho-
dox church. Everything in Kuzman seemed new, un-

used. The trees which lined the market place were spindly and half-grown; the cobblestones had not yet been worn smooth.

Despite all his knowledge of human nature, the mountebank found it hard to evaluate this evidence of new wealth, and difficult to comprehend how so many of the local inhabitants could afford to deck themselves in caracul caps, silk scarves, and ivory buttons. For, though it was almost noon, the villagers hunkered sluggishly outside the teahouses, grinning lazily and puffing on their hookahs as if the day had not yet begun. Indeed, the stranger might never have understood the town's evident prosperity, if some sporadic activity along the dusty side streets had not given him a clue:

Two porters bearing crates of fragrant Mandarin oranges staggered through an alley. A trapper squatted on the ground, surrounded by heaps of russet-colored pelts. In the shade of a doorway, a cobbler stitched delicate embroidery on a soft, leather slipper, so small that it could only have been intended for the foot of a queen.

These sights convinced Judah ben Simon that Jeremiah Vinograd had finally given him some good advice. "Even the air smells of rich women," he thought excitedly, as he passed a perfume-maker's stall. And, eager to take advantage of this perfect opportunity, he rushed to the center of the market place, set down his bench, and began to shout at the top of his lungs.

* * *

Suddenly, Eliezer lowered his head, and, for just a moment, King Casimir glimpsed the traces of a blush on the old man's wrinkled cheeks. "To speak the truth," murmured the rabbi, looking up, "I am reluctant to narrate this scene, which portrays my hero in a somewhat unflattering light. Therefore, I will merely summarize the events which transpired after the mountebank ascended his platform.

"For almost two hours," he continued hastily, "Judah ben Simon delivered a thoughtful, sincere, learned, and unimaginably boring dissertation on pharmaceutical medicine. Most of the village men assumed that only a fool could be so humorless, and did not even bother to leave their seats at the edge of the market place; no one came forward except the most desperate old grandfathers, who, after thirty years of indigestion, were willing to try anything.

But the response of the local women was not nearly so lukewarm. Too thunderstruck to comprehend one word of Judah ben Simon's speech, they stood motionless until he had finished; then, coughing, spitting, holding their heads and moaning in pain, they stormed the platform with a battery of ailments. The mountebank treated their ills with smiles and placebos, but found himself unable to concentrate on their tales of meddling in-laws, thankless children, and insensitive husbands; for he was too busy seeking the lady whose fancy clothes and chronic neurasthenia would brand her as a member of the upper class. However, when night had come without bringing any sign of such a woman, Judah sighed, picked up his bench, and squandered his last few coppers on a room at the grimy village inn.

"Perhaps these noblewomen have no need of mountebanks," thought the young man, tossing on his lumpy straw pallet. "Perhaps they are so lovely that they scorn cosmetics, so wealthy that they need not fear the loss of youth and beauty, so prudent that they never suffer from female complaints."

As it happened, however, Judah ben Simon's prospects were not nearly so dim as he imagined. Early the next morning, he answered a timid knock on his door to discover a fat, teen-aged girl, gazing at him with great moon-eyes and trembling from head to foot. Unlike the majority of dark-skinned, strong-boned mountain women, Judah's visitor had the pale, blotched, unhealthy look of adolescents who have spent too much time fretting indoors.

The girl watched him expectantly for several minutes; her chubby face crumpled in disappointment. "You do not remember me?" she whispered.

"I most certainly do not," replied Judah ben Simon.

"I was there in the market place when you spoke yesterday," she explained, beginning to fiddle with a few strands of oily hair. "I was standing in the front row, the entire time. I was sure that you looked straight at me."

"Then why did you not consult me then?" demanded the mountebank, angrily comparing his dreams of graceful aristocrats with the reality of this lumpish peasant.

"Oh, no, sir!" protested the young woman, curtseying frantically as the words became jumbled in her mouth. "I am not here on my own behalf, sir, but on that of my mistress, the Princess Maria Zarembka. Yesterday, when I returned from town, I told the ladies how handsome you were, how learned, how cultured, how sophisticated and genteel. And I asked them if there was anyone in their households who needed the services of a mountebank.

"The three ladies only laughed," continued the maid; but, before she could utter another word, Judah had taken her elbow and ushered her into his room, as gallantly as if she had been the Queen of Sheba, come on a royal visit. "And what do these 'ladies' of yours call themselves?" he asked.

"Aside from the Princess Maria," she replied, giggling hysterically when she realized that there was nowhere for her to sit but the rumpled mattress, "there is the Countess Catherine and the Baroness Sophia. But, here in Kuzman, people speak of them only as 'The Three Sisters.' "

"Then they are related?" inquired the mountebank.

"That would be as rare as apples, plums, and peaches growing on a single tree," answered the maid, beaming as if she herself had invented the simile which had long ago made the rounds of local wits. "No, they call them that because the ladies keep so closely to themselves, and rarely come to town, not even to attend the Easter mass."

"Then your mistresses are shy?" said Judah. "Slow in adjusting to a new place. Still ill-at-ease in a town full of strangers?"

"No, sir," said the girl, curtseying again, "that is not it at all. During the many years they have lived here, they have had a thousand opportunities to meet their neighbors. And perhaps they would have done so if it had not been for the rude and curious stares which follow them through town, and the vicious lies which gossips spread concerning their unmarried state."

"What lies?" asked the young man, thanking heaven for having sent him such a cooperative informant.

"They are not worth the trouble of repeating," declared the servant, with a note of genuine outrage in her voice. "I will only assure you that they are false and wicked. Of course, I cannot claim to understand why such lovely women should remain unmarried; at certain times of year, their homes are full of handsome suitors, meandering from room to room and complaining of the ladies' heartlessness."

"Ah," sighed the mountebank sympathetically, "with no husbands to protect and amuse them, your mistresses must lead insecure and lonely lives."

"It is not so bad in summer," answered the maid, "when noblemen from all over Poland flock to their balls and parties. But from the first of October to the end of June I do believe their isolation must be almost unbearable."

"Is that so?" murmured Judah ben Simon, scarcely able to suppress an excited grin. "In that case, they must surely have welcomed the news of a cultivated young stranger, newly come to town."

"Not at all," she mumbled, staring uncomfortably at the floor. "As I started to say before, they only laughed at me, and accused me of all sorts of wicked things. Then, when I persisted, the Baroness Sophia became annoyed, and swore that she would not dose her lowest servant with the poisons of a wandering charlatan. But late last night, my own lady came into my room, and confessed that her pet kitten had indeed seemed out of sorts lately, in need of a suitable tonic."

"I see," thought Judah ben Simon bitterly. "These snobbish women dare not trust me with anything more significant than the spirits of a peevish cat." Nevertheless, concealing his emotions, he went immediately to work. He opened every herbal packet and held each colored bottle up to the light. He presented them for the maid's inspection, and explained their contents in a tone and vocabulary which were in themselves implicit compliments to her intelligence. He promised instant recoveries, described miraculous cures, and so dazzled the provincial girl with his radiant smiles that, by the time she clutched up her bag of catnip and departed, she was swaying from side to side and gasping for breath.

That afternoon, she again appeared at Judah ben Simon's door—bearing a gilded invitation to the home of the Princess Maria Zarembka.

Just after sunset, the young man put on his blue mountebank's robe and started towards the mountains north of town; arriving at the huge stone mansion, he

(214)

was ushered to the threshold of the main dining room. "And there," smiled the Rabbi Eliezer, "my hero came upon a sight so exquisite that it might well have blinded the sensitive eyes of your greatest court artist.

"The whole interior of that long, low-ceilinged hall shimmered with a weird phosphorescence, like the strange, silvery sheen which sometimes appears on the surface of the finest silk carpets. The crystal chandeliers seemed to hover in mid-air, casting a pale, unearthly light on the tapestries which lined the paneled walls. Beneath this glow, the colors of the room formed a muted pattern of deep burgundy and purple, moss green and rich, wood brown. These hues were repeated in the woven cloth which covered the long, narrow table and set off the lustrous and harmonious arrangement of pewter dishes, iron candlesticks, plates of hammered brass, and old silver goblets, filled with dark, red claret."

"When does this narrative take place?" interrupted King Casimir, as if he had just discovered an important clue to the rabbi's meaning. "I cannot remember a time when the nobles of our land set their tables in the manner of a tinsmith's stall."

"But it was not these furnishings," continued Eliezer, ignoring the boy's question, "which lent the room its opalescent quality. Rather, it was the beauty of the gray-velvet-clad woman standing at the far end of the hall, whose face gave all her elegant surroundings the air of a plain background designed to exhibit a single smoky topaz.

Judah saw that she was tall, black-haired, about thirty, with olive skin and the strong, strangely tragic features of a Corsican or a Greek. But, as she glided towards him, like a figure in a dream, the young man was soon obliged to discontinue his appraisal of the lady's charms. For suddenly, he noticed that his powers of observation had begun to fail, and that the woman's smooth, hypnotic pace was causing him to feel an odd dizziness and nausea, not unlike the final stages of a drunken stupor.

"Was this setting really so strange?" broke in the King of Poland. "Or was your hero just another peasant bumpkin, overwhelmed by the magnificence of ordinary aristocratic life?"

"I swear to you, King Casimir," replied the rabbi, "that even Your Majesty himself has never experienced an atmosphere so dark, so heady, so full of promise, mystery, and danger. Indeed, considering the circumstances, it was remarkable that the mountebank was able to regain his wits so soon. Shortly after the Princess Maria had taken his sweaty hand and led him to the table, the young man's composure started to return. He decided that his faintness had been a simple matter of optical confusion, brought on by the peculiar light of the chandeliers and the gleaming candles. In this same calm spirit, he acknowledged the princess's greeting, gave his name as Stanislas the Physician, and reassured himself that his otherworldly hostess was just another woman—richer and more beautiful than any he had yet encountered, but equally capable of being captivated and delighted. Therefore, he fixed her with his most ingratiating smile, and inquired about the welfare of his patient.

"If you are referring to my servant girl," replied the Princess Maria, smiling slyly, "then I must inform you that she was half-dead of faintness and palpitations by the time she reached our doorstep."

"No," stammered Judah uneasily, "I was speaking of your pet. I hope that you will permit me to observe the creature's condition, since firsthand diagnosis is the only truly reliable method of diagnosis."

"My dear Stanislas," answered the woman, with a musical laugh, "I have not invited you here for an animal show. Come now, we are both experienced in the ways of the world; we both know that this entire catnip affair was merely a charade designed to procure me the assistance of a handsome traveler in whiling away these last evenings before the start of my social season. Furthermore," she continued, wrapping her long fingers around a wine goblet and leaning gracefully towards him, "my friends and I do not pay court to the God of Science."

As Judah stammered in helpless amazement, twelve somber, uniformed servants entered the room, bearing huge platters of roast beef, grilled pheasant, mutton stews, wine broths, and jellied aspics. These fragrant reminders of all the days he had gone hungry jolted the bewildered young man into a desperate attempt at genteel expression.

"Then am I to understand," he said, "that my lady is a devotee of religion?"

The princess's eyes glinted merrily, and her deep voice took on a mocking tone. "In my house," she said, "the image of Cupid is placed above that of Our Blessed Mother."

"But what has that to do with my medicine?" asked the mountebank.

"Simply this," the woman replied. "It has often been said that scientists are among the God of Love's most disobedient servants."

"On the contrary," he smiled, rising to her challenge. And so it happened that Judah ben Simon and the Princess Maria Zarembka came to debate the nature of love and science.

Unfortunately, the young man was such a stranger to this witty and artificial style of conversation that it took him almost the entire meal to learn its rules and patterns. At first, he could not understand why the lady did not inquire about his travels or his studies, and endeavored to engage her on the subject of her day-to-day existence; then, when he began to see that such inconsequential chatter was out of fashion among the aristocracy, he committed himself to the subject at hand. Still, in his efforts to achieve the proper tone, Judah often stumbled, and relied upon the princess's disapproving looks to point out his errors in demanding precise definitions of love and science, and in averring that passion might perhaps be nothing more than an elixir of certain chemicals and animal instincts.

Thus, it was not until the table was heaped high with mountains of frosted cakes that Judah ben Simon felt sufficiently self-confident to lead their discussion down a new and unexplored path.

"Suddenly," he began, helping himself to a fourth glass of claret, "it occurs to me that all our lamentations concerning the incompatibility of love and science have been unfounded. In fact, the two spheres are as harmonious and well-matched as the opals in your lovely earrings. How could I have prattled on so long without confessing that I am something of an expert on human behavior? In this capacity, I have never attempted to banish love into the realm of dim longings and irrational impulses. Rather, I have studied it objectively, and can offer positive proof that passion and science may actually be combined in an effort to understand the gentle workings of the heart."

"And what have these studies taught you?" asked the Princess Maria, suppressing a smile.

"Many things," declared the mountebank proudly. "Many things. For instance: have you not noticed that, when ugly men and women look for love, they consider nothing so much as the physical beauty of their mates? Is it not true that sleeplessness is the surest symptom of passion, that loss of appetite plagues the rejected lover? And certainly, my lady, you do not need a scientist to tell you that, while satiation soon quenches the flames of adoration, an unsatisfied desire can burn throughout a man's whole life. Indeed, madam, these few examples should enable a woman of your intelligence to comprehend my system, and to acknowledge the truth and universality of these scientific laws of love."

At this final statement, the princess burst into delighted giggles, and rushed to the defense of Cupid's boundless variety. "How can you not see," she murmured, in a soft, cajoling tone, "that the God of Love is so brilliantly capricious that he could never restrict himself to a fixed and rigid plan, so infinitely imaginative that he need not repeat the same combination twice? Why, for every rule you have named, I can already cite an exception:

"My late Cousin Wladislaw, whose warts outnumbered the stars in the sky, paid court to a woman twice as hideous as himself. A lady of my acquaintance slept fourteen hours a day so that she might dream of her absent lover; then, when he neglected to return, she consoled herself by gorging her stomach with ten stuffed capons. My Aunt Theresa has been the same man's mistress for sixteen years, yet their passion has not diminished since the first night they spent in each other's arms.

"Besides," she continued, winking mischievously as she refilled her visitor's goblet, "I could tell you about love so strange that your system could never have predicted its occurrence. A courtier of my father's loved two beautiful sisters equally well, and, driven by misery and indecision, married their widowed hag of a mother in the hope that she would embody both her daughters' virtues. A dwarfed young girl in my native

(220)

village was so enamored of a handsome neighbor that she had herself stretched on the rack so that he might find her more attractive. And, only recently, I was forced to dismiss my chief falconer because of his obsessional attachment to my prize hawk."

"But these bizarre passions cannot really be classed among the works of love," argued Judah ben Simon. "In fact, they might even be profitably interpreted as additional proof of my scheme."

"Wait!" cried King Casimir of Poland, interrupting the narrative of this gracious dinner party for the third and final time. "I appreciate the singularity of your hero, of his fascinating hostess, and of his worthy and thought-provoking system. Yet," he continued, anxious finally to display one area of experience which, he hoped, would exclude and consequently impress the old man, "I am so familiar with this sort of debate, which so often occurs within my own court, that I fear I will soon lose interest."

"Perhaps that is true," replied Eliezer, somewhat snappishly. "But perhaps you are not quite so familiar with the way in which this particular discussion ended. For, through a series of events which an innocent old man like myself could not possibly hope to describe, Judah ben Simon's aristocratic debate on the nature of love was finally resolved between the silken sheets of the Princess Maria Zarembka's bed.

"The next morning," the rabbi went on, with a forgiving smile for his red-faced listener, "the mountebank awoke to find himself in the strangest bedroom he had ever seen. For the single candle which had guided their passage from the main hall had not enabled him to perceive that the chamber was decorated in the style of a nomad's tent. Rough canvas hangings, worn rugs, and crude tapestries covered the walls. Hay straws littered the floor, and charcoal braziers smoked in the corners. The bed was piled high with the skins of long-haired sheep and goats; beneath them, the Princess Maria lay wide awake, staring at Judah ben Simon as if he were a dangerous marauder who had somehow invaded her home.

The young man was equally disoriented until he remembered the pleasures of the night before; then, he laughed warmly, and reached out to stroke the woman's black hair. "Good morning," he smiled, hoping to reassure her that she had not bestowed her favors on a lover who would take them for granted. "It would seem that the God of Love has an even greater store of marvels and surprises than I had realized."

Without pausing to answer him, the noblewoman leaped out of bed and ran from the room.

Almost immediately, the same maid who had come to the inn stumbled into the bedchamber. One look at the naked guest caused her such convulsions of embarrassment that she nearly dropped the heavy silver tray —on which the mountebank eventually found six sweet rolls, a pot of coffee, and a note inviting him to bid his hostess good-by in the main dining room. Judah ate and dressed quickly, then rushed downstairs; but, when at last he came upon the princess, he became so ashamed and self-conscious that he could hardly speak. "I am sorry," he mumbled haltingly, "for anything I might have done to offend you."

"You have not offended me at all," she replied. "That is just the problem. And now, if you will consent to keep me company while I finish the remainder of my breakfast, I will tell you a story which may help you comprehend my motives.

"When I was fifteen years old," began the noblewoman, when her guest was seated, "a gang of bandits invaded our family estate. Within a few hours, they had terrified the cowardly royal guards into submission, ransacked our mansion, and beaten my father and brothers to death with barbed whips. The ghastly sights of that morning so stunned and shocked me that two days elapsed before I realized that I myself was among the booty which the gigantic bandit chieftain was bearing off to his mountain hideout.

"In the beginning, I did nothing but curse my captors and spit in their faces; the coarse, brutal robbers, who dressed in swatches of fur and wore their matted hair halfway down their backs, would surely have retaliated, if their captain had not ordered them to leave me in peace. Gradually, however, when the icy winter wind began to shriek through the barren hills, sheer loneliness made me consent to share in their drunken revels and their feasts of roasted horsemeat, to learn to ride bareback on their frothing steeds, and even to help them plan their future raids. At last, at the end of February, I took to warming myself beneath the heavy skins of my protector's bed.

"But I mean just that," insisted the princess, noting her listener's curious look. "For I did not let him have my body. Remember: I was fifteen then, a virgin, with dreams of a pale, perfumed prince who would someday touch me with his cool hands. And I could not bring myself to abandon these dreams for such a muscular and strong-smelling reality.

"For some reason, the bandit obeyed my wishes. Who knows why men act as they do? But, even though he saw that I was also struggling against myself, the waiting and frustration did him no good. He grew distracted, nervous, absent-minded, less boisterous in answering his men when they taunted him about my uselessness.

"Finally, he could stand it no longer. Late one night, on the eve of their long-awaited raid on the city of Cracow, he drank three jugs of wine, and, responding to the jeers of his companions, came charging towards me, in the midst of the camp.

"His pistol was inches from my heart; my legs went numb with panic. Nevertheless, driven by instinct and fear, I threw back my shoulders and tried to make my scant one hundred pounds of flesh seem as stiff and imposing as possible.

"Shoot me if you want!" I screamed. "My virtue will protect me from your bullets!"

"At this point," sighed the princess, "any man of

good society would have seen me for the idiot I was; he would have sneered, turned his back, and stalked away. But my bandit lover flew into a rage, and, shutting his eyes, fired at my breast.

"To this day," she continued, after a short pause, "I cannot understand what happened. Everyone saw the gun's flare, and heard the report. I cringed against the pain, but only for a moment, for I was not hit.

"Perhaps the pistol misfired; perhaps my would-be murderer was too drunk to hit his mark. Perhaps," she smiled, "I was shielded by my virtue. But none of these explanations even occurred to the bandits, who immediately decided that they were in the presence of a witch. Mumbling with terror, they saddled their horses, and set out on their ill-fated invasion of Cracow.

"Two weeks later, when they still had not returned for their belongings, I knew that my robber chieftain was dead, and that I had loved him more than I would ever love again.

"Throughout that spring, I remained alone in the mountains to mourn him; in June, I stole a horse, and rode home. But my mother and sisters, who had finally adjusted to their bereavement, were disturbed by the sight of my face, which reminded them of that tragic day. They refused to believe that I had preserved my innocence, and despaired of finding me a suitable husband. Therefore, they suggested that I retreat to the Carpathians for a short, recuperative rest, and I have been here ever since."

Judah Ben Simon kept silent for what seemed to him a suitable interval, then spoke in a kind and gentle tone. "You are not the only woman who, after a night like ours, has awoken with a strong desire to speak of her first love," he said. "Yet, though your story has moved and fascinated me, I cannot see how it justifies your hasty exit from our bed."

"When I was fifteen years old," the princess explained patiently, "I gave my heart, but held on to my body like a miser. Now, though I give my body a thousand times over, I will keep my heart set aside for that one man, for I do not want to be prodigal with the only thing I ever gave him. For this reason, I am terribly afraid to spend too long in the company of a guest who pleases me. And that is why I must now ask you to leave my house forever.

"But," she continued, turning her smiling face towards him, "I am certain that the citizens of Kuzman have little to offer traveling mountebanks in the way of financial reward, and I would hate for you to leave our town with so little to show for your efforts. Therefore, so that you may at least have the pleasure of one more good meal before your departure, I am extending you this invitation to dine tonight at the home of my friend, the Countess Catherine Landowska."

Grateful for this second chance to improve his lot, Judah ben Simon rose from the table, bid the princess a gracious farewell, and hurried back to the inn for a few more hours of sleep. Thus, it was not until that night, when the mountebank discovered the exterior of the Countess Catherine's mansion to be an exact replica of the Princess Maria's, that he first began to comprehend the damage which his spirit had sustained.

Chilled by cold waves of anxiety, he hesitated at the bottom of the steep carriageway, wondering if the evening's entertainment was to be another witty play of discomfort and deception, in which he would again be cast as the fool. These thoughts so undermined Judah's confidence that he would surely have retreated to the village, if a sudden fancy had not entered his mind and enabled him to find a source of hope in the very familiarity of the thick stone walls.

"By now," he muttered, attempting to fire up his courage as he climbed the cobbled path, "I have had some experience with houses like this one, and with the sort of women who inhabit them. I am no longer the blundering simpleton whom they can intimidate with their stylized debates and fancy manners."

As soon as Judah reached the threshold of the dining room, however, he realized that none of last night's lessons would help him at the countess's table. For, despite a certain similarity in decorative style, no two rooms could have seemed so different as those of the aristocratic neighbors.

The same muted tapestries covered the walls; the same narrow table occupied the center of the hall. But, in contrast to the pale, silvery phosphorescence of the princess's public apartments, those of her friend gleamed like a bracelet of burnished gold. Here, the chandeliers were set with thousands of tiny candles;

the brass had been replaced with delicate china, the dull pewter dishes had been supplanted by plates of sparkling crystal; and the goblets of dark claret had given way to pitchers of bubbling champagne.

Once again, however, the atmosphere of the room owed less to its furnishings than to the presence of its owner. And, if the mood and appearance of the Princess Maria had suggested a smoky topaz, then the Countess Catherine Landowska could only have been described as a diamond of unspeakable brilliance. Blue-eyed, fair-skinned, with high cheekbones and long, blond hair curled into ringlets, the lady seemed a perfect Slavic beauty. Her body was frail and doll-like, her nose slightly snubbed; her small, heart-shaped mouth wore a flirtatious smile.

"Perhaps," thought Judah ben Simon, as she rushed forward to take his hand, "this one will prove less dignified and aloof, more open, simple and direct."

But this impression was soon dispelled when the countess led him to the table, and began to speak.

"I have been told that you are a fellow of keen intelligence," she said, "a mountebank and a man of science. Therefore, I am sure that no one could be better qualified to tell me this: what is it that we catch and throw away, that we cannot catch and keep?"

Unnerved by this peculiar form of greeting, her guest was unable to imagine any fit response, until, recalling his conversation with the Princess Maria, he turned to his hostess with a knowing grin. "Can you be referring to love?" he murmured suggestively. But the smile froze on his lips when he found the lady staring at him as coldly as if he had uttered the most shocking obscenity.

"No," she replied. "That is not even a remote possibility."

"Then I am afraid I do not know," he said, feeling more and more bewildered.

"Ah, well," sighed the countess after a while, "I suppose it was unfair of me to begin with such a difficult question, an unsolvable riddle which is said to have driven the great poet Homer to a death of sheer frustration. Now, to resume on an easier and more congenial note, let me pose you another: what was four weeks old at the birth of Cain, yet has since grown no older?"

Judah ben Simon labored desperately to summon up his few remaining memories of the Rabbi Joseph Joshua's school, but, in his growing consternation, could think of nothing but the Sin of Adam, and the Exile from the Garden of Eden.

"The moon!" cried the countess, interrupting his puzzled reverie. Although she had begun to giggle, Judah could plainly see the first signs of doubt and impatience beneath her charming smile. For this reason, when the lady offered him a third and presumably final opportunity to redeem himself, he employed more logic and concentration than he had ever applied to his scientific research, in a single effort to find the most likely solution.

"What is it that watches us constantly, though we

are afraid to look at it in return?" she asked.

"Death?" he ventured hesitantly, after a silence of almost five minutes.

A mixture of delight and relief flooded the countess's face. Only then did she clap her hands and order that the servants bring on the meal; only then did she introduce herself, and explain that, over the years, she had developed a passionate fondness for all manner of riddles, enigmas, puzzles, problems, games, and paradoxes.

"For example," she whispered coyly, "have you ever heard the story of the thirteen Jews?"

"No," answered Judah tensely, anticipating some racial slur.

"Long ago," began the lady, leaning forward so that the mountebank could see the tops of her breasts above her dark blue satin gown, "Josephus and twelve companions were pursued into a cave by hostile Romans, and decided that mass suicide would be a nobler fate than certain slaughter. Unfortunately, they were unable to devise an equitable order in which to die, and turned to Josephus, who was striving to invent some means of saving his own life."

"With the aid of pencil and paper," interrupted Judah, who, though still perplexed, was beginning to comprehend and join in the spirit of the evening, "I could soon find the great historian a solution."

"I am sure you could," purred the noblewoman, her cheeks growing steadily more flushed. "Luckily for Josephus, however, he did not have to wait for you to come along.

(230)

"Finishing his computations, he persuaded his friends to form a circle, and eliminate every third man, counting around and around. They would proceed in a clockwise direction, starting from the fellow on Josephus's left. Naturally, Josephus himself was the last one remaining, and quickly escaped from the cave."

Thus, as the dinner progressed, the Countess Catherine led Judah ben Simon in a lively discussion of the history and meaning of puzzles. She told him of magic squares, Chinese rings, Alcuin's ferry, the tower of Brahma, and the great wheat game invented by the Grand Vizier Sissa ben Dahir. She amused him with the riddle of the sixteen larks and that of Mohammed's camels; she narrated the legend of the sphynx, and recounted the paradox of Achilles and the tortoise.

Her tone grew steadily warmer, more seductive, so that the mountebank was often unable to perceive any relation between the things she said and the manner in which she said them. After the servants had cleared away the last dishes, she posed the problem of the four jealous husbands in a tone of unmistakable invitation. Judah managed to make use of all his wits and solve it—a feat unmatched by any of the lady's previous guests. The champagne gradually disappeared; their games became intimate and childish. At last, they investigated the mystery of the hidden treasure, which, amid much laughter and accidental brushing of hands, was finally discovered to be a lavender sachet, concealed beneath the coverlet of the Countess Catherine's bed.

"The next day," said the Rabbi Eliezer, "Judah ben

Simon awoke to find himself in a room made completely of glass, set in the midst of an elegant formal garden. Trying to remember how he had come to rest in such a peculiar environment, he rolled over on his side—just in time to see the Countess Catherine Landowska escaping through the door.

Cursing his stupidity in having let himself be tricked twice at the same game, Judah threw on his mountebank's robe and rushed down to the main hall. There, reflected in the mirrored pendants hanging from the chandeliers, the morning sun produced a light far brighter than the thousand candles. This blinding dazzle halted the young man at the door of the room, and, in the few moments which elapsed before his eyes became accustomed to the glare, his fury burned down to a smoldering bitterness.

"So," he muttered, standing over the countess, "we are beginning our day with a fine game of hide and seek."

"Sit down," she commanded, in a calm, serious tone, "and I will tell you of a puzzle which may help you understand.

"When I was just sixteen," she began, as her visitor reluctantly obeyed, "my mother died, and the count, my father, began his rapid descent into madness. That year, when the young men first came suing for my hand, he took it into his head to be like the lords of old, and to devise a small test by which the would-be suitors might prove themselves worthy of his only daughter.

"The challenge was a hedge-maze made of tall haw-

(232)

thorns, much like those labyrinths which adorn the gardens of many wealthy homes. The contestant had only to reach its center, and inscribe his initials in the loose red clay.

"I assure you that I was much lovelier in those days; my father's fortune was enormous. For these reasons, many handsome nobles were willing to try their skill in a bit of harmless sport. But what they did not know was this: the maze was an impenetrable system of blind alleys, dead ends and vicious traps, through which a man might stumble aimlessly for the rest of his life.

"And that is precisely what happened. Watching from my attic window, forbidden to offer a word of warning or advice, I watched them die, one by one. Of course, the brave aristocrats showed no fear until they discovered the remains of an unfortunate predecessor. Then, the fainthearted boys immediately sat down to await the onset of starvation and exhaustion, while the more spirited young men tore themselves to shreds as they attempted to crash through the unusually sharp and plentiful thorns.

"By the time a distinguished delegation arrived to investigate the disappearance of their favorite sons, the corridors of the labyrinth were littered with drying bones. My father was condemned to an asylum; and, despite my protestations of innocence, I was exiled to the furthest reaches of the Carpathians, where merciful Providence delivered me at the Princess Maria's doorstep.

"Since then," concluded the countess, with a pathetic sigh, "I have become so comfortable and familiar with all sorts of puzzles that I no longer fear the memory of that maze which did my father's gruesome work. But, regardless of the princess's constant persuasion, I have not yet been able to forgive the God of Love, who spurred those poor young men to pit themselves against a lock which had no key. And therefore, I must beg you to leave my home at once, before our hearts become entwined in the webs which our wits and bodies have been spinning."

"Before that happens," snapped Judah ben Simon angrily, stalking from the house, "you will have more than enough time to solve your most baffling paradoxes."

XV

"THAT AFTERNOON," continued the Rabbi Eliezer, "when the Baroness Sophia Majeski's invitation was slipped beneath his door, Judah ben Simon crumpled the gilded parchment in his fist and threw it on the mattress. "I would sooner dine on blood with Satan's favorite hellcat," he muttered furiously, and resumed his preparations to leave Kuzman. But an hour later, as the mountebank considered the tattered garments, chipped bottles and leaking packets which half-filled his cotton sack, he suddenly realized that a man who had no idea when he would eat again might well take his last meal at the home of a baroness.

"It must be possible," he told himself, "to remain unaffected by these noblewomen's tricks and enticements. Now that I am no longer seeking their money or their respect, why should I care if they think me a gentleman of wit or a bumbling idiot? I can simply avail myself of the baroness's pantry, then be on my way."

"But once again," sighed the rabbi, "all of Judah's confidence and resolution vanished on the doorstep of his hostess's dining room.

"King Casimir," said Eliezer, "considering how many years it takes for a man to amass a legion of ghosts behind him, a young fellow like yourself cannot often have experienced the uncomfortable sensation I am about to describe. Among men of my age, however, it is an almost daily occurrence to see someone on the street whom, for just an instant, we recognize as one of the most hated or beloved figures from our past. The knees grow weak; the heart begins to pound; and it seems scarcely possible to keep from fainting until that climactic moment when the long-lost star of our youth turns out to be a neighbor's cousin, from the other side of town."

"I know exactly what you mean," nodded Casimir, who, in fact, had often glimpsed his mother in the faces of obscure relations and foreign ambassadors' wives.

"In that case," continued the rabbi, "you will certainly be able to imagine the shock which coursed through Judah ben Simon's body when he saw Rachel Anna walking towards him across the room.

"Of course," the old man went on hastily, "Judah soon perceived that the baroness's resemblance to his wife was limited to her orange hair and her thin, graceful figure. The noblewoman's face was fuller, her features more regular; both her eyes were a cool, pure blue. But," mused Eliezer, "who can say how much that faint likeness influenced the young man's judgment and helped convince him that the Baroness Sophia Majeski was the most beautiful woman he had seen since the start of his travels?

Indeed, this beauty so disarmed him that several minutes passed before he began to notice the strangeness of her home, which seemed more like a woodsman's hunting lodge than the palace of an aristocratic lady. Everything was plain and bare. A blaze in the granite fireplace and a few dim candles provided the only light. There were no tapestries on the walls, no chandeliers hanging from the ceiling, no fine cloth covering the oaken table. The dishes were made of heavy peasant ceramic, the utensils of polished wood; the tin mugs contained clear, cold water.

"I never expected such chasms of style to separate a baroness's apartments from those of her nobler sisters," marveled Judah ben Simon. "Perhaps this woman will be able to prattle of nothing but needlework, horticulture, and the rising price of mutton." But, as the young man sat patiently at the table, waiting for his hostess to initiate the conversation, he began to understand that the difference between the baroness and her neighbors was far greater than her decorative tastes had led him to suspect:

Unlike the Princess Maria and the Countess Catherine, the Baroness Sophia Majeski did not favor her guest with a single word.

(237)

"Perhaps she is afflicted with a stammer," thought the mountebank, in a sort of panic after ten minutes of uninterrupted silence had gone by. Yet, when the servants carried in the platters of simple, plentiful food, Judah heard the lady issue a series of firm, sharp commands, and realized that her speechlessness was not the consequence of some natural disability.

"I will not be the first to speak," he resolved warily, recalling his humiliation at the homes of the other noblewomen. "Surely, this unnatural reserve is just another trap, another trick designed to deceive and betray me. As far as I am concerned, neither of us need say anything all night; I will be perfectly happy to keep my mouth closed except when I am stuffing it with food."

As the meal progressed, he stubbornly kept his peace; yet, despite his efforts at detachment, he found himself struggling to discern the meaning of this new game, and thus outwit his hostess. The silence between them grew as tense and strained as that of two old lovers, grown restless in each other's company. Judah became steadily more unnerved, until at last, just as he was finishing his second helping of strawberries and clotted cream, all his patience vanished.

"So," he whispered angrily, leaning across the table so that the baroness could not evade his eyes, "are you going to disclose your sad history now, or do you plan to wait until tomorrow morning, like the others? Why not save us both some time and trouble, and reveal the mysterious relation between your behavior tonight and the miseries of your youth. Tell me: were you enamored of some dashing deaf-mute? Did ten thousand men take vows of eternal silence in return for one smile from your pretty lips?"

Startled, the Baroness Sophia glanced up from her plate, then laughed, as if delighted by some unexpected pleasure. "My only story," she said, "is that I alone among the three of us have had no tragic drama in my past."

"What kind of story is that?" demanded Judah ben Simon, dismayed by the girl's refusal to acknowledge his insult. "What kind of noblewoman are you, without a bandit lover, or a hedge-maze in your childhood home?"

"A sad one," she replied, answering both his questions at once.

"I do not believe it!" cried the mountebank. "Life here in the mountains must be paradise for a lovely young woman with no fear of poverty, hunger, or cold. And, if there really are no monsters looming out of your past, then you are even luckier than those two friends of yours."

"I would gladly trade everything I own for one of those monsters," the baroness said calmly. "Listen: for the past three years, I have spent every evening in the company of two women whose lives once overflowed with wildness, magic, and the most delicious suffering. Night after night, when my companions stare into the fire and begin to brood on their glorious sorrows, I am reminded that I have no tragic story to offer in return, that nothing grand or heroic has ever happened to me. How could I presume to trouble them with anecdotes from my rebellious girlhood, with tales of how I slapped my sisters, slept with the grooms, and finally provoked my parents into sending me away? And, without a buried grief on which to blame my frailties, how can I dismiss all those empty-headed suitors after they have warmed my bed?"

"I suppose you can tell them the same things you are telling me," suggested the young man sarcastically.

"I swear that I have never spoken this way before," declared the baroness, her blue eyes shining with tears. Then, she giggled. "Usually, I rid myself of bothersome men by remaining silent as the grave for days on end."

"Then why have you chosen me for this singular honor?" asked her guest, torn between his old distrust and the growing conviction that the lady was sincere.

"Because," she replied, smiling boldly, "I am grateful that you did not try to spoil my meal with boring chatter. I am eager to test the reports I have heard concerning your superior wit. And I am utterly delighted by your beautiful blond hair."

But the mountebank could not repay his hostess's gracious compliments, for he was too disturbed by a vague echo of the past which had sounded in her words. Unable to identify the source of his distress, he attempted to drive it away by introducing some clever new topic of conversation. Thus, when he heard the voice of a solitary cat, howling in the darkness, it was with a deep sense of relief that he seized upon the opportunity which this noise appeared to offer.

"If that is the Princess Zarembka's kitten," he laughed, "it would seem that my medicines have failed to cure its melancholy."

"That is a story I can tell you!" exclaimed the Baroness Sophia happily, recovering from her dismay at the young man's cold response to her flattery. "The Princess Maria's cat!

"The princess and the countess found that wildcat long before I came here," she began, moving her chair closer to Judah ben Simon's and affecting a conspiratorial whisper. "By now, it is a full-grown beast, and only foolish sentiment allows them to speak of it as their kitten. But listen, and I will tell you what they do with that unfortunate animal:

"Sometimes, in the midst of January, when our lives have become more monotonous than the deserts of hell, the two ladies comb their mansions for a plump, healthy rat. Then, they shut themselves in a room with their pet and its natural prey, and, laughing merrily, watch the cat tease and batter its victim until the walls are streaked with blood."

"So that is how genteel ladies pass their time," said Judah ben Simon with a hearty laugh, though the image of the women at their sport had caused him to feel an unpleasant chill.

"These January games are only the beginning," said the baroness. "May I remind you that our winters last

(241)

until the end of April?" And, winking slyly, she began to entertain her guest with a series of scandalous anecdotes, rendered doubly delightful by the fact that they seemed to please the teller as much as her listener.

The stories intoxicated Judah ben Simon more than all the princess's wine and the countess's champagne; giddy and lightheaded, he heard himself repeatedly clapping his hands and shouting with laughter. Two hours later, when the lady collapsed in giggles and leaned her carrot-colored head on the table, the young man realized that he had not felt so carefree and happy since his first years in the forest.

"Now it is my turn to apologize for having nothing to offer in return," he said, after his hostess had raised her head and dried her eyes. "For how can I possibly repay you for the pleasure you have given me this evening? But, if you promise that you will not allow your disapproval of my base, mercenary motives to poison our friendship, I will try to make do with the tale of how I came to visit Kuzman, and of the eccentric mountebank I encountered in the estate of the Princess Maria's father."

The Baroness Sophia Majeski swore to the indestructibility of her affection, then laughed appreciatively as Judah ben Simon spoke of Corporal Svoboda, Jeremiah Vinograd, and the preposterous gypsy cart. When he had finished, however, she stared at him with the confused, quizzical expression of someone who still awaits the end of a joke long after the clown has fallen silent.

"Now that I have heard the conclusion of your story," she explained after a while, "I am doubly curious about its beginning. For I have a strong suspicion that the events which preceded your arrival at the princess's ancestral home were far more interesting than the circumstances of your journey to Kuzman."

"On the contrary," mumbled Judah ben Simon. "Nothing could be duller than my early history." Yet slowly, unwillingly, he let himself be persuaded to speak of his parents, his neighbors, and his native village. Urged on by the baroness's pertinent questions, he confessed to the charade which Simon and Hannah had enacted to bring about his conception. Encouraged by her sympathetic smiles, he began to talk of his marriage, and saw the noblewoman wince with jealousy and embarrassment when he recalled those years of happiness in the woods. At last, he described his final visit home, mentioned the promise which Rachel Anna had extracted from him, and, attempting to dispel the tears which had started to thicken his speech, ended his narrative with a sharp, bitter laugh.

"Something stranger than a child conceived in a dream!" he snarled hoarsely. "Can you imagine anything stranger than that?"

For several minutes, the baroness stared intently at her guest, then apparently discarded the answer she had first intended to give.

"Yes," she murmured, gesturing vaguely towards her open window. "If the moon were to slip down the sides of those mountains and roll through the fields,

(243)

that would be much stranger than a child conceived in a dream."

Once again, however, the young man could offer no suitable response, for the fact was that he had not heard one word of the lady's reply. Instead, he had been stunned and distracted by the distinct impression that one of her eyes was shining with a vivid green light. The mountebank did not stop trembling until he had succeeded in tracing this hallucination to his ill-advised foray into the past. Resolving to prevent the recurrence of such alarming delusions, he hastened to steer their conversation towards the safer and more navigable realm of the present.

Speaking in low, soft voices, Judah ben Simon and the Baroness Sophia began this phase of their talk by sharing their occasional joys. The noblewoman smiled as she attempted to recapture the brilliance of the Countess Catherine's midsummer dances; her guest described the satisfaction of curing an infant's colic. But, within five minutes, they had exhausted their entire store of happy experiences, and were obliged to confess the essential dreariness of their lives. Judah complained of his constant hunger, his pointless journeys, and his total inability to satisfy the crowds of jeering strangers. The baroness nodded understandingly, and spoke of the nights spent alone in her icy bedroom, trying to fall asleep with the pathetic sounds of six-month-old aristocratic gossip still echoing in her ears.

The intimate nature of this last image caused a portentous and somewhat nervous silence to fall over the couple. Neither the mountebank nor the lady uttered a word until the brassy and painfully discordant bells of Kuzman tolled five times. Then, Judah ben Simon and the Baroness Sophia laughed, joined hands across the bare wooden table, and, with all the unembarrassed haste of new lovers, rushed upstairs to the young woman's bedchamber.

"I am afraid," said the Rabbi Eliezer, "that I now find myself faced with the necessity of making a rather rude and brash intrusion into my hero's privacy. For I must tell you that, during his night with the Baroness Sophia, the young man began to remember the difference between true pleasure and the tired battles he had fought in the other noblewomen's beds. Indeed, he was so overwhelmed by passion that quite some time passed before he noticed that the princess's cat had resumed its raucous yowling. It was this unexpected distraction which momentarily cooled his ardor and allowed him to perceive a most disturbing sensation.

"In the instant before the force of his desire returned and obliterated his detachment, Judah ben Simon felt the familiar touch of a hand with six fingers, pressing against his back."

XVI

"THE NEXT MORNING," said the Rabbi Eliezer hastily, before his listener could interrupt, "Judah ben Simon awoke in a drowsy, pleasant mood. But this sense of well-being gradually disappeared as he became aware that the walls of the baroness's bedroom were covered with illusionist murals, depicting the elm grove in which he had first met Rachel Anna. He recognized the arrangement of the trees, the shrubs, the flowers; even the shelf-mushrooms were in their accustomed places on the trunks. Yet, before the young man could even attempt to comprehend this unsettling discovery, his uneasiness and confusion were multiplied by the realization that the Baroness Sophia Majeski had already gone from the room.

"So I have been tricked again," muttered the mountebank disconsolately. Numb with disappointment, he lay beneath the blankets, trying to understand how he could have let himself be so completely deceived, wondering why the three women had gone to such great lengths just to torture him. He searched through his memory for some clue which might help him understand the meaning of the bedroom murals, and taxed his imagination to explain the strange reminders of the past which had disturbed him on the previous night. Again and again, the Baroness Sophia's image appeared before his eyes. He re-examined every word of their conversation, and, each time he recalled the dreams and confidences with which he had so foolishly entrusted her, he heard himself utter an involuntary groan of shame.

Eventually, however, as Judah tossed back and forth, he began to hear a dry, rustling sound beneath his head, and reached beneath his pillow to find a sheet of plain, gray paper, inscribed with a precise and delicate script.

My dearest mountebank, read Judah ben Simon,
If you are the man of intelligence and sensitivity which I believe you to be, you must know by now that my love for you is more profound than the deepest valleys of the Carpathians. Therefore, I have decided to escape from this prison of Kuzman and go away with you. Do not be afraid: the money I have saved from my parents' remittances will support us for many years. After that, I will gladly learn your business, and assist you in the mountebank's trade.

Indeed, the only obstacles to our perfect happiness are the princess and the countess. Over the course of those long winter evenings, they have grown fond of my company, and would certainly oppose the idea of my departure. They are powerful, unpredictable women; I have seen them be quite mean to the unlucky men who have tried to cross them.

For this reason, I suggest that we tell no one of our plans. Do not try to find me now, at this bright and public hour of day. But, if you have any love for me, come back at midnight, when I will be waiting, and prepared to go.

Until then,
I am,
Your devoted mistress,
THE BARONESS SOPHIA MAJESKI

The mountebank read this note four times; then he put on his clothes, tucked the letter safely inside his robe, and left the house at once, without seeking to consult his hostess. Thoroughly preoccupied, oblivious to his surroundings, he passed blindly through the streets of Kuzman and returned to the inn. There, he sat down on his mattress, and scarcely moved all day as he considered the obvious advantages of accepting the baroness's proposal.

"My worries would be over," thought the young man hopefully. "I will no longer need to scrape for pennies, sleep on the hard ground, and wander for days on end without a decent meal. With such a beautiful, adoring woman by my side, my loneliness would vanish. No one could accuse me of abandoning one woman for the sake of another just like her, for the baroness has told me with her own lips that *she* would never believe in anything so stupid as a child conceived in a dream. Should our union prove discordant, I can always redirect my path towards Kuzman and return the lady to her home. And, within a few short hours, I will be able to see if my mistress really has six fingers on her left hand, and to learn the name of that countryman of mine who painted those disturbing murals on her walls."

By the time the village clock showed half past eleven, Judah ben Simon had not yet been able to find one drawback in the lady's plan. Who could have blamed him for the perfect confidence with which he gathered his belongings and headed towards the north edge of town? Indeed, as he turned up the road which led into the mountains, he could hardly keep himself from beaming with happiness.

It was a lovely spring evening, bright with the glow of the full moon and the stars. The sky was clear, the air cool, the leaves full and fragrant on the trees.

"On a night like this," thought Judah excitedly, "it is almost shameful to keep to this barren and well-trodden path. It must surely be possible for me to cut through the forest, and reach the baroness's home by a more pleasant route."

But, a few moments after he had turned from the

(249)

highway, Judah ben Simon knew that he had made a mistake, for the heart of the forest reeked with the fetid smell of decomposing flesh. "I can hardly arrive at my mistress's house stinking of the grave," he murmured, and decided to return to the main road. As he attempted to retrace his steps, he found that the cobbled path was nowhere in sight.

Having spent half the nights of his life in the woods, Judah was not particularly alarmed by this temporary disorientation. Certain that the highway must lie somewhere to his west, he resolved to take his bearings from the stars. Yet soon, he realized with anxiety that the heavens seemed to have changed their shape, and that, in place of the constellations he had known as a child, the bizarre, twisted forms of starry lizards, dragons, and horned toads filled the sky.

It was then that Judah ben Simon first began to perceive how different this wilderness was from the comfortable forest in which he had passed his youth. The foliage was thicker and blacker than any he had ever seen; gnarled branches, overhanging ferns, and moss-covered vines were knit into a canopy which screened out all but the faintest rays of moonlight. The loud, incessant chirping of the crickets had a forced, discordant sound, like an orchestra obliged to play the death march of a tyrant; tense, frantic animals scurried through the underbrush with sharp noises, and high-pitched shrieks.

Suddenly, out of the corner of his eye, the mountebank noticed the shadow of a monstrous, black shape, passing across a clump of dead-white birches. "These fancies of mine are absurd," he said to himself, experiencing a faint, fluttering sensation at the pit of his stomach. But, no sooner did he utter these words than he realized that he had somehow wandered into a section of the forest so overgrown and dense that he could no longer see.

Tripping over a fallen tree, the traveler lost his balance and fell to the ground; moving on all fours, he began to grope his way through the blackness. The stench of decay grew steadily more powerful; roots and sharp stalks scratched at Judah's arms; a bank of dank, sticky moss gave way beneath his knees. As he attempted to keep himself from slipping further into the mud, his right hand clawed through the damp, spongy layers of leaves, and came to rest on the wet, putrified fur of a dead rodent.

Judah ben Simon jumped to his feet and stumbled forward, walking more and more quickly as the unending darkness intensified his fear. He did not stop when the thick brush caused him to lose his footing in the dark, nor even when he crashed against the trunks of half-grown pines. Some branches scraped the side of his face; the mountebank reached up to feel the warm blood trickling down his neck.

In a blind panic, he started to run, and did not pause for breath until he had reached a patch of sandy ground, where the sparse foliage permitted a few rays of light to filter down. There, in a grove of tall, spindly firs, was an abandoned wooden shelter, not un-

(251)

like the one which Judah had shared with Rachel Anna.

Panting with exhaustion, the young man crept stealthily towards the hut. He peered in through the chinks between the logs and saw one small room, filled with cobwebs and a greenish, phosphorescent mist. Although several beams had fallen from the ceiling, the frame of the structure seemed sufficiently reliable and sturdy. Therefore, despite the shelter's unprepossessing appearance, the mountebank decided to take refuge there until dawn.

But, when he reached the opposite side of the house, Judah ben Simon was presented with a sight which made his knees grow weak with terror.

The door of the hut fronted on a large, barren clearing. On the floor of this meadow was a thick carpet of bones—sharp-toothed, hollow-eyed rat skulls, gleaming stark white in the moonlight.

Once again, Judah started to run, trembling with nausea as the bones snapped and crunched beneath his feet. Just beyond the far edge of the clearing, stabbing pains in his chest obliged him to slacken his pace. He stood doubled over, struggling to regain his strength. Then, when the blood had stopped pounding in his ears, he began to notice that the forest had fallen perfectly silent.

The crickets had ceased their chirping; the animals nestled close to the ground and remained motionless. Even the cool spring wind had stopped rustling the leaves. The young man took a few tentative steps forward, watching for the slightest movement, listening warily to the silence.

At that moment, Judah ben Simon realized that he was being stalked.

He had distinctly heard the footsteps, moving in rhythm with his own, pacing behind him, stopping when he stopped. "My imagination," he whispered tensely, and started to walk faster. The footsteps sped up. Judah broke into a run, and heard the animal running after him.

For almost an hour, the mountebank eluded his unseen pursuer. He knelt in dense thickets, ducked behind trees, crouched in the icy hollows of damp boulders. At times, he attempted to quiet his terror by scheming to discover his hunter's identity, for he could not imagine what sort of creature could combine such an earthshaking tread with such agility and poise. But, despite all Judah's efforts, the animal held back in the shadows, lurked behind in hidden corners of the woods, teasing its prey, awaiting its chance. As he tried to lure his enemy into showing itself, the young man grew calm and clearheaded, distracted from his fear by the notion that he was involved in a clever game of wit and instinct. Yet gradually, as he came to understand that he would soon be overtaken, sweat began to wash down his forehead, and spasms of panic ripped through his chest.

Finally, Judah reached the middle of a wide meadow, and knew that he would never reach the other side. He could no longer outrun his pursuer;

there was nowhere for him to hide. He turned around, took out his knife, and prepared himself for battle.

At that moment, Judah ben Simon saw an enormous, coal-black cat emerging from the edge of the forest. Its huge, gleaming eyes shone like blue-green lamps; its pointed yellow teeth dripped with spittle. Its back arched and rubbed against the lower branches of the pines, and, as more and more of its body appeared from out of the trees, Judah realized with horror that the creature was more than ten feet long.

"I am dreaming this," thought the terrified young man. "Such monsters do not exist in nature." But, as the cat shook its hindquarters and leaped towards him across the plain, he knew that it was no dream.

With a shrill, piercing scream, the animal pounced on its prey. Locked together, Judah and the wildcat rolled over and over through the high grass. The cat spat, and clawed at the young man's neck; the mountebank slashed at the thick, glossy fur. There was screaming, snarling; Judah felt the beast's teeth bite into his hand, and the sharp nails tear at his breast. The struggle grew fiercer, more intense and vicious.

At last, too exhausted to continue fighting, Judah ben Simon relinquished his hold on the creature, lay quietly on his back, and felt the cat begin to bat his helpless body from side to side. "So this is what death is like," he thought in the instant before he spent his last strength in a desperate stab at the wildcat's throat, and slipped into unconsciousness.

XVII

KING CASIMIR of Poland stared at the Rabbi Eliezer with round, mystified eyes. "What is happening?" he cried, running his chubby fingers through his pale blond hair.

"I assure you," nodded the old man, "that is exactly what Judah ben Simon wondered when he awoke the next day to find himself covered with cuts and bruises, flat on his back in the midst of an open meadow. His flesh felt raw and tender, as if it had been scraped with bristles; twinges of pain shot through every nerve and muscle. Slowly, with great difficulty, he turned his head, and saw the carcass of the gigantic black cat, lying dead in a pool of blood which had apparently flowed from the jagged wound in its thick, furry neck.

Only then did Judah remember the events of the previous evening. "So I have met the Princess Maria

Zarembka's kitten," he thought, with a shudder of revulsion. A few moments later, he began to recall the mission which had led him from his comfortable room at the inn to this cold and dewy meadow.

"The baroness has been awaiting me all night," he whispered excitedly, scanning the sky and realizing that it was almost noon. "By now, she must be half-dead with fear." And so powerful was Judah's concern for his mistress that it enabled him to gather all his strength and stagger to his feet.

In the cheerful morning light, the woods appeared lovely and benign, without a trace of danger or malevolence. The ferns were a deep, rich green; the vines drooped with colorful spring flowers; nowhere was there any sign of the abandoned hut or the field of bones. The warm sun acted as a salve on the mountebank's wounds, so that he was gradually able to quicken his pace. The eager lover soon found the road, and, after kneeling briefly at a wayside stream to wash the caked blood from his face, set off for the Baroness Sophia Majeski's home.

But as Judah approached the steep carriageway, he discovered that the stone walls of the mansion had been draped with somber black and purple bunting. "So there has been a death in my lady's family," thought the young man uneasily, aware that this unexpected turn of events would surely place new obstacles in his path. "No servant would ever allow a man of my bedraggled appearance to enter a house of mourning. Besides, it is certain that the princess and

(256)

the countess will have come to offer their condolences, and will not be particularly delighted to see me." For these reasons, Judah ben Simon resolved to wait beside the gate until he could find some surreptitious means of announcing his presence to the baroness.

"As luck would have it," smiled the Rabbi Eliezer, "the first person to happen along the road was the Princess Maria Zarembka's goggle-eyed servant girl—who, by then, had taken to wearing a crude, hand-painted portrait of the mountebank in a locket on her breast.

Recognizing Judah's form, she gasped, as if amazed to discover that the dearest figure of her dreams still existed in reality. Immediately, she raised her meaty fingers to cover the lower half of her face; but, when the necessity of answering Judah ben Simon's request obliged her to remove her hand, the young man saw that her cheeks were even more mottled than before, and that her bulbous nose was red from weeping.

"No," she replied mournfully, "there's no way I could get a message to any of them now, unless I had wings to fly with."

"What do you mean?" demanded the mountebank hoarsely, grasping the maid's plump shoulders.

"Oh, sir," stammered the girl, in a breathless, choking whisper, "last night, just before twelve, my mistress and the Countess Catherine took it into their heads to go for a short drive in the mountains. After a long stop at the baroness's house, all three of them set out in a single coach. When they had not returned by dawn, we servants became alarmed, and took the liberty of forming a search party.

"Three miles to the east of here," she continued, as the tears began to flow down her bumpy cheeks, "we came upon a horrible mess. At the base of a high, rocky cliff, lay the beautiful painted carriage, reduced to a heap of splinters. And the ladies' bodies were sprawled on the boulders, all broken and crooked, like a baby's rag dolls. As soon as we could bear it, the maids and kitchen girls came home to dress the corpses, while the butlers and grooms went on to hunt the culprit."

"The culprit?" cried Judah ben Simon. "Then that devil of a drunken coachman abandoned them to die?"

"No, sir," replied the girl, "the princess's driver never drank. God rest him, he was killed along with the others; indeed, the whole affair was quite peculiar, considering how well he knew those mountain roads.

"No, sir," she repeated, sobbing softly, "there was something else, which I have forgotten to mention—something horrible, which led us to raise the cry of banditry and murder. For, as we approached the Baroness Sophia's poor, twisted frame, it became clear to us that her lovely white throat had been sliced straight across, laid wide open from ear to ear."

All at once, the maid appeared to notice Judah's bloodstained, tattered garments, and recoiled in horror and suspicion. But, as she hesitated, torn between her heart's infatuation and her sense of public duty, the young man started to move away; then, grown suddenly oblivious of his painful wounds, Judah ben Simon ran headlong up the mountain road.

"For almost two months," sighed the Rabbi Eliezer, "my hero roamed the hills like a wild man, sleeping beneath the trees, subsisting on mushrooms, berries, and raw greens. The sweeping vistas which the Carpathians offered him were far more dramatic than any he had ever experienced, but now the naturalist took no notice of his surroundings. Instead, he squandered all his energy in an effort to puzzle out the riddles which had begun to plague him, to understand the mysteries and strange patterns of coincidence which had shattered his peace of mind.

Each day, however, he grew more confused and uncertain, increasingly inclined to doubt all his principles and convictions. Finally, at the beginning of August, Judah ben Simon realized that he had neither the knowledge nor the wit to answer his own questions, and that there was only one man who might be able to help.

"Judah the Pious?" whispered the King of Poland tentatively.

"King Casimir," grinned the rabbi, so obviously delighted that the young sovereign could not restrain himself from smiling with pride, "I can see that I have not been telling you this story in vain. And, if I have taught you to repair your own errors as well as you mend my hero's, then my mission will have been a total success.

"Three weeks later," continued the old man, "Ju-

(259)

dah ben Simon entered the famous gates of Cracow and soon found himself even more ill-at-ease than he had been in Danzig. For the bustling, preoccupied city dwellers had little time or goodwill to waste on an ill-clad stranger who had clearly come to swell the already unwieldy ranks of municipal beggars.

As the ragged mountebank wandered through the twisting alleys, children taunted him with insults, dogs nipped at his heels, and adolescent boys, draped casually across their doorways, pelted him with rotten fruit. Gradually, however, the stranger began to notice an odd phenomenon: each time he asked directions to the court of Judah the Pious, the stern, icy faces of the Cracovites grew momentarily open and warm. Matrons smiled on him as if he were complimenting their favorite daughters; young girls blushed prettily; old men could not have been happier to discuss the talents of their newest grandchildren.

But it was not until Judah ben Simon finally entered the court itself that he began to understand why the religious assembly occupied such a favored place in the citizens' hearts.

Although the interior of the crowded canvas tent wore not the slightest frill of man-made luxury, it still appeared clothed with all the trappings of paradise. Sweet music and flowery incense filled the air; mountains of oranges, dates, and pomegranates were heaped on the long tables which lined both sides of the enormous enclosure; above them, ropes of gardenias and chrysanthemums hung from placards engraved with the most beautiful verses of the Torah and the Song of Songs.

Seated on hard wooden benches in the center section of the tent were the same shabby students and exotically-dressed foreign scholars whose presence had so thrilled Hannah Polikov and her neighbors. But it is doubtful whether the spectators at Rachel Anna's trial would have recognized their argumentative visitors— whose faces now seemed perfectly tranquil, like those of men presented with a vision of eternal bliss.

All their attention was riveted on a single point at the front of the assembly; and, as Judah followed their gazes, he began to blink his eyes in amazement: on the small, raised dais was a man bathed in splendor, surrounded by a brilliant, many-colored radiance, not unlike the northern lights which the mountebank had seen in Danzig.

"So that is Judah the Pious," thought the young man, as all his confusion of the last months was peculiarly intensified by the expectant hush of religious awe within the tent. "I will stand quietly for a few minutes and hear what this fellow has to say for himself."

As it happened, Judah the Pious was telling his congregation about the meaning and power of miracles.

"There are thousands of miracles in the air above my head," said the holy man, "but I have no desire to reach up and grasp them.

"So I said to that unfortunate unbeliever who came to me many years ago, offering to embrace our faith if I would only show him one of the marvels for which

(261)

I was then so famous.

" 'Go look at those violets on my table,' I told him. 'Notice the deep purple color of the petals, their velvety softness and sweet fragrance. Then, if you still have no understanding of miracles, I will know that no wonder in the world can make you a religious man.'

"And that very day," concluded the saint, "I decided that my own miracle-working career was over."

During this speech, Judah ben Simon edged slowly through the large crowd at the back of the tent. Despite the mass of spectators blocking his view, he was able to catch several brief glimpses of the sage. Little by little, the mountebank began to perceive that the head of the Cracower court was a thin man of gigantic stature, with strong shoulders and a massive chest; his huge hands were dusted with liver spots and curling reddish hairs. Beneath a broad-brimmed black felt hat, his yellow-white hair flowed in a thick mane down his back; together with a pale, waist-length beard of extraordinary wildness, it seemed to form a cape which cloaked the upper half of his body. His face was bony, broad, and swarthy, dominated by a huge beaked nose. Yet the saint's most impressive features were indisputably his great blue eyes, which seemed to glow and crackle with the energy of thunderbolts, and which were apparently responsible for the weird, luminous aura which encircled their owner.

The mountebank was unable to obtain a complete, uninterrupted view of the holy man until he had pushed his way through the mob to the back of the scholars' benches. Standing at the edge of the crowd, he endeavored to make a detached, careful study of the sage's unique and striking presence. Yet this attempt was soon disrupted; for, at that instant, the Cracower rabbi fell silent, and startled his audience with a deep, booming command.

"Judah ben Simon!" he called out, staring directly at the newcomer. "I have been awaiting your arrival all day; I had even chosen a topic for today's discussion which I hoped might interest you. Move closer. Come here and tell us what your scientific research has taught you!"

"I-I am not yet certain," stuttered the astonished young man, feeling himself being drawn down the center aisle as helplessly as if he were possessed of a dybbuk. With each step, he saw the sage's features from a new perspective, a different angle; and slowly, very gradually, he began to apprehend a most astounding fact.

Included in the rabbi's rich, complicated physiognomy were the unmistakable, unforgettable faces of Jeremiah Vinograd and Dr. Boris Silentius.

This discovery so stunned the mountebank that his head began to swim with a nauseating dizziness; his knees almost buckled beneath him. Propelled steadily forward, he did not stop walking until he stood within inches of the wise man, where he saw that his impression had been correct.

"So," he whispered, in a voice which quavered with anxiety, "you are also a master of disguises."

"Or a great miracle worker," replied Judah the Pious softly, deliberately imitating the thin, reedy giggle of the Danzig doctor. Then, his voice resumed its naturally deep and mellow tones.

"We have here a shy and retiring young naturalist," he began, addressing his congregation. "Accustomed to the privacy of the deep woods, he is understandably hesitant to reveal his most cherished theories before a crowd of strangers. Therefore, if you will excuse us, we will retire to my private chambers."

As the audience buzzed with wonder and excitement, Judah the Pious ushered his guest through a tattered black curtain beside the stage, into a bare room containing two hard wooden chairs.

"Why did you do it?" demanded the agitated visitor, barely giving the rabbi a chance to sit down. "Why did you put on all those disguises just to ruin my life?"

"I am sorry if that is how you interpret it," replied the saint, smiling tranquilly. "All I can say in my own defense is that it is not such a terrible thing for a father to try and teach his son a worthy lesson."

Judah ben Simon collapsed into the other chair, and began to breathe deeply. Overcome by panic and confusion, he felt as if he were suddenly discovering his whole life to have been a deceptive and senseless story, invented just to indulge the whims of one man. "So you are my father," he murmured in a low, tired voice. Then, he sighed. "With all due respect for my mother," he continued, after a while, "I must admit

(264)

that I suspected something like that all along."

"My son," replied the holy man earnestly, "if only you had been open-minded and patient enough to perceive the logical implications of your suspicion, you could surely have spared yourself a lifetime of misery and error."

"What do you mean?" asked the mountebank uneasily.

"Let me tell you a story," said Judah the Pious, "a tale which I heard from a Hindu brother on one of my first pilgrimages to the East. According to that worthy sage, his countrymen firmly believe that unfailing devotion to God insures one's entry into heaven. In order to illustrate the meaning of such devotion, their wise men love to quote the fable of King Sisupala.

"This powerful sovereign, it is said, was born with a fierce and implacable hatred for all religion, a passion which caused him to spend every moment of his life cursing God. He scorned and abused the Lord from his cradle, his marriage bed, and even his funeral pyre. He chastised the heavens for each drop of rain which fell, each thunderbolt which disturbed his sleep; he shrieked at the deities whenever one of his subjects sickened and died.

"Naturally, all those who loved the king also dreaded the hour of his death, for they were certain that his soul would be condemned to roast in the hottest ovens of hell. But, as it happened, Sisupala's soul was admitted to heaven the very instant it departed from his body.

(265)

"For all the celestial judges swore that they had never seen a man who kept the name of God so constantly in mind.

"So it was with the miracle of your conception, Judah ben Simon. Clearly, your mother never believed in it; neither did I. And, from everything I have heard about Simon Polikov, I would imagine that he was clever enough to have soon guessed the truth.

"Indeed, you were the only one among us who was devoted to the memory of that long-forgotten miracle. You alone gave it credence by hating it so bitterly, and by molding your entire life to contradict the principles on which you believed it to be based."

"Then I am the most religious man of all," laughed the young man bitterly.

"Exactly," replied Judah the Pious.

Judah ben Simon lowered his head and said nothing for several minutes. "But why did you make my parents humiliate themselves that way?" he whispered at last. "How could a great saint stoop to such a petty sin, and devise such petty deceptions in order to conceal it?"

"I am not a great saint," answered the Cracower rabbi, gently shaking his head. "I am merely a charlatan like yourself, a charlatan who has been lucky enough to perceive the miraculous warmth of God's love." The sage smiled genially, and reached out to pinch his son's flushed cheek.

"I am still completely human, I assure you," he went on. "Do not condemn me too harshly. Try to imagine, Judah ben Simon: suppose, in your declining years, you were suddenly tormented by a last temptation of the flesh, an unexpected, irresistible attraction to a lovely middle-aged matron. You fight it for a while, then give in: who can say how these things happen? But tell me this: could you possibly think of a better way to enable the woman, her husband, and her neighbors to continue their lives in untroubled contentment?"

"No, I could not," agreed the mountebank, amazed to feel the tears well up behind his eyes. Despite himself, he was beginning to believe his mother's tales of the sage's boundless wisdom, and to experience a strong affection for this calm and powerful man.

When Judah ben Simon spoke again, all the arrogance and obstinacy had vanished from his voice and given way to a new tone of meekness and humility.

"I have come to ask you a question," he said, then stopped. "No," he corrected himself, "I have come to ask you to explain the meaning of my life, to reveal the significance of my experience among those three strange women, to interpret those weird coincidences, to describe the origin of that monstrous cat. And, most important of all, I am asking you to tell me whether these things might not be considered stranger than a child conceived in a dream."

Judah the Pious laughed out loud, as if his son had told him a hilarious joke; but, when he realized that the young man was serious, a spark of irritation became visible in his burning eyes. "Clearly," he muttered, "you mistake me for a boy with scientific notions, like yourself. Otherwise, you would never expect me to label and explain each event in your life as if it were some cog or wheel in a mechanical clock.

"I am neither a clockmaker nor a scientist, Judah ben Simon; I am a man of God. And frankly, considering all you have experienced, it disappoints and astounds me that you can still request a precise, orderly, and final explanation of His marvelous and mysterious plan."

"No," interrupted the mountebank hastily, "you misunderstand me. I am no longer searching for conclusive proof of anything. But I would be inexpressibly grateful if you would consent to shed just one ray of light on this dark mystery, if you would offer one possible—one remotely probable—method of solving this baffling puzzle."

"That is something I can certainly agree to do," smiled the sage. Grown cheerful once again, he paused for a moment's reflection.

"I suppose," he began, "that one might attribute the last ten years of your life to a careful plan of mine, a lesson aimed to disabuse my son of some overly scientific notions. With this end in mind, I entered the body of Dr. Boris Silentius—"

"Or disguised yourself as the ailing scientist," Judah could not help interrupting.

"Whichever way you choose to see it," sighed the old man patiently, "I attempted to teach you the truth with the aid of a few strange stories and moldy bones.

(268)

Then, when this failed, I resumed my role as Jeremiah Vinograd, and sent you out on that greatest of all follies, the mountebank's quest for success."

"But really," the young man broke in again, "all this must have been a great deal of trouble for you to undertake, even for the sake of a son."

"Not at all," replied the saint, smiling slyly and gesturing with his head towards the main tent outside his room. "I would have done the same for any of them out there.

"Indeed, to tell the truth," he continued, "the worst bother was yet to come: let me assure you, it was no easy task to locate a woman who resembled your unique and extraordinary wife. And it took every bit of my political influence to have her installed in the hunting lodge of two dotty noblewomen, and to persuade them to let me refurbish one room with some evocative murals."

"All this makes perfect sense," pronounced Judah ben Simon slowly, "yet there are still too many things which cannot be explained in this manner. I refuse to believe that you would have slept with your own daughter-in-law, and fathered her dream child. I am unable to imagine how you could have created that enormous wildcat, nor do I understand the nature of its relation to the Baroness Sophia, and the creature which used to howl in my native woods. Finally," he concluded, watching the old man carefully, "not even the most wicked villain would murder three young women just to prove an abstract philosophical point."

(269)

"And so we have come to the very heart of the matter," said the head of the Cracower court, smiling radiantly. "I am absolutely delighted to see that my only son is at last becoming the wise and perceptive young man I had always prayed he would be. For I will tell you, Judah ben Simon, you could not be more correct.

"As much as I hate to admit it, my miracle-working ability never progressed to a level which would permit me to fashion a child from the airy vapor of dreams, or a gigantic cat from the fears of a dark night. No, the plain truth is that these things happened, and I had nothing to do with them. What else can I say?

"All I can do," he went on, after a while, "is offer you another possibility, an alternate explanation which completes and surpasses the one I proposed a few minutes ago. By now, Judah, you yourself must realize that these odd chances which have befallen you can only be interpreted as separate scenes in the strange and miraculous play of God.

"Despite my flawed understanding of His ways, I will still venture to guess that He was acting out of motives much like mine—shaping and molding your destiny in an effort to make one of His children see the truth. Right from the beginning, in fact, I knew that he was moving me to take the form of Jeremiah Vinograd—for I *do* possess the essentially simple power of being in two places at once—and to steer you to Danzig."

The holy man fell silent for a long time, then shook his head in wonder. "When I heard about the dream-child," he continued, "I realized that He had grown impatient with my feeble efforts, and had resolved to step in Himself. From then on, things were no longer in my control. I did my best to help out, with that business of the mountebankery, and the three women.

"But, in the end, he outdid me again: the black cat proved beyond a doubt that none of us mortal miracle-workers have achieved one-millionth of His divine skill and accomplishment."

"So this God of yours would cheerfully wreck a man's life just to teach him a lesson?" demanded Judah ben Simon, in a voice which quaked with fury.

Judah the Pious looked sharply at his son. "To tell the truth," he said quickly, "I would never have thought so; but that is the way it appears to be. Indeed, I will have to give some consideration to this problem of God's unpredictable nature. Yet, be that as it may, I must still maintain that the hand of God is the only force which could have directed your fate in this way. What other explanation can you give?"

Once again, the young man bowed his head. He suspected that his father's words were true, but could not yet bring himself to accept them. "I can blame it on the laws of coincidence," he answered weakly, unable to abandon all his convictions without some time to reconsider.

"Blame it on anything you want," replied the saint placidly, aware that his son's dilemma would not be instantly resolved. "As for your second question," he continued, "I cannot possibly presume to tell you

(271)

whether these phenomena are stranger than a child conceived in a dream; I do not often worry about one thing being stranger than another. Such fruitless and time-consuming questions of comparison can only be subjectively resolved. It does seem obvious, however, that there is sufficient doubt in your mind to merit a return journey home, and a few years of reflection."

Conscious that the sage's wisdom could not be faulted, Judah ben Simon felt so much excitement that he could no longer sit still. "You are right," he said, beginning to pace the confines of the tiny room. "I am grateful for your advice. And now, if you will permit me, I will be on my way."

Then, in an instinctive, almost involuntary gesture, Judah ben Simon fell to his knees and kissed the wrinkled palms which lay upturned in the old man's lap.

"Farewell," said the saint, grasping his son's shoulders and staring deep into his eyes. "My heart is calmer now, for I feel quite confident that your troubles have come to an end. One thing is certain," he went on, smiling wryly, "and that is the fact that *I* will no longer be tampering with your life. I am more than ninety years old; my time is almost over. But, if you should ever be in need," he concluded, running his fingers affectionately through the young man's long blond hair, "do not hesitate to call on me."

"Thank you," replied Judah ben Simon tearfully, and hastily preceded the rabbi through the entrance to the main tent. As the mountebank rushed breathlessly up the center aisle, and into the crowd of onlookers at the back of the assembly, he realized that the great wise man of Cracow had already begun to address his congregation.

"Wonder of wonders!" boomed the saint, causing smiles of warmth and affection to appear on his listeners' faces. "Today, I have met a most interesting fellow, a brilliant young naturalist who has taken the trouble to study every line and detail in nature's magnificent plan. And, at the end of all the mazes and labyrinths which he has explored in the course of his painstaking research, he has discovered yet another testament to the miraculous power of God."

XVIII

"AND RACHEL ANNA?" asked King Casimir, so eager that he could hardly keep himself from squirming on the carpeted steps. "How long did it take Judah ben Simon to find her and persuade her to forgive his sins?"

"I am afraid that it took him an eternity," replied Eliezer sadly, and fell into a long, melancholy reverie.

"When my hero returned to his rebuilt, relocated village," continued the rabbi at last, "he found his entire family reduced to one small boy, the two-year-old dream-child who had been placed in the care of Joseph Joshua's young and liberal replacement.

Several weeks passed before Judah was able to extract any information from his old neighbors; in the beginning, the townspeople turned their faces from him in fear and embarrassment, as if his anxious, questioning expression was the symptom of some fatal illness. Gradually, however, he managed to piece together certain fragments of overheard gossip, and began to understand about the plague and its cure; as the villagers grew accustomed and oblivious to Judah's presence in the tavern, they slowly returned to their favorite conversational topics, and once again spoke of Rachel Anna and her departure with Jeremiah Vinograd.

Finally, in the midst of winter, as the townspeople grew more and more desperate for amusement, a few loquacious citizens could no longer resist the temptation to tell Hannah Polikov's son about the rumors which had filtered back from Warsaw.

It was then that Judah ben Simon began to hear how Rachel Anna had entered the capital city in the mountebank's employ, and how her remarkable performing ability had transformed her into a local celebrity. He learned how Reb Daniel of Warsaw had haunted her tent, driven by a fierce desire which had plagued him ever since the days of the dream court, and how bitterness and exhaustion had made her take the ugly old rabbi as a lover.

"Then," concluded the villagers, "she left the mountebank's service, despite the violent protests of Jeremiah Vinograd."

"And after that?" demanded the distraught young man, again and again. "Where is she now?"

But even the most dedicated gossips would fall silent and refuse to reply, until, one night, Judah met the apothecary's daughter, who had inherited all her mother's good humor. Frowning dourly, she told the anguished husband how his son had been mysteriously sent home from Warsaw, with an anonymous letter explaining his orphaned state.

The boy's mother, said the letter, had died in childbirth, as she struggled to bring forth Reb Daniel's stillborn baby. But Rachel Anna's was no ordinary maternity death; there was no infection, no uterine hemorrhage, no puerperal fever. Instead, the strains of labor had somehow opened an old wound on her neck, and caused the young woman's blood to flow in torrents down her breast.

"And what does it mean!" cried Casimir passionately. "What does it mean that Rachel Anna, the Baroness Sophia, and the monster wildcat all died in the same way?"

"In the words of Judah the Pious," shrugged Eliezer, " 'These things happened. What can I say?' "

During the full, thoughtful silence which ensued, King Casimir of Poland rubbed his eyes until the rims were red and teary. "Rabbi Eliezer," he began at last, regaining a shaky hold on his composure, "it is true that I feel no regret at having taken your advice and sent my courtiers away."

"Casimir," interrupted the old man brusquely, "I am going away soon, and you will never see me again. Say what is on your mind."

Shocked by the boldness of Eliezer's request, the king hesitated for several minutes. Then, he felt overwhelmed by a sense of tranquillity and relief.

"Before you came this morning," he murmured tentatively, "I was in a most unsettled state; I had lost almost all my faith, for I had begun to scorn it as a worthless system of injustices and improbabilities. But I will confess that your story has shown me the dangers of such a narrow and scientific view. I am nearly tempted to repair to my royal chapel, to see if I can recapture any of the old emotion. Perhaps nothing will happen," his voice trailed off. "It is impossible to tell. . . .

"At any rate," he continued pompously, straining to pronounce his official decision in a properly ceremonious tone, "you have clearly won our bargain. Your people may continue with their custom. But one thing still bothers me.

"How shall I defend myself when my advisors accuse me of having based my royal decree on some charming but fantastic fairy tale, told by an obscure old Jew?"

"King Casimir," said Eliezer, slyly raising one eyebrow, "what I have told you today is factual history. Let me explain: in my father's old age, he lived in such fear of the spirits that he consistently referred to himself in the third person, as Judah ben Simon, in the hopes of throwing the demons off his track."

Attempting to evaluate this new information, the king kept silent until he had reached the obvious conclusion. Then, he began to stare at the rabbi with an intent, dumbfounded gaze, as if he were seeing some supernatural curiosity for the first time.

"So you are the child conceived in a dream," he said, in a low, awe-struck whisper.

"Yes, I am," nodded the old man proudly.

"But how do you know?" demanded the boy.

"By now," replied Eliezer, "there can be absolutely no doubt that I am Judah ben Simon's son."

"And how do you know that?" insisted the King of Poland.

"Ah," said the Rabbi Eliezer of Rimanov, "that is another story, much longer and more complicated than the one I have told you today. That is the story of my fine, exciting life, a story which I regret to see so near its end."

Embarrassed by this disquieting and morbid turn, the King of Poland half-rose from his seat. "Well," he muttered nervously, "at least you will have the consolation of knowing that your body will be buried with all the proper ceremonies."

"I do not care about that ritual!" exclaimed the Rabbi Eliezer. "I need no mourners to tell my spirit it is free to leave this earth. Not for one moment did I ever give a thought to those filthy handfuls of stony graveyard dirt; as far as I am concerned, they can leave my body out in the open, and let the crows pick out my eyes. No, my dear Casimir, I came here because I wanted to see the sovereign of Poland, just once before I died.

"That is the truth," the old man chuckled happily. "And it is something you would never have predicted."

Leaning down from the throne, Eliezer kissed the king's pale forehead with his dry, wrinkled lips. Then, with a laugh just as boisterous as the one with which he had entered the court, the Rabbi Eliezer of Rimanov stood up, walked through the mirrored halls, and departed.

Three years later, a group of Cossacks, grown poor and restless during the unprecedented peace of King Casimir's reign, descended on the town of Rimanov and massacred nine hundred people. During the general slaughter, the troops invaded the home of Rabbi Eliezer, who harangued and insulted them until the very moment of his death. In revenge, they cut out his tongue and nailed it to the lintels of his doorway—thus displaying the organ which, unbeknownst to them, had once so sweetly addressed their sovereign.

After the pogrom was over, the Jews of Poland realized that they still knew nothing about the man who had made it possible for them to retain one of their dearest customs. The people wept with vexation and dismay when they learned that their newest saint had carried his history with him into the grave. Eventually, they began to make up stories concerning the sage's early life, and at last, in an effort to understand and preserve the Rabbi Eliezer's heroic achievement, they invented this legend of his meeting with the king.